C000008935

WILD KISS

KINGDOM OF WOLVES

C.R. JANE

MILA YOUNG

CONTENTS

Dedication	v
Join Our Readers' Group	vii
Kingdom of Wolves series	ix
Wild Kiss Soundtrack	xiii
Chapter 1	1
Chapter 2	14
Chapter 3	40
Chapter 4	54
Chapter 5	67
Chapter 6	78
Chapter 7	109
Chapter 8	121
Chapter 9	127
Chapter 10	155
Chapter 11	160
Chapter 12	176
Chapter 13	195
Chapter 14	208
Chapter 15	220
Chapter 16	236
Chapter 17	248
Chapter 18	261
Wild Forever	267
Author's Note	271
About C.R. Jane	273
About Mila Young	275

Wild Kiss Copyright © 2022 by C. R. Jane and Mila Young

Cover by Aura

All rights reserved.

No portion of this book may be reproduced in any form or by any electronic or mechanical means, including information storage and retrieval systems, without written permission from the author, except for the use of brief quotations in a book review, and except as permitted by U.S. copyright law.

For permissions contact:

crjaneauthor@gmail.com

milayoungarc@gmail.com

This book is a work of fiction. Names, characters, businesses, places, events, locales, and incidents are either the products of the author's imagination or used in a fictitious manner. Any resemblance to actual persons, living or dead, or actual events is purely coincidental.

Proof: Jasmine Jordan

DEDICATION

To all of us who don't want to be tamed... don't let anyone
tell you how to live. Follow your wild and love hard...

JOIN OUR READERS' GROUP

Stay up to date with C.R. Jane by joining her Facebook readers' group, C.R.'s Fated Realm. Ask questions, get first looks at new books/series, and have fun with other book lovers!

www.facebook.com/groups/C.R.FatedRealm

Join Mila Young's Wicked Readers Group to chat directly with Mila and other readers about her books, enter giveaways, and generally just have loads of fun!

www.facebook.com/groups/milayoungwickedreaders

KINGDOM OF WOLVES SERIES
FROM C.R. JANE AND MILA YOUNG

Wild Moon

Wild Heart

Wild Girl

Wild Love

Wild Soul

Wild Kiss

Wild Forever

These stories are set in the Kingdom of Wolves shared world, but our Wild series will follow Rune's continuing story with her alphas.

WILD KISS
REAL WOLVES BITE...

Just when I thought all was lost...my enemy saved me.

My past has returned with a vengeance.

And my enemies won't stop until I'm six feet under.

They close in from all sides, threatening to destroy the love I've found...and my future.

And just when I think, I'm going to lose it all, the man who swore he'd end me, shows you can walk in the dark and still be an angel in disguise.

I'm now on a new path, one I don't recognize.

I don't know who I am anymore.

And as I learn to embrace what it truly means to be wild...

I just hope I can be strong enough to survive the storm coming my way.

PILLBX
Grace Gaustad

I Wanna Be Like You
KR3TURE

Control
Halsey

Run
Northern Lite, Chapeau Claque

Plouă
Holy Molly, Tata Vlad

Labyrinth
Taylor Swift

Infinity
Jaymes Young

Kiss Me
Dermot Kennedy

War of Hearts
Ruelle

Love You to Death
Chord Overstreet

Listen to the **Wild Kiss Soundtrack** on Spotify

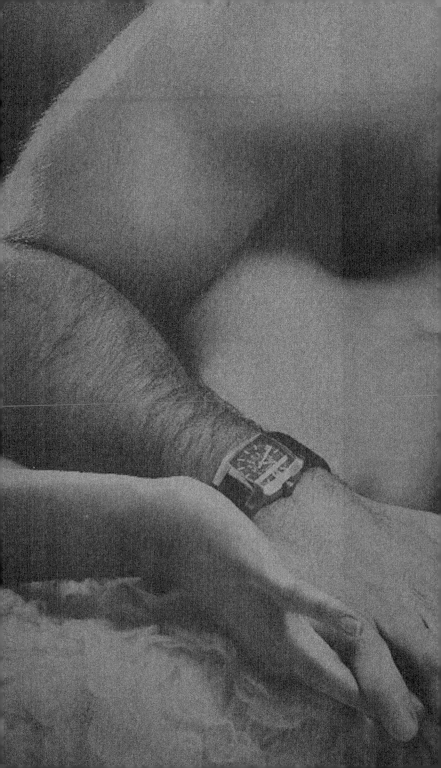

CHAPTER 1

RUNE

Love. That was what I felt when the sharp pain of Daxon's bite faded away.

Overwhelming love. And possession. And gratefulness.

Daxon's feelings rushed over my senses like a wave caressing the sand as it slid back to the water.

I hadn't known you could feel like that.

Like you were someone's beginning and end. Like there was nothing you could do that would make them stop loving you.

I'd thought I'd known love.

But I hadn't. I hadn't even had an inkling of what it was like when two souls intertwined so closely together you had no idea where one ended...and the other began.

Our mating bond crashed over me in a single, throbbing, heart-stopping moment.

It was like I was caught in a snow globe, the world settling slowly around me as pieces of our past flashed between us. A tableau so beautiful, tears slipped down my face.

There was the moment when I'd first seen him. How the golden light of the sun had reflected off of him on his bike, and I wondered how it was possible for there to be such beauty in the world.

There was the moment at our first dinner, when he'd stared at me like I was everything. I could see the wonder in his gaze. The promise even then.

There was our first time making love, our fight with Alistair's enforcers... the way he'd taken me against the car hood.

There was the way he'd promised me he'd never hurt me after Wilder had walked away.

Moment after moment streamed through my consciousness. And through it all...I felt him. That overwhelming sensation that he would never betray me, never break my heart...always place me above all others.

I could feel it, in the dark space of my heart that belonged to him...that had always belonged to him...he thought I was perfect. A miracle he would spend his whole life holding on to.

His love was mad. Obsessive. All-consuming. It wasn't the love you read about in fairy tales. It was more. So much more.

The sensations were almost...too much. My brain wanted to say that something like this couldn't be real, but the emotions crashing over me pushed the doubts away.

This love was so much more than I had ever dreamed.

I'd closed my eyes, just concentrating on allowing myself to...feel...and when I opened them, there he was.

My mate.

He stared at me with that golden adoration he'd always had...but I'd somehow missed the intensity of it along the way.

"Rune," he murmured, so gently that the tears tracked down my face even faster. He slid one of his hands around the nape of my neck, and the other one tangled in my hair.

"Hi," I whispered, my voice choked with everything I was feeling. He pressed his face against my cheek, his scratchy jaw brushing against my skin. He moved until we were staring at each other, our lips a centimeter away.

And we just breathed.

In and out, until I was sure his essence was settling into my veins.

I was faintly aware of Ares and Wilder nearby, but I couldn't move my head to look at them. There was nothing inside me that would allow me to look away from Daxon.

Finally, his lips touched mine, exerting the softest pressure, like the brush of a butterfly's wing against my skin. He paused again, and I whimpered, because there was a heat rising up inside of me different from the one I experienced before on that fateful car ride with Wilder...but also the same.

There was the same desperation, the same need for Daxon now.

But those emotions were for different reasons.

His tongue pressed between my lips and electricity bloomed inside of me. The long sloped drag of his tongue against mine. Had he always tasted like this, like moonshine and shooting stars and a million whispered dreams? Our tongues tangled together, as his hands worked to move my head just where he wanted it. The kiss quickly moved from soft, and then he was feasting on my lips, like he was already taking me.

I could feel his need like it was a tangible thing. I could feel the filthy, obsessive thoughts filtering through our kiss, like a kiss could talk. Our tongues intertwined, and I sucked lightly on him, wanting him deeper. He growled at my move, a delicious, rasping sound that echoed through my veins and had my panties wet with need. That's all we were at this point, a frenzy of desperate hunger.

"You love me," he gasped, like he'd never believed it before this bond.

And I understood that feeling.

Because it was one thing to hear someone say they loved you. It was another thing to see that someone loved you in how they behaved. But to feel it...to really feel the passion someone felt for you, the all-consuming need, the love that meant they'd do anything for you...It had to be experienced.

And I was realizing that I'd never really experienced it before this moment.

A hand touched my back. Daxon ripped his mouth away from mine and growled like an animal, a clear threat that whoever had dared to touch me needed to run as far away as they could.

"Rune," came Wilder's anxious voice, but something passed over me, something unrecognizable, a livewire flashing through my veins. And then there was a yelp and the sensation of strong wind bursting through the room. I heard the large doors open and then slam closed, and then we were alone. In the back of my mind, I knew I should think deeper about what had happened, but I couldn't. Because now I was alone with my gorgeous mate, and all I wanted to do was wrap myself around him and feel his kiss again.

As if he could read my mind, his arms pulled me against him, lifting me up until I could wrap my legs around his waist and feel his heartbeat against mine. We were walking somewhere, but I couldn't pay attention to where, because his lips were on mine again, that all-consuming kiss threatening to break my heart because it was so perfect. His kiss was reverent and deep, his tongue caressing mine as he explored every inch of my mouth. Our kiss was a claiming one. One that left no doubt that he owned me, and I owned him right back.

I opened my eyes, and he was watching me, their gleam vividly gold, like they were shining from the inside.

He lowered me down against something downy and smooth, before pressing the full weight of his body against mine. And he just stayed there, my body softening around him as we continued to kiss.

"You're everything, my perfect girl. Everything I could've ever dreamed," he murmured between our breaths. He moved my shirt from between us and started to work it up over my chest, only taking a small break from my lips as he pulled it over my head.

We'd done this a million times, but the way he stared at me, it was like it was our first time. There was hunger there, and the assurance he thought I was the most beautiful girl he'd ever seen. His hands massaged my breasts over my bra. He was in no hurry even though I could somehow feel he was just as desperate as I was. But he was also desperate to make this moment last. To make our mating claim extend for as long as possible.

And I could appreciate that, especially as he finally unhooked my bra and threw it somewhere away from us. His hands were back on my breasts, and he rubbed his fingers over my nipples, the calloused touch sending shockwaves through my body. His lips moved from mine and he seemed determined to kiss every inch of me as his hot breath against my skin only added to the sensations coursing through my body. His hands plucked and pulled at my nipples until my cries were echoing around the room. His mouth took its time, leisurely sliding up and down and across my jaw, and then down my neck and chest before he finally licked at my taut nipple.

I whimpered as his teeth and tongue began to lap and bite at the sensitive peak. The orgasm building inside of me felt... life-changing, like everything about this experience did.

"You're mine, sweetheart. My mate. My goddess come to life." He continued to pull at my nipple before moving to the other one, suckling like he was trying to draw my lust out through the tip.

I was wearing a pair of leggings, and while his mouth continued to work on my chest, his free hand pulled them down, his fingers catching on the band of my panties, yanking on them until I was completely bare underneath him.

He was still wearing all of his clothes, and it somehow made the moment even hotter, even if I was desperate for our skin to touch.

His gaze danced across my skin, absorbing every inch of me as if he couldn't get enough.

"Fuck, sweetheart," he groaned suddenly. "I love every part of you. You're so fucking hot. So fucking perfect."

I moaned in response, my hand sliding between us, gripping his cock tightly through his jeans, desperate for him to give me what I wanted. Even if he just put his lips on my nipples one more time, I'd come. More than that, I'd crash into an entirely different stratosphere.

"Tell me you want me," he murmured.

"You can feel that I do."

His fingers traced over my slippery folds, and that was it. I came so hard, I indeed saw the stars. I forgot how to breathe. Pleasure like I'd never experienced before crashed over me in a profound, earth-shattering climax.

I was faintly aware of my screams echoing around whatever room he'd brought us to, but I didn't care how loud I was. He'd just given me something life-changing.

Daxon brought his fingers from my folds, and licked at his gleaming fingertips, closing his eyes as he moaned at the taste. When he opened them again, his gaze was feral, the gold glow of them even brighter than before.

"Never tasted anything so delicious until I met you," he purred. His hands pushed my thighs wide, and although sometimes I could get self-conscious, none of that was present at that moment. My body felt perfectly safe, at home with him. His feelings for me were still pulsing through my veins, and I absentmindedly wondered if that would fade with time, or if it would always be like this.

I wouldn't mind. I loved his quiet confidence pulsing through me. His confidence in me. In us. Carrying that feeling through life would definitely help with my own confidence.

Daxon moved further down until his head was lowering between my thighs.

My heart was still racing out of control from the orgasm I'd had, but I knew I was just a few licks away from another one.

He lapped at my core in long, slow, delicious movements, like he was truly savoring every taste he got.

"You're going to cum for me again, sweetheart. I want to make my mate the happiest you've ever been."

He feasted on me, nuzzled into my folds like he was starved. There wasn't a dip he didn't explore, a crevice he didn't taste. His stubble was rough against my inner thighs as pleasure built inside me. I grabbed onto my golden god's hair, riding his face shamelessly as he growled against me. His tongue circled my clit, pressing on it as he slid two fingers inside, immediately finding that perfect spot. He suckled on my clit as he rubbed, and that was all I needed to fall again...over and over, my pussy sucking his fingers into me, milking him like I would his cock.

He didn't stop; he continued licking and sucking until it felt like I might set a record for longest orgasm with how much he was extending it. He licked down around where his fingers were thrusting, lapping up the juice running down his hand.

"Sweetest fucking girl. My perfect girl."

And I felt perfect in that moment, something I'd never experienced in my life. He swiped at my clit one more time, tremors sliding up my body, and then he withdrew his fingers and moved back over me, pressing his lips against mine.

My taste on his lips felt right. I wanted to smear it all over him, mark him like he'd marked me. I whimpered again at the thought. "Sure, sweetheart. Anything you want," he murmured randomly...like he could read my mind. "But you have marked me. It's right here."

Okay...that definitely felt like he'd seen into my thoughts. I made a mental note...one he could maybe hear, to follow up on that.

But not right then...right then I needed...more.

Daxon moved away from my mouth and slowly pulled up his shirt, inch by delicious inch revealed. I followed the path of his shirt up, until something caught my eye. There, above his heart, was an eternity symbol, etched into his skin like a tattoo artist had carved it there.

"Mine," I whispered fervently, reaching towards it and softly tracing its edges.

"Yours," he affirmed.

My gaze danced from his sculpted shoulders to the mating mark, to his bronzed, ripped body, and then back to the mating mark, like there was a thread connecting my gaze to it, and I couldn't move away for long. His eyes tracked me, and I could feel the pride he felt that he carried my mark.

"I'm going to worship you now, baby. Show you you're everything to me. Would you like that?"

"Yes," I murmured.

He unzipped his jeans, and his hot, swollen dick immediately popped out, because of course he wasn't wearing briefs.

"I'm going to make you feel so good," he growled.

Without thinking, I leaned forward and lapped at the milky liquid seeping from his tip. And he moaned. My core clenched as my mouth and tongue licked it up before moving back to gaze at him.

"My new favorite taste," I murmured, and he growled even louder.

After he'd gotten his jeans all the way off, he took himself in his hand, rubbing the tip against my soaked folds. My muscles spasmed as they readied to let him in. I was desperate for it.

The slow glide of his cock inside me felt like coming home. Like he *was* my home now. Pleasure soared through my veins like liquid fire...and I was crying again. Because how could I not? The moment was so profound. So everything.

I arched against him, needing him deeper. I was hot and wet and so ready for him, his huge length could just slide right in, if only he'd let it.

He finally pushed deep. Deeper and deeper, the slippery

friction sending pleasure and pain through my body. But it felt like I was finally whole when he sunk to his hilt. And just that feeling shattered me into another awe-inspiring orgasm.

My head thrashed back and forth, and I moaned his name as I clenched and tightened around him.

Usually Daxon could last forever if need be, but this was different, this moment was different. Everything was heightened beyond both of our experiences. And while I held him inside me, my body milked him, and he suddenly came, just from the sensation. Daxon groaned and his teeth came down on the bite he'd given me. As he licked and sucked at it, I came again.

Somehow harder.

The pleasure was too much. I wondered in the back of my mind if either of us would survive it. My breath was coming out in gasps and we were holding tightly to each other as our pleasure spirals finally ended. A trickle of moisture slid down my inner thigh from his cum.

He grinned at me beautifully, awe in his gaze the same I was sure was in mine.

And he was still hard, no sign he'd just cum at all. He stroked the back of his fingers along my cheek. "Prettiest girl I've ever seen," he murmured roughly.

Daxon thrust back and forth slowly then. I was sore from cumming so many times, but the slide of his cock inside of me felt like heaven. I felt high, endorphins pumping through me. I never wanted the moment to end. I wanted to stay like that with him forever.

Our panting breaths, the slap of our skin, and the smell of...us drowned out the mustiness of the room we were in. The sounds coming out of his mouth were the sexiest I'd ever heard, and I moved eagerly against him, lost to the pleasure we were creating.

The moment seemed to drive on and on, until I was clenching him tightly once again. I leaned forward and bit down on that space between his neck and his shoulder, slicing down hard enough that I broke the skin, and I could taste the salty sensation of his blood as it trickled into my mouth.

He moaned wildly, and his thrusts grew harder. "Yes, bite me. Just like that, my perfect mate. Make me feel you forever," he purred.

I groaned at his words, lapping at the bite and wanting it imprinted on his skin for eternity.

One of his hands moved to my breast, and he pinched my nipple while he continued to impale me.

"Best day of my life. This moment. I never could've dreamed of anything more," he whispered, his voice coming out pained. He came again, his cock jerking inside of me as heat filled up my core even more, so much that it dripped out. Our eyes were locked against each other as his hips slowed.

"I love you," he whispered, as a tear trailed down his face.

"I love you too," I murmured.

We lost track of time after that, lost in each other's bodies...and lost in each other's souls.

———

The Queen was standing in front of me, staring in the mirror as she played with the blue stoned necklace hanging around her neck. "There are rumors the unrest is growing," she said anxiously, wisps of her hair falling out of her elegant updo.

"We'll face whatever comes," a man's voice answered. I looked back to see the king I'd seen in the castle's coffin, sitting in an armchair, a little girl playing at his feet.

"We have to protect her at all costs," he murmured, watching as she scooted toy cars around a toy track.

The King and Queen both looked exhausted, like they carried the weight of the world on their shoulders.

"I don't understand why we haven't figured out who's behind it yet." The Queen paced the room back and forth, fidgeting with her dress. "Even the fae haven't heard anything."

The King's voice darkened. "I'm not so sure King Cantor would tell us if he knew."

The Queen nodded at that, only looking more concerned.

"Whoever's behind the unrest, they won't be able to outweigh the good we've done for our people." The King was trying to reassure her, but I could see the tension in his gaze. He wasn't sure if he believed his words.

"What if we sent an emissary to the Hunters? Maybe they've heard rumors of what's going on," the Queen offered.

The little girl made a honking sound as she pretended to crash two of the toy cars together.

That only seemed to worry the King and Queen more, like her innocence was too much for them to bear.

The King nodded slowly. "I'll send Hendrick," he said, standing up, his eyes distant as he thought about the plan. "He was adopted into that family of vampires, so he'll be more adept with their ways." The Queen nodded, her lips pursed as he strode out of the room. Staring after him for a long moment, she walked over to the chair he'd abandoned and set herself gracefully on it. She reached out and tenderly played with the little girl's hair. The girl glanced up at the Queen, and my blue gaze stared out from her face.

"What's wrong, Mama?" she asked in a soft, sweet voice.

The Queen straightened her shoulders and pasted a fake smile on her lips. "Everything's fine, my darling. Your daddy and I are just stressed about a few things."

The little girl laid her head against her mother's knee and smiled at her. My heart pinched inside me; it was obvious the little girl loved the queen very much.

"Sing our song, Mama," she pleaded.

The Queen quickly hid her grimace and gave her another false smile.

She hummed a hauntingly familiar melody, but as she opened her mouth to sing the actual words, the room disappeared and I found myself once again huddled against Daxon's chest, wondering why I could still hear the melody ringing in my ears.

CHAPTER 2
RUNE

Coming out of the mating frenzy was like coming out of a deliciously erotic dream. I knew I had in fact dreamed after I'd finally fallen asleep after hours of lovemaking, but for the life of me, I couldn't figure out what the dream had been about.

"Hi," Daxon purred, pressing a soft kiss against my lips. I could feel the fluttering of arousal inside of me, but my body was completely sore...destroyed, in fact. There was no way I could go for another round.

I watched as he slid off the bed, his muscles carved perfectly like a god's.

Okay... I at least couldn't go for another hour or so.

I sat up, bleary-eyed, glancing around the room, wide-eyed at the space. It was a testament to the strength of the frenzy that I hadn't been aware of how creepy this room was.

Like the other rooms we'd wandered into before, this one was perfectly preserved, with a thick layer of dust on the nightstands and dressers, and photographs hanging on the walls. There was a giant painted picture of the King and

Queen, but I didn't think this had been their bedroom. The room was much smaller than I would expect for royalty; not that I knew that much about that.

I really hoped this hadn't been their bedroom.

I slid off the bed, noting the dust that moved through the air as I pushed the covers back. Daxon shrugged sheepishly. "I probably should've looked for...a cleaner place to settle into," he murmured. I lifted my arms and noted the dirt streaks across them, across my entire body...and his, where sweat...and other bodily fluids had combined with the dust.

"You think there's any running water still in this place?" I asked.

I'd been joking, because the castle had been abandoned for a very long time, but Daxon still strode into the accompanying bathroom, and a few seconds later I heard the sound of water running.

He peeked his head back through the doorway. "I guess you don't shut off water to a castle, no matter if no one's lived in it for years."

"No one but the ghosts," I joked. It was funny how the room had gone from our passionate love den to something from the beginning of a horror movie. As soon as I washed the dirt and sweat off of me, we were leaving. I walked into the bathroom, and my thoughts drifted to Wilder and... Ares. I winced thinking of how they'd been pushed out of the room.

Wait a minute...

I stepped under the water with Daxon. "Was I just imagining something, or did some kind of magical wind blow Wilder and Ares out of the room when Wilder touched my back?"

Daxon's forehead wrinkled as he thought back.

"Now that you mention it... I'm not exactly sure what happened."

We were both lost in our thoughts as Daxon stroked his fingers through my hair. Of course there wasn't any soap in the shower...or at least there wasn't soap in the shower we were willing to use, so getting cleaned with water was the best we could do.

A nervous tension flittered through my veins and I stared up at him, biting down on my lip.

How would this change everything? I could feel Daxon inside of me. I was head over heels in love with him, but it hadn't diminished what I felt for Wilder...what I was beginning to feel for Ares as well, I grudgingly admitted.

"There's nothing to worry about," he murmured soothingly, stroking my cheek.

My eyes widened. "You *can* read my mind!" I cried out, thinking of how awkward that would be. While there were some cases I could see that being nifty, I definitely didn't want Daxon knowing everything that went through my brain.

He chuckled. "I can't read your mind exactly...it's more like I get a taste of what you're thinking, the feelings behind it. I know you well enough by now I can generally guess what thoughts are causing you to feel that way," he explained.

That made me feel...marginally better.

"Why can't I feel you?"

He settled a hand on my chest, right in between my breasts. "You should be able to. Just close your eyes and take a deep breath, and try to feel that bond inside of you."

As if his words had given it power, the bond in my chest seemed to grow. As I closed my eyes and tried to connect with it, I could feel Daxon even more. And not just the love he had for me, but other emotions as well, like…amusement. Oh, and there was a flash of heat. I opened my eyes and saw his gaze was greedily devouring my body.

He'd been right. I could guess what he was thinking by the flavor of his emotions. He winked at me cockily. "Told you."

I sighed and laid my head against his chest, the warm water streaming around us as I just…felt him.

Finally, I knew it was time to face reality. And to face Wilder and Ares, something I was extremely nervous about no matter what Daxon said.

"I would never try and take them away from you," he murmured as he turned to shut off the water. "Although we do need to talk about how the bloodsucker suddenly became something to you."

There was a line of tension in the muscles of his back, and I knew he was purposely facing away from me. "I didn't think…I'd ever want to share you. But I've come to peace with it now. Being able to feel you inside of me, I understand better. It isn't that I'm not enough for you. It's that somehow your heart has fallen completely in love with multiple people, but it doesn't change the strength of your love for me."

A hiccuped sob burst from my lips, but I held my tears in. I reached out and trailed my fingers along his back, his skin trembling under my touch.

"No, it doesn't," I whispered.

After a long moment, he turned to face me, shooting me a reassuring smile as he grabbed my hand and led me out of the shower. It was freezing. Because obviously while the water had been kept on, such things as the heater had not, and I had no doubt that I would be covered in dirt again if I tried to use the towel hanging on the rack.

I opened up one of the cabinets and spotted some towels in there, but I could see the dust all over those as well.

Air dry it was.

Once we got our clothes back on, Daxon took my hand and we walked from the room. My stomach chose that moment to growl...loudly.

"My first official task of being your mate will be to make sure you get some food in you," he teased.

I smiled at him, thinking it was hilarious...and somewhat embarrassing how even that made me swoon.

"I think your first task was getting inside of me as many times as conceivably possible," I retorted.

He simply winked, obviously proud that my core felt broken.

It was a wonder how lost to our surroundings I'd been during the frenzy, because we'd wandered down at least three hallways before we were back in the enormous entry of the castle where Daxon had first marked me.

A shot of worry suddenly dashed through Daxon's bond.

"What is it?" I asked, rubbing my chest.

"I—I don't know what came over me...what happened. You have to know I would never have purposely done something like that against your will."

His face was heartbroken as he stood there. I reached out to him and softly held my mate's cheek.

"I do think that you're possessive enough to mark me without my consent," I teased. "But in this case, you just followed your instincts, whatever they were triggered by. And...I'm just glad that whatever had been holding me back before from accepting your bite, didn't this time."

He stared at me in awe, like he couldn't believe his good luck.

Daxon winced. "I am a possessive bastard, aren't I?"

"Baby, I'm also beginning to understand you're a little bit of a psychopath judging by the emotions I can...or lack of emotions I feel in your bond about anything but me. But I can work with that," I said with a wink. He just grinned at me, his eyes dancing with mischief...and a little bit of madness.

Just how I liked him.

"I knew I'd eventually get my bite to stick," he joked as he led me towards the giant doors that led to the outside.

Daxon heaved the heavy doors open, and I took a breath as we walked out into the gloomy day.

"How long have we...?" My voice trailed off.

"How long have we been fucking?" he tossed at me lightly. I rolled my eyes, knowing what we'd been doing had been far more than that.

Daxon pulled out his phone, his eyes widening. "Holy fuck," he spat out.

"What is it?" I asked worriedly, thinking he'd gotten a concerning message on his phone.

He stared at me. "I've been inside of you for three days," he finally said, and the bastard looked so proud of that.

"Three days," I repeated slowly. Well, that explained why I was walking so funny.

"Rune," Ares's voice called from nearby,

I glanced over at him emerging from the woods, that nervous feeling fluttering inside of me. I expected him to look angry or worse...disappointed. But he looked as he always did, kind of cocky, and kind of obsessed.

"There's my girl," he murmured, as he approached and softly stroked his thumb on my cheek.

I was taken aback by his forwardness, because...we definitely hadn't gotten to that point yet. But he evidently had decided my mating bond with Daxon meant he could be more forward with his feelings. If telling someone they were your blood bond didn't do that in the first place.

Surprisingly, Daxon's bond was still in my chest. All I could feel was his love for me, no sign of the undying hatred for Ares I was sure he'd felt in the past.

"I didn't know if you two were ever going to come out," said Ares, and this time there was a tiny bite to his voice.

Daxon coughed, the words "jealous bastard," coming out as he did so.

Okay, this wasn't as awkward as I thought it was going to be.

"What have you guys been doing?" I asked.

"You mean since the mysterious power pushed us out of the room like we'd been swept up in a tornado?" Ares asked lightly, a mystified glint in his gaze.

I bit my lip again, because I was suspicious that the wind had come from me. I could see that kind of power coming in handy, but it just added to the confusion of why I'd have such power in the first place.

"Yeah, since then."

"Are we going to talk about this–" he began, but Daxon cut him off.

"No, we're not. At least not right now. We also have a lot to talk about when it comes to *you* as well. But Rune's hungry, and I promised her some food. Since I don't have food, however, my best chance of providing her with that is through you bastards."

Ares rolled his eyes. "Tell me more sweet nothings," he said sarcastically. But then my stomach growled, and he looked as worried about it as Daxon seemed to be.

Give a girl a break; I'd literally just had sex for three days. I could only imagine the kind of calorie burning that had done for me. Of course I was hungry. Ravenous, in fact.

Ares tipped his head to the right, back into the forest. "Wilder and I have been hanging with the bear shifters while we waited for you. I'm sure they'll be happy to serve you," he teased.

I groaned, remembering how over the top they'd been once they thought I was the lost princess, something I agreed with them I was at this point, but I certainly wasn't prepared for that kind of thing.

Wait a minute...Ares hadn't even been there. How long had he been watching us?

My stomach growled again. Okay, questions could wait while I got a hot meal. Or any kind of food.

Daxon took my hand and marched toward the forest. I could feel Ares's amusement behind us as he followed.

I felt the dark shadow of the castle behind me, and though I fought the urge to look, I couldn't help but glance back.

There were no signs of ghosts. I didn't get any more new visions. But I couldn't shake the creepy feeling dancing down my spine, or the sensation that eyes were on me.

I couldn't get away from the place quick enough, even if the trip had been life-changing in a way completely unanticipated.

We walked farther into the woods, and after a five minute stroll, I inhaled the scent of smoke on the wind. I glanced back at Ares, whose gaze was fastened on my ass.

He met my eyes unrepentantly. "Have you been hanging out at the castle every day?"

"I've been looking around the place, waiting for you two to emerge, wondering if I could find anything interesting."

He shrugged and shook his head. "There's a lot in there, but nothing that gave any more clues to the past."

Again something pushed at my thoughts, a memory that for the life of me I couldn't recall. Hopefully it would come to me sooner rather than later, or I was really going to be bugged.

We made our way into a clearing where the bear shifters were gathered around a large fire. I immediately glanced around for Wilder, but he was nowhere to be seen.

"He's been...going for walks a lot," Ares said, obviously reading the worry in my features. "I'm sure he'll be back soon; he's been checking in about as often as I have to see if you'd returned."

The unease in my stomach grew. Wilder and I already had our problems when it came to the idea of sharing me. I wasn't sure what was going to happen now that Daxon was my mate.

"Do you know how long ago Wilder left?" I asked one of the men gathered around the fire.

"About two hours ago," he answered, the reverence in his gaze making me uncomfortable. The only eyes I liked to see that emotion in were my lovers', as weird as that sounded.

"Thank you," I murmured. Daxon had approached the fire, and belatedly I realized there was a large pot on one side of it, sitting on top of the flames. "What do you have cooking in there?" he asked.

"Rabbit stew," one of them answered gruffly.

My ears perked up at that. I hadn't had rabbit stew, although I knew I'd eaten rabbit when I was shifted. Surely the cooked version tasted better than the raw one, although my wolf had thought it was delicious.

"Could I have some?" I asked hopefully.

It was chaos as they all basically battled to get me a bowl. But of course my mate somehow exited the pile triumphantly, holding an enormous bowl of stew in his hands.

"I love you," I beamed at him, and a blush rose to his cheeks that I didn't think I'd ever seen before.

"Oh, is that all it takes?" Ares asked casually.

And now I was the one blushing.

"Better luck next time," taunted Daxon as I settled onto one of the wooden logs that had been put around the fire, and I devoured the stew. And I mean devoured. The bowl was enormous, and in about two minutes flat, it was completely empty, and I was eagerly hoping to get it filled again.

This time Ares was the one to grab the bowl and get me a second helping.

"Thank you," I murmured as I took it from him.

"Don't you have anything else to say?" Ares teased. I just rolled my eyes at him while I worked on my second helping. Next to me, Daxon was devouring his own bowl just as feverishly. Looking back, it was truly amazing we'd survived without water or food for three days, and I hadn't thought of either once. The frenzy was a crazy thing.

It took three more bowls before I was done. All of the servings had been offered so eagerly that I felt guilty taking so much from the bear shifters.

But the pot was truly enormous, almost like a witch's cauldron in a children's story book, so at least there'd been a lot to go around.

I leaned against Daxon with a groan, holding my now stuffed belly. "I think that's the best meal I've ever had."

"Agreed," replied Daxon, sounding just as satisfied as I was.

At that moment, I glanced up, and there, standing at the edge of the clearing...was Wilder.

"Wilder," I gasped, locking gazes with him.

I couldn't read his face at all. It was completely blank, and chills slipped over my skin at the sight.

"I'm going to talk to him," I said, moving to stand up from the log. Daxon grabbed onto my hand. "He's not allowed to make you feel upset about this," he growled.

I shot him what I hoped was a comforting smile. "There's absolutely nothing to regret," I murmured, earning myself a blindingly gorgeous grin.

Daxon let go of my hand, and I tentatively walked over to Wilder. He hadn't moved from where I'd first spotted him, and my nerves only grew as I got closer.

"Hi," I breathed, because I was nothing if not eloquent.

"Rune," Wilder answered, and that's when the blankness broke. The way he said my name, it was...tortured. I was brought back to that night at the cabin where he'd let me go and walked off into the woods. My lip trembled as emotion tore through me. I reached up to touch his face and he took a step away from me.

"I'm not going to say 'I'm sorry,'" I told him, trying to keep the tears at bay.

"I wouldn't expect you to," he said, his voice pure melancholy. "But he shouldn't have forced you into it." This time there was a growl in his voice as he shot a death glare at Daxon who was watching us both with interest.

"Obviously this wasn't how I envisioned it happening, Wilder. But you know I've been ready for this for quite some time."

He flinched as if I'd shocked him.

I realized immediately how he'd taken what I just said. "I've been ready for it with *both* of you," I added hurriedly.

That caught his attention again. "And now?"

"Now what?" I asked, confused.

"Do you still feel that way? Are you still ready for...both of us?" I realized he was asking about the mating bond. Now that I'd accepted Daxon's, there shouldn't be any problem in accepting Wilder's.

"I might need a day to recover before I enter a frenzy like that again. And maybe we can have food and water nearby this time," I teased, but before my full sentence could come out of my mouth, his lips were crashing against mine, so much relief embedded in our kiss that a hitched sob broke from my chest.

When he released me, I shook my head sadly. "After all this time, you still...doubt me." There was heartbreak in my voice and he flinched from the sound of it.

I was eager to have him bite me, as exhausted as I was. Because Wilder was missing something inside of him, and not in the way that Daxon was. Daxon, perhaps, was missing part of his soul. Wilder was lacking in his ability to feel loved. Whether that was because of his parents, or his bitchy ex, something was missing inside of him. And although I tried my best to fill that part of him up, maybe the only thing that could work was the mating bond, for him to be able to really feel the depth of my love. To understand it wasn't a fleeting, slippery thing that would fade with time. It was real.

I wasn't going to go away.

And after all we'd been through, my love had only grown.

I was suddenly desperate for him to be able to get the same confidence in us as I'd gotten from my bond with Daxon.

Before I could do something crazy, like offer my

exhausted body to him, Daxon was behind me, his hand curling around my waist.

"I am in no way trying to stop the bond from forming, Wilder, but I can see the way that you're eyeing each other. She needs a night of rest...a night to recover. That's the first meal she's eaten in three days. She needs at least three more of those before she goes into a frenzy again."

A flash of disappointment danced in Wilder's gaze, but he quickly pushed it down.

"Of course. We should wait longer than that. We have all the time in the world," Wilder reassured both of us.

And although I didn't doubt he really meant it, a rush of foreboding passed over my skin. Did we really have all the time in the world? There was always something after us, something in the way of our happily ever after. How much longer until something completely prevented us from having our happy future for good?

"Everything's going to be all right," Daxon soothed, rubbing his hand up and down my back. I'd forgotten for a moment he could feel me, and I hurried to check in with how he was doing since Wilder and I had just been eye-fucking each other right in front of him...not that it hadn't happened before.

Again, there was nothing. In three days, we'd evidently achieved a huge level of growth we hadn't reached before. Adding Wilder to that would be amazing.

———

Three days before
Wilder

I hit the ground hard, the door slamming shut behind me.

Flabbergasted, I stared over at Ares. "What the hell was that?" I growled, jumping to my feet and running towards the door.

I couldn't believe Daxon had done that. After how careful we'd been, for him to bite her...a flare of guilt hit me as I thought about something similar I'd done before. The asshole I was, I still flew at the door, wrenching it open. Daxon and Rune had disappeared from the entryway, and I could hear their soft moans from somewhere down one of the hallways. I moved to go after them, and Ares grabbed my arm.

"Get your hands off me, you filthy bloodsucker," I growled, baring my teeth at him.

My anger didn't seem to faze him at all. "You can't go after them," he said calmly.

I shook his grip off my arm. "Why the fuck not?"

He sighed, like he was talking to an errant child, and my anger only spiked.

I moved to run after Rune again, and *again* he grabbed me by the arm.

"Look man, it's not my favorite thing either. But she already accepted the mating bond; you'd only hurt her if you tried to stop her from getting what she needed from it."

"And what is that?" I threw out, even though I definitely knew what a newly bonded mate needed.

He rolled his eyes at me. "Obviously to be fucked for as long as it takes for the bond to settle."

I knew he was right, but it didn't stop the terrible emotions running amok under my skin.

I pointed at him. "This is all your fault. Why the fuck are you here? Why the fuck did you touch her?"

I took a step towards him, fully prepared to go at him again as I was right before Daxon's bite, but Ares just crossed his arms in front of him calmly. What the fuck did it take to get this guy riled up?

"I came back because Rune is my blood match," he announced proudly.

I froze. I'd known he believed that. But I'd refused to accept it. Forgot all about it actually.

"No. Fucking. Way."

I'd heard about blood matches. We'd learned about it growing up in school. It was a vampire's version of a soulmate. There was no fucking way that my girl was this vampire's fucking soulmate.

"That's not happening," I snarled.

Ares grinned and crossed his arms in front of him. "You expect me to care about your problem with that? Rune knows it's real, and that's all that matters."

The world went white around me, and I lost my mind. That was the only thing that could explain me coming back to reality with my hands wrapped around Ares's throat, trying to choke him to death. Something that obviously wouldn't work well since he was one of the undead.

Ares reared back and punched me in the mouth. My lip exploded and blood flicked all over his face.

I roared with rage and let go, stumbling back a few steps before running full speed at him.

We tumbled to the ground, rolling around and exchanging punches like complete buffoons. Finally, Ares pinned me under him, his elbow hooked against my neck.

He snarled at me, his incisors lengthening. "Yield," he spat.

I just glared at him. I'd lost it; Ares never would have gotten me pinned otherwise.

"Yield," he said again.

Finally, I exhaled loudly and released the tension in my

body. He wasn't going to get my words, but evidently, I was lucky today, because he hopped off me with a disgusted glare and strode off into the woods.

I lay there, my chest heaving, feeling exceptionally sorry for myself.

I was the one left out. If Ares was telling the truth, he was one of her mates, and now Daxon was one... What if she didn't want to mate with me? What if they were enough?

I rolled over to my knees and promptly threw up, the idea too much for me to bear.

Rune was everything to me. Did she know that? Had I made it clear?

I'd fucked up...repeatedly. And she'd forgiven me.

But now...

I stumbled to my feet, nausea still sliding through my gut. I didn't go back to the castle. I knew Ares was right, and Rune and Daxon needed time to settle the bond. All I could do was wait...wait and hope she wanted to bond with me too.

I tracked for about a mile before I came to a clearing and saw the bear shifters that had been frothing all over Rune before we'd gotten to the castle. They stared behind me hopefully, like Rune would appear at any moment.

"She's still at the castle," I said glumly, not even asking if I could join them before I flopped myself onto one of the logs surrounding their large fire.

"Did you find anything useful in the castle?" one of them asked. I eyed him suspiciously, thinking of the necklace Daxon had stolen from the Queen's coffin.

"No," I lied, just in case they knew about the necklace and would try and steal it.

"You look like you need this," another of them said, handing me a bottle of whiskey.

"Thank fuck," I snarled as I grabbed the bottle and took a long draw, and then another...and another.

The guys stared at me, shocked, but made no move to stop me as I proceeded to down the bottle for the next hour until I was sufficiently drunk. It was special whiskey, the kind that hit shifters hard, exactly what I needed while I endured the hell of waiting for Rune and Daxon to be done, my thoughts running wild.

Night had fallen before Ares showed up, casually strolling into the clearing.

My jaw dropped as they all appeared to recognize him, all of them shouting out friendly greetings.

"You know he's a vampire, right?" I slurred.

The looks I was getting, it was as though they thought I was an asshole. These bear shifters were idiots.

"My friends don't care about that," Ares commented smugly as he slapped me on the back and settled next to me, smirking when he saw the almost empty bottle in my hands.

"How can you look so fucking happy?"

"What do you mean?" Ares asked, thanking the shifter who handed him his own bottle of whiskey.

"Why aren't you sick at the thought of her with him right now?"

He shook his head confidently. "Because there's nothing that would prevent me from going after her and making her mine."

My eyebrows rose in surprise.

He stared at me, as if disappointed. "By all means, take yourself out of the race; less time I have to share with her.

But I'd gotten the impression you cared more about her than that."

The world was spinning around me, and I was getting a throbbing headache. "It isn't my choice."

He shrugged his shoulders. "You must have missed that Rune hasn't quite gotten on the same page, but that's not stopping me."

"I'm probably going to kill you when I'm sober. There's no way I'm allowing you near Rune again."

The asshole laughed, like I'd told a particularly funny joke. I winced as the sound rattled through my head.

"Okay, killer. We both know that killing Rune's blood mate would only hurt her...and that's not something that's probably best when trying to mate her, now is it?"

I flew off the log, swaying as I tried to keep myself upright.

I knew I was being an asshole right now. A petulant child, really. But there was something inside of me...something terrible...that said everything was not going to be all right.

And I'd learned to listen to those feelings a long time ago.

But unlike in the past, when I'd managed to survive whatever came my way, I was pretty sure what was coming...was going to be the end of me.

Because I was nothing if I didn't have Rune.

———

Rune

My sleep was dreamless and deep. When I finally opened my eyes, it was to the tent's canvas tarp the bear shifters had graciously provided us. I stretched my arms above my head and rolled to my side, promptly encountering a delicious set of chest and abs.

My gaze trailed up to his face.

"Wilder," I purred, delightfully happy to see him.

His smile was warm, and I searched his face for any sign of the unease from yesterday.

Besides the slight line of tension in his forehead, he seemed okay. Or at least better than yesterday.

"How long have I been sleeping?"

"For about fifteen hours. I started checking your breathing about six hours ago," he joked.

I laughed and rolled onto my back again, checking in with my body. Before I'd fallen asleep...I'd been beyond sore. I was pretty sure my vagina was broke, but now... now I was feeling pretty good.

Maybe ready to add one more mate to the mix.

My chest throbbed, Daxon's amusement pushing through our bond. Evidently, he'd felt the pang of lust that flashed through me at the sight of Wilder's naked chest.

That was going to take some getting used to. Even with the threesome action we'd had before the mating bond...I still expected him to rip through the tent and tear Wilder away from me.

"Are you hungry?" Wilder asked, sitting up and revealing a plate of eggs and bacon that had my mouth watering.

"I love you," I breathed, eagerly reaching for the food. I was starving again.

"I knew I was sweating over the fire all morning for a reason," he joked.

I picked up the fork and scooped up a bite of the eggs, practically shoveling it into my mouth. I chewed it slowly while I thought about what to say next.

When I finally swallowed, Wilder was staring at me patiently, obviously knowing I had something to say.

"It isn't just the mating bond that has you feeling out of sorts; you've always had issues with that."

He sighed and glanced away from me.

"Yes... And no. Everything seems to be up and down in my head. One minute I'm doing just fine, and then something more happens and all my insecurities are set off again."

I nodded, understanding that probably more than he knew. I always thought I was healed from Alistair's rejection, but then something would be said, or a wave of insecurity would hit, and all the bad feelings and self-loathing would come creeping back. I wasn't sure those feelings would ever go away. It felt like they were ingrained in my DNA at this point. Was that what it felt like to him?

"I know about your ex obviously, but what else do you think contributes to it?" I asked hesitantly. I didn't feel great about delving into his insecurities. I knew I didn't want to discuss my own right then, but it felt like a conversation we needed to have. I wanted to make sure he knew I loved him, just as much as I loved Daxon. That he was also one of the great loves of my life.

"Life was a series of disappointments until you rolled into town. When everything would be looking up, something would come crashing down. Every time I thought I had it all, the scholarship, the girl...it would disappear." He shook his head bitterly. "I promise I'll get my shit together. Maybe it's just this place. There's a darkness in the land, and it's like it's seeping into my skin. Can you feel it?" he asked.

I nodded. Even though I'd been distracted for several

days, I could feel it, the wrongness, the way that their death had cursed the ground we were walking on.

I ate the rest of my breakfast in silence. Wilder looked pleased with every bite I took.

"What time are we supposed to leave?" I asked.

He shrugged, his eyes beginning to heat as he stared at me. "We weren't sure how long you'd sleep...so there's no set time."

The implication was clear, or should I say the offer was clear. If I wanted to mate with Wilder, no one was going to stop me.

"I want you," I confessed. "I want to feel you inside of me, feel your warmth around my soul. I never want to be without you."

"Thank fuck," he breathed as his lips touched mine. He licked and sucked at my mouth, our tongues tangling together. He was claiming me, and I held onto his shoulders, desperate to get as close as possible to him. His lips eventually trailed down my neck and across my shoulder, the opposite one that Daxon had claimed. He pulled back briefly to stare at me, his green eyes piercing my soul. "Are you sure?" he asked again, and I saw the flicker of fear in his gaze that I would reject him.

I leaned forward and gave him a soft kiss. "Perfectly sure," I murmured against his lips before I slowly pulled away.

His tongue licked at the spot on my shoulder he'd chosen, and then...he struck.

I cried out as the pain tore through me, and I waited for the feeling of blissful heat to block it out as it had with Daxon.

But nothing happened. There was just the cold trickle of blood down my skin. My eyes were clenched when he pulled away, and I was a coward, because it took me a long moment to open them and stare at him.

Wilder was a broken man. His face had somehow paled in the seconds between the before and after of the bite, and his eyes were red and watery. "I don't understand," he whispered desperately, his gaze trailing to the bleeding bite on my shoulder.

"Why didn't it work?"

Panic was streaming through me. Was I the messed up one? Was I the one blocking his bite, or was it him? And what did that mean for our relationship?

He made a move towards the bite again, like he was going to try once more, and a burst of wind flew through the tent and knocked him away, the tent ripping as he soared outside.

I was shaking as I stared in disbelief at the giant hole in the tent. I could hear the shocked voices of my men outside, but it was like I was frozen in place, completely unable to move. I guess that explained who was responsible for pushing Wilder and Ares out of the castle after Daxon's bite.

I pulled at my hair anxiously, wanting to find a hole to climb in and disappear.

A few moments later, Daxon's face popped into view, staring at me, concerned. Concerned and with so much love, I promptly burst into tears.

"Something's wrong with me. I'm some kind of wolf freak," I sobbed.

He climbed into the tent and immediately pulled me into his arms. "You're not a freak," he said staunchly.

I stared into his beautiful golden eyes, tears blurring the view.

"I couldn't accept his bite. And when he tried again..." I gestured towards the hole in the tent.

There was a tic in Daxon's cheek, and his gaze immediately went to the still-bleeding wound on my shoulder. "I can't believe he tried to bite you twice. He practically mauled you," he snapped. "We need to get that necklace back on you, get you healing again. It looks terrible."

I nodded limply. Wilder hadn't come back in, and although I could understand him wanting to avoid me after what had happened–it felt like my soul was breaking.

Daxon winced and rubbed at his chest, and I remembered he would be feeling my pain almost as clearly as if it was his own.

"I'm sorry," I gasped. "I suck at this mate thing."

He growled and licked at the scar on my other shoulder, sending shock waves of pleasure through my body that helped cover up the pain of Wilder's bite. "I think you're the most perfect mate in the world," he purred.

My sobs only grew louder. After giving me one more kiss, Daxon gently sat me on the ground. "I'm going to find a first aid kit and that necklace piece, and hopefully we can get you healing." His jaw was tight as he said it.

"Don't be mad at him," I pleaded. "It was a normal reaction."

Daxon vigorously shook his head. "It's not a normal reaction to maul the girl you're wanting to mate with," he spat before climbing out of the tent.

Frowning, I moved to get up, wincing when I felt the pain of my shoulder. Wilder's bite had been deep.

When I got outside, Wilder was sitting at the campfire, shoulders slumped and his head down as he studiously focused on the soil beneath his boots. He didn't glance up at me when I approached.

"Wilder," I began, but then Ares was there.

"Why are you bleeding?" he snapped, his gaze immediately honing in on my shoulder that was bleeding through my shirt.

My mouth opened and closed.

Daxon was back then, carrying a first aid kit from who knows where.

One of them was evidently more prepared for a camping trip than I was.

Daxon ignored Ares as he moved the shirt to the side and began to dab alcohol on the bite. I winced as the sting of the alcohol hit me.

"Well?" Ares pressed.

"My bite didn't take," Wilder mumbled dejectedly.

Ares's eyes widened, but Daxon continued to work on my shoulder, rubbing some salve on it and then putting a large bandage over it.

"That should help for now, but you might need stitches if this necklace doesn't let your wolf out and allow you to heal."

Wilder winced out of the corner of my eye.

I was done with this day, done with these palace grounds...done with it all.

I wanted to get my wolf back.

And I wanted to go home.

"Where are the necklace pieces?" I asked, my voice coming out choked and despondent.

Daxon growled again, like he was pissed he couldn't make the world perfect for me. He pulled one of the pieces of the necklace out of his pocket, and Wilder stood up from the fire with the other one.

"Alright, now how do these pieces go together?" Daxon muttered, grabbing the necklace away from Wilder who was standing there like he'd been stabbed.

"I'll do it," Ares offered, holding out his hands. Daxon glared at him distrustfully.

"Like I'm going to let you hold Rune's fate in your hands," he snapped. "Why haven't you left yet? Or better yet, why hasn't Wilder killed you yet?"

Ares sighed, rubbing his hand down his face wearily. "Because we've come to an understanding. Wilder understands that since Rune is my blood match, there's no sense trying to push me away. I'll never stop trying to be with her."

I shifted uncomfortably at the reminder. His teeth sinking into my neck ran through my head. How good it had felt...

Definitely not ever going to bring *that* up in front of Wilder.

Daxon's jaw had dropped...I'd never seen him look so shocked before.

His gaze went to me, and there was betrayal in his gaze...and running through his bond. Which only made me feel worse, because it wasn't like I had any say in the blood match.

"Rune, it's true?" he asked softly. And I could tell he was trying to keep the emotion out of his voice. He'd known Ares was claiming we had a blood match. But I guess it was another thing for me to confirm that I believed it too.

"I think so," I answered roughly, wondering how we'd had three such perfect days...and now everything sucked.

Daxon's eyes closed and he looked conflicted, but when he opened them again, there was not a trace of unease or anything else. "Alright, bloodsucker. Put this necklace together."

I was like a woman possessed as I considered mounting

Daxon right then and there for not making this a bigger deal. Maybe the bond was useful...he could tell when I was on the verge of losing it.

Ares tried a few different ways of putting the necklace together before one finally worked. I think I'd expected something to happen, like sparks, or the necklace to glow... but there was nothing.

"That was a bit anticlimactic," mused Ares, as if he could read my mind. He shrugged his shoulders and handed me the necklace.

I took it, excitement and anxiety buzzing through my veins. *Please work.* My shoulder hurt like a bitch, and I was desperate to reconnect to my wolf.

Holding my breath, I slid the necklace on.

Nothing.

Nothing happened.

My wolf was still locked inside of me. My shoulder wasn't healing.

If I had any tears left to cry...I would have started sobbing once again.

"It could just take some time," Daxon cautioned, his features bleak and exhausted with failure, like I'm sure mine were.

"Yeah...that's probably it," I murmured before squaring my shoulders and ignoring Ares and Wilder's equally desolate stares. The stones suddenly disconnected, and I sighed. "Can we get out of here now?"

All three of them nodded, almost in unison, and after packing up our very meager belongings...we headed towards the waiting carriage.

Good riddance.

CHAPTER 3
RUNE

My gaze traveled across the three gorgeous faces of the men in the carriage with me. Three men who would normally be at each other's throats, ready to kill each other. It was a bit strange how things had been less about stabby moments lately and more about bonding marks. In all honesty, I wondered if them trying to kill each other would be less painful. My heart squeezed for Wilder, while a blush of pain ran over his bite mark.

I cleared my throat, gaining Daxon's attention.

I reached for the necklace, and Daxon's palm slid over my thigh, distracting me. I lowered my hand over his instead, sensing his worry in my chest.

"It's okay," I answered before he even asked the question. "Things just feel a bit much, but that seems to be the story of my life."

"I'm here for you, baby," Daxon reassured me, his voice soft. I'd always known I loved him, but this new, deeply affectionate side of himself he was revealing...it was taking it to another level. Everything he did made me swoon.

"Me too, Rune," Wilder added, his voice still depressed.

Ares smiled at me, not saying anything because I knew at this point he had no plans to leave me alone any time soon. The fire in my chest burned. Ares was definitely growing on me. There was still so much unknown between us, and things we had to sort out. But Wilder...he was going to break me before I could get to that. His eyes were darkened with pain, and he was slumped, like he carried the world on his shoulders.

Daxon's hand slid across my thigh, and warmth ignited over my skin, drawing my attention away from the others and back to him. Sparks of a thousand stars danced inside of me as we locked eyes.

He was my mate, and the urge to crawl onto his lap and kiss him as the rest of the world faded intensified.

Movement came from the seat across from us in the carriage, and I turned back to Wilder and Ares, who both watched me. Ares grinned, enjoying the show, happy for me because he considered me securely his now. But it was obvious Wilder would struggle until we figured out why the mating bond wasn't working. So I moved quickly to sit between them both, our sides pressed together.

"Hey you," I murmured to Wilder, coaxing a weak smile out of him, while Daxon watched with a pout. Ares had his hand against my leg now, fingers stroking slowly in small circles. I wasn't sure how I felt about that.

"This is rather amusing, don't you think?" Ares murmured.

"Why the hell are you in the carriage with us?" Wilder snapped, the tension around him thickening.

I ran my hand down Wilder's thick arm, caressing his tense muscles, wanting to calm him because fighting amongst ourselves wouldn't solve anything right now.

"Calm down, asshole," Daxon butted in, looking ready

to tackle Wilder into submission if he kept upsetting me. "If it'll make you feel all warm and fuzzy, I'll kick the blood-sucker out for you."

Ares laughed hysterically, leaning back, unable to appear more relaxed if he tried. "I think it's pretty obvious the big bad wolf is crying from his inability to perform."

Daxon made a strange huffing sound that came out as a suppressed laugh, and I eyed him intensely. "Wilder," he began. "The more pressure you put on yourself, the more you're blocking the bond."

"Shut the hell up," Wilder snarled.

"Okay, let's talk about something else," I pleaded, my gaze sweeping from the two grinning hyenas to Wilder, who was rolling his eyes at both of them. On the bright side, he wasn't leaping over me to break their faces. At least not yet, anyway.

It suddenly felt like a furnace in the carriage, and as much as I appreciated Daxon attempting to put a chink in the invisible wall Wilder wore as armor, I didn't think pushing the point would work.

"So, that was a crazy adventure," I said, completely changing the topic and leaning in against Wilder as he slipped an arm behind my back, holding me possessively.

"That's one word for it, but we found the second piece of the necklace, and that's what matters," he muttered. He looked tired, his hair rumpled.

I held his gaze, trying to hide that I was breaking inside. I hated that I couldn't give Wilder what he yearned for the most—to mark me. He turned to stare outside, and I sighed, twisting towards Daxon who wasn't helping the situation by lounging back, his legs crossed at the ankles, grinning, studying me, reading all my emotions.

Ares, on the other hand, still had his fingers dancing

against my thigh, not giving up on claiming his spot along-side me. With him reclined in the gothic-looking carriage with tiny wolf motifs running along the top paneling, it made him appear every bit a dark lord. An extremely sexy one at that. But I shook my head, needing to not complicate things.

When he blew me an air kiss though, I flashed on how far we'd come, how quickly he'd engrained himself into my life, and how it felt like it was destined. From him tracking me down with the other hunters to kill me, to then giving me half the stone pendant to save me. Which reminded me of something...

"Ares, where did you get your half of the necklace from? I never asked you, but I'm curious now that we've found the other part." I remembered the tale he'd told me about his family living with the royal family, but he never revealed how he'd gotten hold of the stone.

"Good question," Wilder quipped, shifting around to stare at the vampire, a challenge in his gaze.

Ares blinked, not responding quickly, but the corners of his mouth were curling upward. "A friend had gifted it to me. They insisted it was the stone of Atlandia, once belonging to the royal family. It carried healing powers, especially when merged with the broken half. So I kept it with me, until the stone started to emit a low humming sound that mortals couldn't hear. And the closer we got to you, little dove, the louder it grew. The stone was drawing me to you, so I figured you were related to the royal family somehow and you'd know where the second piece was."

Daxon bristled as he glared at Ares distrustfully. "You were using Rune to find the stone for yourself?"

Ares's expression tightened. "Not exactly. The

Atlandia royal family took so much from me, and there were rumors the princess had survived the family execution."

I felt sick thinking of Ares coming after me in revenge, even if I'd already known about it. He had taken me to the tavern with the other vampires and bitten me, and he'd called me...*Your Highness,* and when he'd told me I'd pay for what my family took from him. I didn't want to be the long-lost princess he'd been searching for...but all signs were saying I was.

I wanted to believe the strange visions I'd been having meant something else...that there was no way I was royalty. But I didn't think I could get that lucky.

"I'll never forgive you for trying to kill her," Daxon growled, and my insides tightened as I examined him... wondering if I could really trust Ares's intentions.

Wilder snarled, the threat clear. This was getting out of control...fast. I was suffocating in the tense air.

Ares raised his palms defensively. "That was before I met Rune, before I tasted her blood, before I realized she was my blood match. After that, I swore my life on protecting hers. Now, I would never harm her."

"I'll never trust you with her," Wilder spit, his shoulders rising.

But Ares had to be the most confident person in the world, or the best poker player, because he didn't react once. Instead, he went on to explain what he'd told me a while ago. How his parents had been found guilty of betraying the Atlandia royal family and beheaded as traitors. That Ares was only six when it happened, which still broke my heart to hear. Then he told them how the entire royal family was wiped out many years later by an enemy that no one had identified even to today. They even took out the extended royal family with only one assumed survivor—a young princess.

As they threw question after question at Ares, I frowned and fidgeted with the chains around my neck, something heavy curling around my chest. My breathing heightened, and the louder they got, the harder it was to draw in breath.

A strange sensation came over me. My hands trembled, the need for fresh air gnawed at my insides.

I continued nervously fingering the chains around my neck, pulling back from the billowing argument that seemed like it would burst into violence any second now.

I examined the blue stone pendants in my palm, trying to distract myself because it felt like I was about to have a panic attack.

The stones looked like they didn't belong in this world —the blue was almost turquoise and glinted even without sunlight on them. The two pieces gave a sudden jiggle, and my eyes widened in astonishment. They snapped together like two magnets drawn back together, a clicking sound filling the carriage as they merged. I gaped at the necklace, all three men silencing their argument and glancing over at me...at the stone.

"What happened?" Ares asked.

"I-I..."

Where once there were two stone pieces, now only one sat in the palm of my hand, perfectly merged without a single fracture. It shone brighter too.

Then it started—a buzz across my hand. It moved through me with lightning speed. My heartbeat quickened, my gaze flickering in and and out.

I cried out, shuddering in Wilder's arms. Daxon and Ares lunged towards me...as the world went black.

I ran.

That was all I knew, all I'd been told to do by my new mother —the woman who'd saved me and whisked me away from my home. From the men who'd broken in and butchered my parents.

Shadows shifted in the woods around us, trees rustling from the wild wind, while screams and shouts boomed behind us. I kept wiping the tears from my cheeks, my heart growing heavier every step we took away from our castle. It was my home, a place where my parents had promised me the world, taught me how I'd rule in their place one day, and where we were supposed to be safe.

I sobbed, tripping over a tree root. I hated running while my home was torn apart.

Fighting for breath, I sniffled, then stopped. "We need to go back." My breathy words grew raspy. "Maybe they're not dead and it's not too late."

Our family doesn't let their emotions control them, *Father would say, and I straightened my back.*

Despite struggling for air, I couldn't back down, and I curled my hands into fists.

"Hush now and run," she urged worriedly, grasping my arm, hauling me alongside her to move faster. "They can't see us, can't find you. This is no time to be a hero."

"Mama might still be alive," I cried, fighting against her grasp. She swung around toward me. Shadows danced over her face, hiding most of her in it, but her eyes found mine.

"I'm sorry, little one, but she wouldn't have survived, and even if she did, they wouldn't let her live. They'll come for you next. They'll hunt you down, and slice your throat. I made her a promise I wouldn't let that happen. We have to run."

"Who are those men? Why are they——" I burst out crying, her words like blades, cutting into my heart.

"I don't know who they are," she whispered, her grip on my arm squeezing as she pulled me into a run again. "But I do know

these woods will be swarming with the enemy in no time because they didn't come here just for your parents. They came here to get rid of the entire Atlandia family. Now, run for your life!"

I snapped back to reality with a whine on my throat. Where the world sharpened in colors around me, and where smells were so intense, they let me know instantly I was next to Daxon, Wilder, and by the faint smell of death surrounding me–Ares.

My body shifted, a whimper fell from my lips as I tumbled onto all fours.

I was back in my wolf form, a sense of freedom rippling over me, but with it came a jumble of emotions desperately surging through me, voices of my men calling to me, their hands on me.

Staring down at myself, I moved around in a small circle, unable to believe that I was in my wolf's form.

The stone had broken the fae's curse, and I yelped with joy, the sound coming out as a singsong howl.

But being confined in the carriage was all too much, and I still couldn't get enough air into my lungs. I threw myself at the door, which slammed open, and I hit the ground hard as I jumped out of the moving carriage.

I didn't care that it hurt, or that I rolled on the dirty ground, not when the cool air brushed through my fur. After she'd been locked inside me all this time, frantic to escape; she needed her space.

Scrambling to my feet, I jolted right into the woods just as a deep, raspy voice called out after me. "Rune!"

I glanced back as the three men poured out of the moving carriage frantically, and heat licked my insides at seeing them. Giving a small groaning sound, I dove forward, leaving them behind.

My heart leaped, and I never stopped running, unable

to believe I finally had my wolf back. Warmth slipped across my body, and the light was fading fast as night approached, but stopping wasn't even an option.

I scrambled forward when heavy footfalls smacked into the earth behind me. Swinging my attention around, three dark figures sliced through the woods.

Adrenaline surged as excitement for the run...for the chase...coursed through me. I knew it was my three men before they emerged from the shadows. Wilder and Daxon, in their huge wolf forms, Ares moving like the wind, coming right for me.

Excitement burst in my chest, my heart thundering as I threw myself faster, my white paws hitting the ground.

I'd missed running so much, and nothing soothed stress like a long jog, but a chase... Well, that was even more delicious. My wolf had no problem being the bunny these monstrous men hunted.

Cold wind hit me, whipping the strands of my white fur, and I skirted around a cluster of dense pine trees. There I threw myself up an ascending hill, claws digging into the hard soil for purchase.

A swoosh of air rode right past me, and I growled at Ares, knowing it was him, then snapped at the rippling current he left in his wake.

Abruptly, I swung to the left, darting around the trees, dried pine needles crunching under my paws.

My two wolf alphas were closing in, both fanning out, flanking me on either side. So I speared through the overgrown underbrush and swung to an abrupt halt as both men sprinted right past my position.

I threw myself back out the way they'd just come, and I ran, my heart beaming with adrenaline, with excitement, with having my wolf back. The earlier weight in my chest grew lighter, and I settled into a steady beat, not spotting the wolves behind me.

I loved that I'd outsmarted them, and pivoted around just as something dark and big came at me from my side so fast, I barely had enough time to respond.

In a flash, I was whisked off my feet and into Ares's arms as he flew with me across the woods, then settled me down by a great pine.

He stood there, not even breaking a sweat, while my wolf heaved for breath.

"You're the prettiest creature I've ever seen," he murmured. "Your fur is as white as Alpine snow, and the sparks you leave on every paw-print are magic. You aren't an ordinary wolf, are you, my little dove?" He dropped to his knees in front of me, ruffling my fur, and I couldn't help it, I leaned in against him because his touch felt incredible. I might have even drooled a bit, wagging my tail.

As I contemplated transforming back, Wilder and Daxon burst into the scene, tongues out, gasping for air. They came at me, practically bowling over Ares in the process. They were against me, pressing their heads to my ribs, my head, my neck. Powdery, masculine wolf and woodsy scents flooded me, and I preened as they kept moving around me, rubbing along my fur. I couldn't remember ever feeling so loved and protected. My wolf ruffled her fur, and if she could've smiled, she'd have been the wolf version of the Cheshire cat.

"I do believe I won that match," Ares gloated, to which Daxon snarled at him.

Wilder ignored Ares and clung to my side. That was when my wolf retreated, fur sliding away, bones shifting. I was back in my human form in moments. Completely naked.

Ares grinned, his gaze sliding down my body. "I'm loving this side of you," he teased, taking my hand and drawing me towards him.

It was at that moment the air shifted with the electricity of Wilder and Daxon shedding their wolf forms. And suddenly, they pressed up against me, too, naked. Their erect cocks pushing on my hips.

"You forced my wolf to come out without the full moon," Wilder murmured in awestruck bewilderment. My eyes widened. I hadn't even thought about that. He had changed without the full moon.

What kind of freaking power was that?

"Okay, I feel like I'm wearing too many clothes for this party," Ares teased, breaking my thoughts before sliding closer and softly grasping the sides of my face, kissing me. Wilder and Daxon had their hands all over me, their lips on my neck...and I was pretty sure I was the luckiest girl in the world.

I moaned, softening against them, ready to take everything further...when they abruptly pulled back.

Ares took off his shirt, handing it to me to put on. And I realized I might have misread the situation.

"Well, that's a bit of a letdown," I groaned, a smile on my lips.

"I know, baby," Daxon whispered in my ear gravelly, grinding his cock against my ass. "I want to fuck you so badly, but we're not alone out here. And I'm not risking your life."

I flinched at his words, frantically glancing around. Only then did I notice figures emerging from within the forest. Wait, who was that? And how long had they been watching us?

Moments later, half a dozen brown bears walked into

the light. Enormous beasts, with round ears, long snouts, and hot air floating out from their nostrils in wisps.

One of them rose up on hind legs, easily standing five feet tall, unleashing a huffing, jaw-popping sound.

A shiver rushed down my spine, knowing I was dealing with the local pack, but that didn't put me at ease. We'd almost got into a fight with them on our arrival into their forest. And when I said, *we*, I meant Wilder and Daxon.

"Is it just me, or is he warning us?" I murmured, as the three of them closed in around me.

Wilder sniffed the air, his nostrils flaring, a growl rolling in his chest. "It's just the pack we met earlier. Why the fuck did they follow us?" He squared his shoulders and marched toward them...butt naked.

I wasn't sure if I should laugh or be scared, seeing as we were outnumbered and Wilder was in a dark mood. "Did we do something wrong? Maybe these woods are protected?"

"I'm going to enjoy this," Ares said, rubbing his fingers along his jawline, watching Wilder.

Quickly, I pulled the shirt over my head and down my body. Daxon took my hand in his, and we all just stood there. I, for one, had no clue what to expect.

A few bears approached Wilder, their noses high, sniffing his scent. I swallowed hard, pushing myself up on the balls of my feet and back down in a readiness to rush to his side should the bears attack. I figured the last time I crossed paths with them, they all fell to their knees in front of me, so maybe I'd have that effect on them once more.

But as fast as they arrived to stand in front of Wilder, the six bears all shifted into their human form, also naked. One of them said something to Wilder, but I couldn't hear anything.

"Talk about a sausage fest," Daxon mocked under his breath, coaxing a chuckle from Ares. Daxon glared at him, like he was annoyed Ares had laughed at his joke.

I couldn't stop staring, unsure what they were doing. Suddenly, the biggest bear thrust his pelvis out, then seemed to be measuring his cock with the length of his hand. The others did the same. I snorted in disbelief at what I was seeing. The bear shifter leaned in towards Wilder's groin with his outstretched hand, and Wilder jumped back...shaking his head at the bear shifter.

"Are they comparing dick sizes?" I gaped at the sight.

"Well, to be fair, he did approach with his jewels out on display, and bears *are* a proud race of shifters," Ares said. "It's pretty commonplace for them to compare sizes with newcomers though, and Wilder's challenged them on who had the bigger cock by being naked."

Daxon burst out laughing. "I better go in there and save him then. One look at my cock and they'll faint with jealousy."

I snorted and rolled my eyes, gaining a narrowing gaze from Daxon. "Babe!" he said indignantly.

"I'm not laughing at you...I'm laughing at the bear shifters comparing cock sizes with visitors..."

"I better take my pants off then," Ares added, and heat burned through me, searing my cheeks at the thought of them all naked around me at once.

Wilder suddenly stormed towards us, his eyes dark... and embarrassed. My gaze dipped to his huge dick hanging there because I had zero control and knew first hand how delicious it was. He'd have no problem comparing to the bear shifters who weren't even close to his size.

Daxon and Ares were still laughing hysterically.

"So, how'd you size up to them, big boy?" Daxon asked between gasping breaths.

"Fuck off. And for your information, they were so impressed, we've all been invited to spend the night in their camp so they can show us their hospitality," he huffed, his brow furrowing.

"Does part of their hospitality include more cock comparisons?" Daxon snorted.

"It's going to be a long night then," I groaned, rolling my eyes as I pictured it. I guess if the challenges continued for the rest of the night...I'd at least be entertained. As long as the invitation didn't come with any strings attached, then I was ready for whatever the night delivered.

CHAPTER 4
RUNE

I woke up with a gasp on my lips, unable to remember my dream, but it still startled me nevertheless. Sweat had my hair sticking to the back of my neck, and I didn't want to know what I'd seen in my dreams if I'd woke up like this.

Wilder and Daxon remained on either side of me, snoring softly. I got up, moving quietly so I didn't wake them. Stepping through the tent opening, I searched for Ares, but he wasn't anywhere to be seen. I pushed my arms into the air, stretching my back, unable to believe I'd slept so well on the ground in my men's arms.

Sunlight stretched out over the landscape, reds and oranges drenching the sky. There was something beautiful and tranquil about being out in the woods, and I made a mental note to camp more with the guys.

I needed to pee, so I moved to the edge of the campsite where I had at least a little privacy.

At the same time, a tingling buzz surged through me, identical to what I'd sensed right before Wilder had touched me in the castle and gotten thrown out of the room with Ares.

Apparently, I gained power from my mating mark with Daxon.

And I'd never heard of someone growing more powerful with a mating mark. Just another thing different about me from other wolves.

That left me with more questions than answers on all the strange things about me...but answers seemed to be in short supply.

One of the guys made a grunting noise in their sleep, and I grinned to myself at the thought of crawling back in the tent. Everything in me hoped I could wake up between them for the rest of my life.

I really needed to relieve the pressure on my bladder first though, and I rushed towards the shrubs to take care of business.

There was a gurgling river right behind the camp. After I'd peed, I wandered over to splash my face with the crisp water.

I knelt by the shore, still feeling sleepy, thinking over the wild day we'd had yesterday. We'd found a way to remove the curse, and my wolf was free again. I really was getting tired of these assholes messing around with my gorgeous wolf. She huffed inside me, in total agreement that everyone should leave us alone.

With my wolf back, we could return home to Amarok. It still amazed me how I'd stumbled onto that town after I crashed the car in my escape from Alistair–that was a life-time ago, and so much had changed since then.

I was no longer the meek girl I'd once been. Now, I had a home, friends I cherished, and men I loved.

Twigs snapped behind me, and I smiled to myself that one of them had followed me out to the river.

I twisted around to see which one it was, only to be stopped dead in my tracks.

It wasn't my men.

It was *her*...

She stood there, her appearance pristine as usual. With her perfect black hair that trailed to the ground, perfect porcelain face, and a perfect transparent dress revealing everything. Her silverish skin glowed in the morning sunlight, and her crystalline green eyes glinted. She was stunning. Her beauty would always make me slightly jealous when I thought of Wilder dating her.

"Daria," I murmured at the sight of the Fae Queen, trying to sound brave as fear pummeled through me. "I would say it's good to see you, but I don't like to lie."

The last I'd heard, Alistair and Daria had partnered up, both of them wanting to win the award for my worst nightmare. Apparently, that quest extended to Romania...

Excitement flickered across her expression, her gaze glinting with malice. "And here we are, all alone, Rune. Isn't this just wonderful?"

"No, not at fucking all."

There was no pause, nothing but me darting away from her frantically. But I'd barely taken a step when she spoke magic words, and something dark burrowed beneath my skin. It came at me so fast that my knees buckled out from under me. Before I could scream, I hit the ground, unable to move. The last thing I saw was Daria, that bitch, bending to stare into my face with a smirk.

"Be a good little dog and stay down this time."

Then my world went black.

———

Something wet dragged over my brow, and my pulse throbbed in my head like I'd been run over by a semi-truck. My breath rushed in, and my chest tightened. A dry cough racked my body. I opened my eyes to darkness, blinking with confusion, unsure where I was, or even what the last thing I did was.

"Oh, good, you're finally awake," a female's voice snapped impatiently.

I raised my head from the seat I was slouched in, searching the dark shadows of the room for who was speaking. But I couldn't make anyone out.

"Where am I?" I whimpered, trying to move, only to find my hands were tied at my back and my ankles to the seat legs...which of course threw me into a panic. I thrashed for release, fear spiking through my veins.

A click sounded, followed by a bright light flooding the room, blinding me momentarily.

I squinted, then slowly blinked to make out that I was in a bathroom sitting in a chair. Sickness rose through me, confusion fluttering in my chest like a caged bird with nowhere to go.

I kept licking my dry lips, shaking terribly.

In front of me stood the most beautiful woman I'd ever seen. Long black hair that seemed to curl around her, a flowing white dress that was transparent, revealing her heavy breasts and the apex between her legs. She stood there proudly, a cruel glint in her gaze. I hadn't thought such beautiful people existed outside of magazines.

I searched her face for any sympathy, for a clue as to what was going on.

"D-Do I know you?" I asked.

"Unfortunately for you, yes." Venom filled her voice, and her smile resembled something I'd expect from a psychopath.

My throat tightened, and I squirmed in my seat. "Why am I here? Please...let me go," I begged.

"Now why would I do that...when I have so much fun hurting you?"

I shivered under the malevolent stare she gave me.

The woman strolled towards me and snatched a fistful of hair on top of my head, wrenching my head back. "I've had enough of you ruining my plans. Things are going to change. I've taken everything from you...and you won't even remember what you've lost."

"What?"

"I've taken your memories, Rune." She grinned at her confession. Sadistic bitch.

I knew my name was Rune, who my mother was, and that I grew up listening to her reading Harry Potter to me. There were other things, just out of reach in my mind, blurred out by fog, but I couldn't make anything out.

"What are you?" My head ached as I struggled to remember anything...even yesterday.

"You can call me 'Your Fae Majesty.'" She smiled wickedly, rather enjoying herself. Her shoulders curled forward, and I shoved to get away from her, the chair skipping over the tiled flooring in my attempt.

"Get away from me, you bitch."

I screamed for help, but she slapped me, nails digging across my cheek, tearing flesh. I cried out, the sharp pain flaring across my face, and tears streamed out from the corners of my eyes.

Her ice-cold eyes dipped to my chest, widening with

surprise, and she let go of my hair. "Now, what is that you've got there?"

I glanced down, finding myself wearing a necklace I didn't recognize. The chain partially stuck up and over the neckline of my shirt. And attached to it was a beautiful blue stone, giving off a light glow. It was spectacular. How could I not remember owning such a gorgeous necklace?

Glancing back up, the woman's eyes darkened, and her features morphed into something hideous, a scowl that made me think of a demon. Was that what she was?

She lunged at me, hands greedily snatching for the necklace.

Panicked, I screamed, doing my best to pull away from her. But in that same split second, a blast of air came out of nowhere, blowing right past me from behind, ripping at my clothes and tossing hair into my face.

The powerful wind collided into the woman with the force of a bullet train, tossing her backward. She slammed into the door so hard that it ripped off its hinges, sending it swinging outward. She then, in turn, banged into the wall out in the hallway.

I screamed, and savagely thrashed against my bindings. The world blotted in and out of darkness, until I lost the fight.

"You must hurry, the guests have already arrived at the ball," Amina said, holding my gown in her hands. *A violet dress with long sleeves, a tight corset, and flowing layers of satin.*

I huffed, exhausted from a day of riding in the countryside with my parents. "I don't want to attend the gathering tonight." Throwing myself onto the bed, I flopped onto my back. "No one will notice I'm gone anyway. Father holds these so regularly...it's the same event on repeat."

When Amina didn't respond, I craned my neck to see her

studying me with an unimpressed expression, her lips thinning. She laid my violet dress on the bed across from me.

"Shall I inform your mother then, you've chosen to spend the night in your room?"

I groaned under my breath, frustration bubbling in my chest. "Yes, fine. Go ahead." I knew the moment Amina left the room, Mama would storm to my bedroom, but I didn't want to get dressed up tonight.

Once she left, I pushed myself to my feet. Then I staggered across the room to the window and stared down where carriage after carriage lined up along the driveway to drop off important dignitaries, extended families, and other boring old people. I huffed at the sight.

Father would say his functions were to unite all the different supernatural families, to avoid division. But that didn't mean I had to attend each one.

A man I'd never seen before climbed out of a white carriage. Lean and tall, with flowing silvery hair cascading over his shoulders, he held himself proudly, completely ignoring everyone who bowed in his presence. Even from up in my room, I could see the sneer on his face, like the castle was beneath him. Why was he attending then?

No one else emerged from the carriage, but he scanned the place like he might be imprinting it onto his mind. When his gaze rose to my window, our eyes clashed, and I froze. A shiver danced down my spine with the intensity behind his pale eyes.

There was a glint behind them, and his pointy ears slipped out from behind his white hair.

Fae—he was the Fae King. Father had told me he'd be attending tonight and why the function would be important.

It had taken him a long time to gain the Fae King's acceptance to join our ball.

My skin crawled the longer he stared at me, but when the

*thundering footsteps sounded outside my room, growing louder,
I knew Mama was about to burst in here any moment in a
flurry.*

*The Fae King was still watching me when my door flew
open. I glanced at my mother.*

*"You're still not dressed?" Mama demanded from the door-
way, her voice rushing like it always did when she was stressed.*

*But I snuck another glance outside to watch the Fae King
stroll into our castle. I knew with everything in me, I didn't want
to be anywhere near that man. And for the rest of the night, a
sickening sensation rose through me each time I remembered
those pale eyes seeming to stare right through to my soul.*

I flipped open my eyes, trembling because I must have
passed out. What an insane dream.

I was still tied to the chair in the bathroom with the
door ripped off its hinges. I peered into the hallway ahead
of me at the beautiful woman slumped in the hallway. A
smear of blood streaked the wall she'd hit before she fell.
The reality that I'd been kidnapped by a crazy woman came
at me in panicked waves.

I pulled at my ties...but they didn't loosen at all.

The air felt heavy around me, and fragments of the
dream about a fae king flared over my thoughts. Nothing in
that dream had made sense. She must have hit me in the
head at some point. It was the only explanation I could
come up with.

I did the only thing I could think of—I attempted to hop
out of the room in my chair. Small jumps that at first had
me staying in the same spot. Leaning forward, I used my
body's weight and shoved myself forward on each hop. It
was working until I leaned a bit too heavily on one side.
Suddenly, the whole chair was lurching to my right.

I cried out as I fell over. Hitting the tiled floor with my

shoulder, I groaned from the pain, thankful that at least I hadn't whacked my head into the side of the ceramic toilet.

But I ended up in a worse situation. I cried out in pure frustration, shaking with anger over what that bitch had done to me. My whole body was shaking as adrenaline coursed through me.

Once I'd gotten control of my emotions again, I shoved myself closer to the doorway, thinking maybe I'd find a knife or something on my kidnapper.

Before she woke up.

Once I escaped, I would work out how to get my memories back.

The room kept spinning with me. The arm I'd fallen onto screamed with pain every time I moved. But I couldn't stop now. And I sure wouldn't be found dead, starved to death, still tied to a chair in a bathroom.

By some miracle, I shuffled awkwardly all the way to the doorway, frowning when I realized how hard it would be to get the chair through. I scanned the woman for any weapons, for something sharp I could use to cut the ties... but I couldn't see anything. I also took a quick glance up and down the hallway that led to other rooms. Nothing seemed familiar.

I turned back to the woman, and her eyes flipped open. I screamed out of pure fright, flinching backward.

She groaned, rubbing her head, then glared at me. "What did you do to me?"

"I could ask you the same question. Now let me go before I do it again!" I was completely bluffing, seeing as I had no idea what happened earlier and where the gust of wind came from.

Climbing to her feet, she groaned, her face twisting with pain as her fingers came back from her head bloody.

"You did this to me." Her hoarse words echoed through the bathroom.

"Then you better let me go," I said, hardening my voice.

"I've underestimated you, but that's fine...I can change plans and leave you here to rot."

It hit me what she meant, and terror gripped me.

On her feet, she pushed her foot against the edge of my seat and shoved me deeper back into the bathroom. "Have fun, Rune."

She flicked off the lights and slammed the door shut, the click of the lock sounding.

"Fuck you. Let me out!" I yelled, then kept on screaming, hoping someone would hear me.

I didn't know how much time had passed, or how long I remained on the bathroom floor, still tied to the chair on my side. But I was crying. My arm I leaned on had gone numb, and no amount of screaming had brought back the psycho woman. I passed in and out of consciousness, still alone every time I woke up.

Darkness swallowed me, and I might as well have been trapped in my own mind, because I couldn't see a thing.

When the door finally opened, I tensed all over, expecting the worst. Light poured through the doorway, and I blinked at the figure standing there. When I tried to talk, only a groan came out of me, my throat raspy.

My vision slowly returned with the light, and there was a man standing in front of me.

"Help," I croaked, and he came towards me. Strong arms lifted me off the floor and set the chair upright. I almost cried as the pain eased off my arm.

"I'm going to get you out, my moon." He started to cut me loose from the ties, and then I did cry, out of pure relief that I wouldn't die in that bathroom.

His voice sounded familiar, but with the bathroom still remaining dark, I couldn't see his face properly. "Do I know you?"

"I sure hope so, since I'm your fated mate," he murmured, wrapping me in his powerful arms and carrying me out of the room. "We need to go before she returns."

Fated mate? There was a memory there, but it felt out of reach...just like all the others. "How did you get past the crazy fae woman?"

"I snuck in when she left," he answered as sunlight poured over my savior's face, and I lost my breath.

He was incredibly beautiful, with messy hair around his face that added to his rugged appearance. Smooth olive skin, and something forbidden flashing across his dark eyes.

I couldn't look away, couldn't do anything but stare at him...inhale his features. I had the crazy urge to reach out and trace my fingers over his sexy lips, to close the distance between us, and bite down on those lips. I had no idea where those thoughts came from, but this man was crazily handsome. Heat flushed over my skin as his entire presence swallowed all my attention. Those broad shoulders, sculpted chest, corded muscles on the curve of his neck and shoulders.

He must be aware of the effect he had on me by the way his smile curled upward.

The longer I stared at him, the more snippets of my memory slipped forward, and I suddenly remembered him.

"Alistair?" His name streamed from my lips, memories of the party where I'd last seen him pouring through my mind. I barely knew him, but I did recall his kindness to me, the way he grinned at me like only I existed.

"What are you doing here? How'd you find me?" I

breathed, awe in my chest that he'd come to rescue me. Who did that? Heroes? White knights? Rich millionaires in romance movies?

"Hush now." He placed me on my feet, cupping my face, studying me like he was searching for injuries.

I kept blinking at him, trying to shake off that surreal feeling. I reached for his face. My fingers tenderly ran over his cheek. "Thank you for coming for me. Now, please take me with you. Don't leave me here, please." My fingers curled around his, a faint flutter of fear in my chest that she'd return any moment and find us both.

Alistair didn't say another word, but he took my hand in his. We moved quickly through the house, emerging in a front yard with an overgrown lawn, weeds, and a once white-picket fence rotten and half fallen over.

There was a second when Alistair stilled and turned his head towards me, staring at me like he was going to say something, like a million thoughts whirled behind his gaze.

"Is something wrong?" I asked, grasping onto his hand, grateful beyond words that he'd been the one to come rescue me. Maybe he'd also be able to help me gain my memories back.

"Do you believe in second chances?" he asked.

I shrugged because I'd never given such things any thought. "I guess."

He smiled, then we were off again and he rushed me into a black SUV parked out front of the property. He scooped me onto the passenger's seat, then he jumped into the driver's side and we were racing down the road. I glanced at the house I didn't recognize, at the surrounding suburb that I couldn't recall.

But the man sitting across from me, who'd come to my

rescue...I remembered something about him. Enough to give me confidence that he'd help me.

When he glanced over at me, our gazes clashed and he smiled. "I'll take such good care of you, little moon. You'll see."

There were a myriad of emotions flicking through me. But with those emotions, something new rose as well...an unease deep in my gut that something wasn't quite right.

But for the life of me, I couldn't work out what that was.

CHAPTER 5
WILDER

I dragged myself out of sleep to find I was alone in the woods. No sign of Rune, Daxon, or Ares.

Groaning, I ran a hand through my hair to tame it. Rolling my shoulders, I smacked my lips, wondering if there was any food around. If not, I'd make sure we headed off into the nearest town and find somewhere to shower and grab a hot meal.

I turned on the spot, not seeing any sign of anyone. When I glanced out towards the dirt pathway, the carriage still sat there, the horses grazing on the grass. Okay, so Rune must still be near.

Making my way toward the sound of running water, I hoped to find everyone down there, preferably Rune taking a skinny dip.

I barely made it a few steps out of camp when Daxon appeared from deeper in the woods, rushing toward me like a madman, his eyes wild, hair messed up. He looked fucking terrified, and that ominous feeling I hated slithered over my spine.

What the hell happened now?

I sped up to meet him, words pouring from my mouth like lava. "Tell me Rune is with you?"

"She's not. And I can't find her or Ares. He took her. That fucking belly-slithering demon stole her from us again." Daxon heaved for breath, pacing in a circle like a caged wolf, the air around us electric. "Fuck. Fuck." He was whacking the palm of his hand to the side of his head. "How could we be so stupid?"

"He wouldn't," I said slowly. I'd felt like Ares had told us the truth yesterday. Was I a fool to have believed the bloodsucker?

"Are you a fucking idiot?" Daxon snapped. "Of course he did."

"Calm down," I growled, my head spinning, my heart thumping with terror as I tried to figure out what to do first.

Fear for Rune rippled through my chest, shattering my thoughts. Panic wound me tight, and I fought the urge to lose my shit like Daxon was clearly doing.

"If he wanted to take her, why here? Why now? Why the fuck did he wait? What if she'd gone for a walk in the woods? What if the bear shifters took her?"

Daxon's face scrunched at my ideas. "Nope. Ares waited for the perfect moment, Wilder," he yelled. "Use your fucking brain. He's stolen her from us before. And look around you...we're in his stomping grounds...he would know where to hide her."

He paced faster now, in a circle, murmuring, "I can't sense her. Why can't I sense her?"

"Could she be too far out of reach?" But even as the words spilled from my mouth, I knew they were wrong. Once you mark someone with a mating bond, the connection was strong enough to call to one another from almost any distance.

He was shaking his head, clutching at his chest like he was about to go into cardiac arrest. "I can't feel her. Does that mean–"

"Don't fucking say it. She's alive and we'll find her. Your mark is fresh and might need more time to strengthen."

"Fuck!" Daxon bellowed, dropping to his knees, and I swallowed hard because I'd never seen him so defeated. Shoulders curled forward, spine bowed, he was in agony. His whimpers were cruel sounds of grief, bringing with them a reminder of what I didn't have with Rune.

Something savage rose through me...My wolf demanded release to scour the whole damn forest until we found her. That was going to take some getting used to...the fact that my wolf could evidently come out without the full moon after whatever Rune had done to me.

"We search for them in the woods, pick up her scent, any fucking thing it takes."

I kept wondering if Ares had taken her...was everything he'd said a ploy to trick us?

A sudden crunch of foliage drew my attention, and I spun around. Speak of the devil, Ares was strolling towards us like the world was at his feet, his smile huge, his gaze scanning the campground.

"Where's my little dove?" he asked casually. "I have a gift for her." He produced a bunch of wildflowers in his hand from around his back.

I was going to be fucking sick.

A growl thundered behind me, and a sudden gust of air buffeted into me as Daxon lunged himself at Ares.

"You fucking bastard." Daxon slammed into Ares,

taking him completely off guard, the flowers ripped out of his grasp.

The pair hit the ground, tumbling so fast, they knocked into a tree. Daxon wound up on top of Ares, slamming fist after fist into his face.

"Daxon!" I bolted to his side, then threw an arm around his throat and wrenched him off Ares. "Fuck, we need him conscious to find Rune."

Daxon shoved an elbow into my gut and ripped out of my grip. He swung toward me, throwing his palms against my chest. "What the fuck do you think I was doing?"

Anger lashed across my chest, and I shoved him back, fury burning through me.

"Lover's squabble?" Ares asked, not appearing perturbed one bit. "Now use your words, wolf boy, and tell me where the hell Rune is before I kill you both."

I swung toward him, snatching him by the throat, my panic taking over. "You took her, didn't you?"

Ares shoved me off him with ease. "Rune's missing? Why the fuck didn't anyone tell me?"

And in a split second, he darted out of the campsite, leaving behind just a wisp of his shadow.

"Where'd he go?" Daxon's brow narrowed, a nerve twitching at the corner of his eye.

"He's gone to find her I'm guessing." I didn't even bother explaining that we should do the same.

Darkness rose within me, sinking its fangs deep. The urge to give into the panic, to lose my head was strong. But that wouldn't help me find Rune.

I threw myself into the woods, rushing to find the bears and discover if they took her, if she went to them, or if they knew anything.

My desperation burst forward, clenching my throat,

forcing me to run faster because I was certain Rune's life depended on it.

DAXON

Madness swallowed me.

I couldn't stand being in my own skin as it stretched over me while my insides were on fire. *Rune, where are you?*

My heart pounded like it was trying to break my ribs, and I couldn't breathe, couldn't think, except for Rune. Heartache ripped across my chest, striking me like the crack of a whip. My wolf whined for her, shoving against me to come out.

Her absence stole the colors from the air, shredded me to pieces. I couldn't bear a life without her.

Tearing my clothes off, I called to my wolf. He poured out of me with urgency, tearing skin, snapping bones. His growl darkened, turning into something primal and feral.

Rune. I'm coming for you.

I lunged into the woods even as fur still sprouted over my body. My heart felt like shards of glass, bleeding me to death from the inside out.

I didn't get far when I inhaled her scent, and I paused, drawing in a lungful of her sweet honey smell. It was faint, but it flooded me with hope that I'd find her. I jerked my head up to scour the woodland and the shadows that clung to them.

Frantically following my nose, my nostrils flared with each inhale, her scent hard to pinpoint, but I found it once more down by the river's edge.

Desperately, I darted up and down the river, but each time, her scent faded. She hadn't gone that way, and the same happened when I splashed across the water to the other side.

Retreating to the way I'd come, I decided she hadn't taken another path but stayed around camp.

Rune, where are you?

I turned inward once more, reaching deep down for that low hum that came from our bond, and felt nothing.

Only silence and devastation.

I sniffed the air once more and kept going in circles. I couldn't smell her anymore. It was as if she'd disappeared into thin air.

My world crumbled, collapsing in on itself, and for the first time, I didn't know where to turn. I'd always found a way to deal with any situation. I attacked it with brute force. I tore it to fucking pieces. But what was I supposed to do if I couldn't find her?

I drew in the bitter, morning air, coldness seeping into my bones. A deep guttural howl wrenched from my throat, and determination to find her filled me. I trembled with fury, because once I found out who took my Rune, he'd to be sorry he was ever born.

I would tear apart the whole fucking world to find her. My rage erupted, and I hurled myself into the woods, about to obliterate everything that stood in my way.

ARES

I couldn't remember how long I'd been scouring the woods for Rune.

And still no sign of her.

Something was wrong with me. I realized I couldn't exist without Rune. She consumed every inch of me. I hated myself for leaving the camp this morning to take a walk. I should have stayed by her side.

With not one clue on where she'd gone, with Wilder and Daxon also madly racing through the woods, I came to the conclusion that I had one possible ace up my sleeve.

Standing in an empty part of the woods, I fell to my knees, my fingers extending into claws. I frantically started digging at the earth. Soil flew in every direction as I desperately scooped out handfuls.

In my mind, I was drowning, and flashes of Rune kept popping across my mind. It was pure torture to remember her smile, to remember the sound of her laugh. What I felt for her was an all-consuming obsession.

I couldn't hide from the overwhelming feelings I'd developed. The little wolf girl was so much more than I'd expected. I ached for her, my body ached for her...my dead heart needed her.

Doubt crept in that I'd ever find her, and with it...came terror. I shook my head. I couldn't think like that. Not now, not fucking ever.

I kept digging like a madman while the pain of not having found Rune sifted through me like venom in my veins.

"What the fuck are you doing?" Wilder spit from behind me.

I raised my head at his words, his gaze narrowing on the grave I was digging. He was staring at me like I'd lost my mind.

"You can waste your time standing there...or you can help me. I need to find a way to connect with Rune, and since I draw my strength and healing from the earth, it might help me reach out to her."

Wilder grunted, but instead of being a smug asshole, he threw himself down on his knees next to me.

"How deep are we going?" he asked, his arms partially transforming into that of a wolf's, a nifty new party trick that Rune had somehow given him with her powers.

"Enough for me to be buried completely."

Wilder didn't even hesitate. He started digging madly, both of us burrowing deeper.

"The bears haven't seen her since last night. They're searching the woods too. Daxon lost his shit and vanished somewhere in the mountains. For all I know, he could have made his way into the city, burning it down. For once, I don't care to stop him if it helps us find Rune."

I ground my jaw every time I thought of Rune in danger. "Who would have taken her?"

Wilder wasn't faring any better, his heavy breaths sawing in and out of him like a beast. "If we were back home, she had her enemies, but we're in fucking Romania, as far from our town as possible. Aside from the bear shifters, no one else even knew we were here."

I muttered an expletive under my breath, digging manically. "Fuck, just keep digging, and let's hope I pick up something."

Wilder growled, heaving for breath as he worked manically. "She really does mean a lot to you, doesn't she?"

I paused at his question, thinking it didn't come close to covering how I felt about her.

"I'd die before I lost her. I know it's not what you want to hear, but whether I intended it or not, I've lost my heart to her."

Wilder didn't respond, and when I glanced over, his lips were thin, his face pained.

"I don't mind sharing," I offered him, which only gained me a grunting sound.

"Just fucking dig and find Rune. We don't need to get emotional," he finally snapped, ever the moody bastard.

And that was exactly what we did, furiously making me a fresh grave. Once it was complete, Wilder drew back, kneeling alongside the piles of soil.

"Well, here goes nothing." I hopped into the grave that came up to my thighs and lay on my back. It was shallower than I liked it when I healed in the earth, but it should work. "Cover me up."

Wilder started pushing the soil over my body with his bare hands, its weight growing heavier.

"You finally did it," Daxon barked, emerging from the dark woods around us. "You killed the fucker. About damn time."

Sticking my head up, I gave him a deadpan glare, then murmured, "In your wet dreams."

"Fucking asshole." Daxon swung his attention to Wilder. "What exactly are the two of you doing?"

"Shut up and come help me," Wilder muttered as he shoved a pile right over my face, seeming to enjoy himself, just as he rattled off what I'd told him about me trying to find Rune.

With more soil heaped on top of me, I soon felt something heavy stomping over the top of me. Daxon's voice streamed down, "Got to get it nice and compact, asshole."

Blastard furball. I took his weight, then heard the arguing murmurs of him and Wilder. I tried to block them out, and I laid there, my fingers wriggling in the soil, my mind focused on feeling Rune.

My skin buzzed like it always did when I slept underground, and I remembered the taste of Rune's blood on my tongue. Sweet coppery flavor, with a hint of spice, and a slice of magic.

I reached through the soil, sending my feelers outward for her.

A familiar darkness, one of death, rose over my legs, my waist, my chest. It fed me, but that wasn't what I sought. The arguing grew louder above me and I focused harder, searching for my Rune with everything I had, desperate to pick up on her power.

Where are you, little dove?

Concentrating, I kept reaching and reaching out for her, but I kept coming back with nothing. Not a single drop of her energy.

And no matter how long I stayed underground, it didn't change the situation.

I was left empty, like someone had scooped the dead heart out of my chest.

I was broken.

Shattered.

A groan rumbled over my throat, and anger laced my thoughts. *Where had she gone?*

Having had enough, I shoved my way up through the soil, breaking the surface with a fist. I dragged myself out, all under Daxon's and Wilder's wistful stares.

"Anything?" they asked eagerly.

"She's not in the forest, that's all I can tell."

"Fuck this, fuck everything." Daxon muttered, before turning and punching a tree with a snarl.

Up on my feet, I dusted myself off. Wilder was still watching me, his jaw clenched.

"Someone's going to hurt her, and I can't let that happen." The words slipped from his mouth angrily, his face twisted with a savage heartache. "Daxon, get your shit together. We're going to tear up the damn country until we find her. We've got to go now!" Wilder glanced at me. "Are you joining us, or doing this on your own?"

"I'm with you."

The three of us took off, all while a sickness churned through me that I couldn't sense Rune. I should have picked up a clue, something...but nothing...that left me terrified.

And I was an immortal, I didn't fear.

My stomach twisted in on itself, and acid scraped the back of my throat.

All I could think...

How could she have just vanished without a trace?

CHAPTER 6
RUNE

The bed I woke up in wasn't familiar. Neither was the sunlit view of the outside streaming through the window to my left.

I sat up, bleary-eyed, staring around the unfamiliar room. It was lavish; the sheets bunched at my waist were made of silk, and there were fine rugs all over the gleaming wooden floor. The end tables next to the bed were marble and the light hanging above me was a chandelier. I tried to rack my memory for where I could be. I remembered going to the ceremony to meet Alistair, my fated mate...but everything was a blur after that. Did I drink too much? I could only remember a few sips of champagne because I'd been so nervous. So that idea didn't feel right.

My eyes widened as I remembered the beautiful woman who'd kept me prisoner. She called herself a queen? And then Alistair...he'd appeared in the doorway while she left the house. He'd saved me.

Warmth flooded my heart at the idea he was already so caring towards me when I'd just met him, but why did that idea feel so wrong as well?

Just then, there was a knock on the door, and I stiffened, dread flicking through my insides. After taking Alistair's hand, everything had gone blank again. I didn't understand why there were so many glitches in my memory.

"Sweetheart, it's me," Alistair said gently through the door.

I glanced down at what I was wearing, grimacing when I saw the unfamiliar silk nightgown I'd somehow ended up in...that showed way too much of my body. I glanced around the room for a robe, but I couldn't find anything.

Okay, he was my mate...this wouldn't be a big deal. I anxiously tugged at my hair, trying to smooth it down.

"Come in," I responded finally. I winced at the squeak in my voice.

The door opened and Alistair's handsome face peeked in. He shot me a bright smile. "There's my gorgeous girl," he purred.

I smiled back hesitantly.

"How are you feeling?" he asked, concerned.

"Offkilter. Confused. I—can't remember anything."

His eyes brightened for a moment, like he was excited about that. But then he quickly shuttered his emotions and his features sombered.

"We had just met at the party when the fae invaded and stole you away. I've been searching for you for over a year."

I reared back, pulling the sheet up to my chin, nausea building up inside of me.

"A year?" I gasped. "But all I remember is a day." I squeezed my eyes shut, trying to remember...anything. But every time I tried, sharp pain would snarl at my brain.

"How did I lose a year of my life?" I whispered hollowly.

Alistair approached and tentatively sat on the edge of the bed. I tried not to flinch away from him, not understanding why I was feeling like this. I guess it was probably because I'd fucking lost my memory. I'm sure the elation I'd felt when I first saw him would hit me again. I studied his face, noting the exquisite beauty of his features. I just needed to get to know him. I mean, here he was, my knight in shining armor, having risked his life to get me back.

Those feelings would come again.

Right?

I turned away and stared blankly at the wall, a flood of emotions threatening to drown me.

"I'm so sorry this happened, Rune," he murmured to me sympathetically, reaching out and pulling my still-clenched hand away from my chin and the sheet it was holding.

I reluctantly turned back to him, wishing I was alone... and I jumped when I saw the heat in his gaze as he greedily raked his eyes over my skimpy nightgown.

It felt inappropriate from a stranger...but, we were more than just strangers, weren't we...

I guess I was going to have to get used to that. He was... my mate after all. Why did the idea of him touching me make me sick? I could distinctly remember how attracted and excited I'd been when I'd seen him that night.

"The Fae Queen has magic, I'm sure that has something to do with your time with her blurring together," he soothed, answering the question I'd forgotten I'd asked. "It's probably for the best that you don't remember, darling. I can't even comprehend the horrors you've been through." His hand went up to gently stroke my cheek, and again my insides were screaming about the wrongness of his touch. I recognized him inside me as my fated mate, so why did I feel like this?

I needed...some space. But how did you ask for space

from someone who had just saved your life after searching for you for over a year?

My mother. Her face flared through my thoughts, and I winced, because I should've thought about her the second I'd opened my eyes. She would've gone mad losing me for a year.

"Have you told my mother of my return yet?" I asked anxiously. "When can I see her? Is she here already?" I peered through the open door like she was going to appear at any moment.

There was a long silence, and my attention snapped back to Alistair...because I could feel the tension that had suddenly crept into the room.

"Alistair?" I asked, my voice trembling. "Where's my mother?"

"Rune, I'm so sorry. I was hoping I could tell you this when...fuck, I don't know when. I don't know what I was thinking–of course you would want to speak with your mother right away. I'm so sorry, Rune..." he repeated. "But she's passed away."

A brittle sob slipped from my lips as I stared at him incredulously. There was no way. She was going to appear in that doorway at any moment. There were no other options.

"Why would you say that? My mom's young, she has years and years left."

His hand gripped mine and I saw only truth in his gaze. "She got sick with something...maybe it was a curse from the fae queen when she grabbed you. But her wolf powers never took over and there was nothing our doctors could do."

My hands went to my face and I sobbed into them, my cries bordering on hysterics.

I was faintly aware of him rubbing my back and murmuring soft words that I couldn't make out through my tears.

"She's buried nearby. I'll take you to her grave as soon as you're feeling up to it."

I nodded numbly and lifted my face, one of my hands brushing the necklace hanging down between my breasts. I squeezed it and then froze when I remembered I had no idea where the necklace was from...and also remembering what had happened when the queen had tried to grab it. I picked it up, staring at the stone closely.

"What is it, darling?"

I hated how the word "darling" grated on my ears.

"Nothing," I murmured. "Just trying to work through everything."

I didn't know why I was lying to my fated mate, and I really didn't have any idea why I would have a necklace with magical powers. But for some reason, I didn't want to tell him about it.

"Can I use the restroom and take a shower?" I whispered, feeling more drained than I could ever remember feeling before.

"Of course, Rune. This is your home now. Whatever you need, I can get you." I shot him a sad smile and let him help me off the bed, his gaze still racing over my bare skin in a way that made it crawl.

He led me towards a closed door on the far side of the room, and my eyes widened at the opulence of the bathroom behind it. Everything was black marble and shiny silver fixtures. I could feel under my bare feet that the floors were heated. There was an enormous bathtub to the left, and the shower in front of it could fit five people. There were two large sinks, and I realized there was an array of dark bottles by one of them. I glanced over at Alistair and found him watching me intently. Panic bounced around my gut, and I pushed it down.

"Is this...your bathroom?" I asked, praying his answer would be no.

"Of course, my mate wouldn't sleep anywhere but my bedroom," he responded as if any other idea was preposterous.

I wanted to cry at his pronouncement, but I held it in, sensing he wouldn't be happy about that. Instead, I forced a smile, my head beginning to ache as I kept trying to find any pieces of my past year.

"Of course," I murmured. "I'll just take a shower now... or maybe a bath." I glanced over at the tub, thinking that might soothe my spiraling emotions better than a shower would.

"Take as long as you need, my moon. And when you're done, I'll have breakfast for you." He pushed a tendril of hair out of my face and gave me another winning smile.

And I felt nothing.

I waited until the door closed and his footsteps had faded away before I locked it, not wanting him to walk in while I was unclothed. I turned on the bath, changing the temperature until it was so hot it would scald my skin.

I slipped off my nightgown, not wanting to think about how I'd gotten it on in the first place, and then I gingerly stepped into the boiling hot bath.

I sighed as I sank into it, wanting to stay there forever and escape from everything.

"Rune," a voice jolted me from my daze, water splashing over the sides of the tub.

I gazed around the room, expecting someone to pop out

from the closet or the toilet or the bedroom...but there was no one there.

Obviously, the stress was making me break.

I settled back into the water, deciding I'd just imagined the voice...or something. Steam rose up from the water, coating my face with moisture. The burn felt good on my skin, centering me from the chaos of my thoughts. A sob slipped from my throat as I once again thought of the reality that my mother was gone. I squeezed my eyes closed, wishing I could open them back up and it would all just be a dream. She would have wanted me to be strong. I knew that. But the fact that she'd been underground for almost a year was gut-wrenching.

"Rune!" My eyes ricocheted open and I once again stared around the room. The voice was so loud...so real.

Like it was being spoken in my head.

The Queen had probably tortured me while I'd been gone...and I'd cracked. That had to be it.

But why had the voice sounded so upset?

And why had I felt the urge to make the owner of the voice feel better?

Evidently, the bath wasn't the answer. I grabbed some shampoo and conditioner and methodically washed my hair before grabbing the washcloth I'd pulled from a cabinet and cleaning my body.

I only felt slightly better as I pulled the plug on the water and got out, wrapping myself with a fluffy towel that had been warming on a heating rack. I thought of the simple way my mother and I had lived. It was like I'd stepped into a whole new world.

And the crazy thing was, I desperately wished I could have the old one back.

Pulling the towel tightly around my body, I walked into

the closet, thinking I could at least grab one of Alistair's shirts and maybe tie some drawstring pants tight enough to stay up, but I was shocked when I saw that one whole side of the closet was filled with designer women's clothing. Everything looked to be pieces that showed a lot of skin, not something I was used to wearing.

I found a dress that would probably cover at least some of my chest, and then I grabbed some underwear and a bra, somehow in my perfect size. That was kind of unnerving. Had I had a discussion that night with a member of his staff about my sizes? Everything in the closet was new with tags and perfectly my size, so I assumed they hadn't been bought for another woman.

Why did the thought of another woman not make me as upset as it should have?

I groaned, wanting to dive back under the covers and forget today had ever happened. Although evidently, today was much better than the life I had been living over the past year.

Once I was dressed, and I'd found a comb to run through my hair, I tentatively walked out into the hallway, wishing something looked familiar to me. Had he given me a tour the night of the party, or had I seen him, realized he was my mate, and that was the last thing that happened before the Fae Queen had invaded the party?

My wolf growled inside of me, clearly as upset as I was, but at least she was there. She'd been quiet up until now.

It was quiet, alarmingly so. And every footstep I took echoed down the hallway. The place was like a maze, and I took several wrong turns, ending up in a broom closet at one point. Finally, I turned a corner and heard the low din of voices.

Except, I had no idea what door they were coming from.

"What took you so long?" Alistair's voice came from my left. I jumped, almost tripping on a chair behind me.

His features were tense, suspicion in his gaze. What did he think I'd been doing?

"I—I finished my bath and then it took a while to find you. This place is huge. I didn't know I would need directions," I tried and failed to joke.

The fierce snarl on his face faded, something like relief in the depths of his gaze.

Maybe he'd been worried I'd been kidnapped again?

"Right. I'm sorry, I had a phone call I had to get to, and when I went to the room to find you, you weren't there. I just panicked."

Hmm. It hadn't looked like panic, but maybe I was just seeing things. Maybe that was how he panicked. It's not like I would know since we didn't know each other at all.

"I'm sorry," I offered.

"Nothing to apologize for," he murmured, taking my hand and brushing a kiss across my skin.

Goosebumps skittered up my arm...but they weren't the good kind. It was all I could do not to flinch.

"Ready to eat?" he asked, obviously missing my unease.

"Rune!" the mysterious voice called again, and I barked out a surprised yelp.

"Darling?"

"A weird cramp in my leg," I explained quickly.

He seemed to take that as the truth and held out his arm for me to hold.

My wolf growled the moment I slid my arm through his. What the crap was going on?

I knew this man was my fated mate. I remembered the feeling I'd had as clearly as if it had happened today...so what had changed?

Alistair led me two doors down, where a lavish dining room lay. There was no one in the room, meaning I still didn't know where the voices had come from that I'd heard in the hallway. A table that could hold at least twenty people took up the majority of the room, but there were just two place settings.

The feel of it was awkward...and stilted. Like everything with Alistair had been thus far. He pulled out my seat for me and I slid in, staring down at the myriad of forks and knives lying on the table in front of me.

I guess at least if I was going to embarrass myself by not knowing which fork was which...it was in front of my mate and not a room full of people.

There was an entryway across from the door we'd entered through, and a woman dressed in a stiff white apron and brown cotton dress bustled through it carrying a bottle of wine in a small silver cooler, and two wine glasses.

I was carrying a tray with wine and glasses. One of Alistair's men put out his foot in front of me as I passed, and I tripped and dropped the tray. Glass and wine went everywhere.

"You stupid little bitch. Clean it up!" Alistair snarled, his hand whipping across my cheek and sending me flying to the ground.

"What is it?" Alistair asked, his face a picture of concern.

I was clammy, my hands shaking as I grasped at the napkin on the table in front of me.

"I was walking, carrying a tray...and I dropped it." I searched his face for any sign of recollection, but he just looked confused. "One of your men tripped me, and afterwards...you hit me."

He gasped. "I would never," he breathed, reaching out

to try and take my hand. I moved them both into my lap, out of his reach, still trying to read him.

You would have to be a psychopath to be that good of an actor, I thought to myself. There was nothing in his gaze... in his features at all, to show any sign he'd done what had just flashed through my head.

"Rune," he began, his voice hurt. "I talked to the doctors, and they said your memory might never be right after what the Queen did to you."

"What do you think she did to me?" I interrupted him. "Because I have no bruises on my body, and I don't look like I haven't been eating. So what happened?"

"You've been in a comatose state for three weeks, Rune."

I gasped and almost fell out of my chair. "What?"

He shook his head. "I didn't want to scare you, but the way we found you..." He stared off at the wall. "I don't know that I'll ever recover from that," he said hollowly.

At that moment, more of the staff came in with trays loaded down with food. They set down platters of roasted chicken, mashed potatoes and gravy, dressing, and roasted carrots. I should have been over the moon about the food, but it felt like my brain was broken. I couldn't trust myself. I'd lost so much time. What if I lost more time? What if my memory continued to struggle? Is this how I would have to live from now on?

Alistair began to spoon food onto my plate, acting like the perfectly attentive mate. He prodded me to eat, and once I mechanically began to pick at it, he proceeded to talk about various things, filling the silence I was giving him.

I finished off my whole plate, forcing myself to eat since it felt like I needed to keep up my strength the best I could.

When we were finished, the staff came and cleared off

the table before setting down plates of carrot cake with cream cheese frosting.

"Take a bite, darling. It's your favorite," he murmured gently, as I heard my name called again in my head.

That voice. Why did it sound like home? Was this place really my home?

I was falling apart. That was clear.

Alistair ignored the tears streaming down my face as I ate pieces of the cake until finally I could do no more and pushed it away from me.

"Let's get you some more rest," he said gently, and I nodded, trying to wipe away the tears. He didn't seem bothered by them. I guess it could be expected after what I'd been through. I could only hope that eventually I became comfortable enough to not feel like I'd done some-thing wrong every time I cried.

He once again took my arm and led me back towards the bedroom. I tried to take note of where he was taking me this time. Maybe he could get me a map or something.

We made it to the bedroom and Alistair released my arm. I stood there awkwardly, realizing what was ahead.

"I'm going to change," he murmured casually, like this wasn't a big freaking deal.

He slowly lifted up his shirt, showcasing a set of abs that should have had me drooling.

But I felt nothing. Again.

I knew objectively he was good-looking, but it was like staring at a piece of artwork at a museum. I could admit it was pretty, but it didn't spark any heat inside me.

I must not have given him the reaction he was looking for, because he stalked towards the bathroom and disap-peared before giving me the rest of the show. A few minutes later he came out, dressed in a low-slung pair of pajama pants and nothing else. I kept my eyes on the ground as I brushed past him to get ready for bed.

Unfortunately...there was nothing in the closet to wear to bed except for scraps of nightgowns that amounted to lingerie. So I grabbed one of his t-shirts and a pair of his boxers, figuring that would make him happy, and give me an easy excuse to explain why I wasn't wearing the nightgowns he'd provided me.

I washed my face and stared in dismay at my reflection. Again.

How long would I look haunted?

Taking a deep breath, I dragged myself from the sink and walked out of the bathroom, trying to appear confident.

Alistair was already in bed, his nightstand lamp on, a book in his hand.

I strode towards the bed, wishing with every step that we were sleeping in separate rooms.

Just until I adjusted...however long that would take.

I slid into the bed, situating myself as far from him as I could without it being completely obvious. Pulling the covers up to my chin, I settled into the pillow. His scent was all over the sheets, and I wondered how it could smell so wrong. What I knew about fated mates said that everything about them was supposed to attract you. The look of them, the scent of them, the sound of their voice... Right now we were zero for three. But surely that would change?

I glanced over at what he was reading, my eyebrows lifting when I saw it was *The Art of War*. Interesting bedtime reading.

I was exhausted, even though I'd been apparently sleeping for what amounted to forever. But it was going to be hard to sleep with a stranger in the bed.

He glanced over at me. "The bed comfortable enough?" he asked kindly.

I nodded and tried to give him a real smile.

"Tell me what the last year's been like for you?" I asked, shocking myself because I'd just blurted it out.

Alistair froze, thinking for a long moment before closing the book and setting it on the table next to him.

He turned off the light and settled into the bed.

"Awful," he finally said, but the way he said it came across as more of a snarl than anything else. Like he was furious. "When something that belongs to you gets taken away like that, something that's the most important thing to you, it's hard to see past the rage."

I could feel the rage in his words, the meaning in their depths...but something still felt off about it. Even if I couldn't remember my time with the Fae Queen, the distrust I had built up in that situation was leaking through my consciousness.

"But I have everything back now," he whispered, almost to himself. "And I don't intend to ever lose it again." A shiver trickled down my spine at the way he'd said that. I felt like property rather than a cherished mate, but surely I was reading into that wrong.

"Go to sleep, my moon. Everything is going to be different now," he murmured. Alistair promptly rolled over without another word, and within just a few minutes his breathing turned into soft, steady snores...as if he didn't have a care in the world now that his mate was back.

And still I laid wide awake, racking my brain to try and figure out and remember...anything. Anything at all. Eventually, I fell into a fitful sleep...and when I did, I dreamed...

His lips closed over mine, the kiss quickly turning from sweet to more... I melted against him, wanting to get as close as I could while he devoured my mouth, his hunger desperate and echoed in my response.

The way he kissed.

It was what I'd always wanted, what I'd always needed. Every caress of his tongue spoke to his need for me, the possessiveness he would always have for me. I was soaking wet, and as his hands glided across my hips and thighs, I only got wetter. My moans were swallowed in his mouth as his tongue dominated mine.

"Every day I think about this," he purred. "Bending you over, pushing my cock into you. Making you come..."

"Yes, I want that," I breathed in between our decadent kisses. He pushed my skirt up my hips and pulled away from me, admiring every inch of my body.

"All of this is mine."

"Yes," I whispered.

"Say it," he demanded, his dark hair falling in his face and his emerald green eyes staring straight into my soul.

"Yes I'm yours."

He unbuckled his jeans slowly before sliding down the zipper and revealing his hard length. He slid his thick, steely length through my folds, the slide of it easy with how wet I was. He made quick work of the rest of my clothes as he continued his torturous movements, until I was completely bare except for the skirt bunched around my waist. I shivered as his hands closed around my breasts, cupping and massaging them as he stared down at me with a look of wonder.

His tongue licked his full lower lip. And I sighed.

"I'm going to take such good care of you, sweet girl," he murmured, his gaze feverish and wanting. His hands ran all over me as he leaned forward and suckled my nipple. His finger slid through my folds and I moaned as he gently caressed my pussy.

"You're going to marry me," he said, no question in his voice.

His gaze hardened as he moved away from my breast and grabbed my ass with both hands. I automatically wrapped my legs around him, the move as easy as breathing at this point, and I reached up to put both arms around his neck.

"Kiss me," I pleaded as his gaze roamed my face.

"Marry me then," he repeated. But he gave me what I wanted, bringing his face close to mine so I could feel his warm breath on my lips before he gave me a heart-stopping kiss.

"I love you. I want this. Forever. I don't want to lose you..."

He held onto me tighter, so tight his fingertips would probably leave bruises. But I was fine with the desperation laced through his emotions.

"But what about..." I asked, my gaze flicking away from his, because I wasn't sure if the guilt would ever go away, the guilt that although I loved him with every ounce of my heart, my soul demanded Daxon as well.

"Whatever you want. Whatever will make you happy. Then I want that."

His kiss turned fierce, stealing my breath as he suddenly reared back and slammed his cock into me.

His kiss caught my cry as he buried his length deeper.

His muscles quivered under my touch and when his lips moved away from mine, my breath was ragged and choked.

"Sorry, baby," he whispered. "The way you make me feel. What you make me want...it's hard to control myself."

I understood that. I struggled as well. The depths of what I felt for them. I stroked my fingers through his hair soothingly as I dug my heels into his ass, urging him to start moving.

I panted as he slid his cock in and out of me.

"You feel so good...so perfect."

His hips sped up, and the rhythm of it had me practically sobbing.

Our eyes were locked, and the smile on his beautiful face was just as potent as his dick moving in and out of me. His hand moved to my throat, closing over it just enough so I could feel his possession.

"Someday, you're going to marry me. Someday, you're going to accept my bite. Mine. Forever." Every word was punctuated with his sharp thrusts, and I was writhing underneath him.

I loved what he was saying, his words were arousing me just as much as his body. His every thrust seemed to go deeper, until it felt like he was battering against the entrance of my womb.

Images of him holding our baby flashed through my head, and I came...hard. I never thought I would be ready to be a mother with what I'd been through, but I wanted it all with them. I wanted to marry them, be their mate, be the mother of their children...

I threw my head back as one orgasm led into another.

"Yeah, so fucking good." He buried his face into my neck, and his body shivered as he came, the warm wetness of him spreading through my core.

"Love you, baby," he said again with a soft kiss.

I woke to the pressure of Alistair's heavy body on top of me, his lips pressed against mine. His hands were stroking my skin, grabbing at my breasts. I could feel his length pressing against my core through our clothes.

"Fuck, you're hot," he breathed. I was frozen for a minute before I frantically pushed at his chest.

"Get off. Get off," I cried. My core was aching, but everything inside me blanched at the idea of *him* being the one to fill it and give it what it wanted. My chest was heaving, and sweat slicked on my skin.

Alistair stiffened for a moment, like he was warring with the lust pulsing through his body.

He finally slid off of me as tears fell down my face. I had

no idea what just happened. I tried to catch on to snippets of my dream, but they all faded away before I could hold onto them.

"Rune? I'm so sorry," Alistair huffed, not actually sounding that apologetic at all. I wiped my face and glanced over at him to see what he looked like. His gaze was on fire, his grip tight against his raging hard-on through his pajama pants. "You were making the sexiest noises I'd ever heard. I guess my body just responded to you. I'm sure we're trained as mates to innately have that reaction when we see our mate aroused."

His tone was accusatory by the end of his sentence. Like I'd done something wrong, and it was perfectly normal for him to be on top of me like that.

Which, hell, probably it was.

"What were you dreaming about?" he pressed, his face frustrated as he continued to hold his dick as he stared up at the ceiling.

"I don't remember," I said sheepishly, telling the truth... for the most part. Because as he rolled out of bed, "to take care of his erection," I knew one thing for certain...my dream...

It hadn't been about him.

———

Alistair was gone when I woke up, and I was glad of that.

I lay there for a moment, staring outside, hoping that not every night was going to be that eventful. I finally dragged myself out of bed, determined to be a better mate that day.

After taking a quick shower, I threw on a pair of shorts and another one of Alistair's t-shirts. It drowned me, but it at least covered more of my skin than the tank tops hanging up in the closet. I found my way to the dining area much quicker this time, but the room was empty except for platters and plates filled with various muffins, bagels, fruit, and bacon on the table like there was a breakfast party about to start.

I sat there for a few minutes before deciding no one else was coming, and I was going to be eating breakfast alone.

After I was done eating, without seeing even one of his staff, I decided to explore my new home. I wandered down a few hallways until I finally came to a large set of stairs leading up. I walked them slowly, seeing nothing familiar, wondering where everyone was. As I wandered down another hallway, I saw Alistair's father, the alpha, through an open door, sitting at a large desk.

He didn't look surprised to see me. He leapt up from behind the desk, a large smile on his face as he practically jogged towards me, his arms outstretched.

I gulped. I remembered very little interaction with the Alpha the night of the party. I remembered walking into the room and him and his wife and Alistair watching me as I got...a blood test? Was that the last thing I remembered? Why was I getting a blood test?

"Rune, it's so good to see you. We've been so worried," he said gruffly as he held out his hand. He had the same green eyes as Alistair, and like Alistair's, they were cold. I thought I remembered him not seeming happy that night, but the man in front of me appeared completely on board with my presence.

"It's good to see you, sir," I nodded respectfully, tentatively putting my hand in his. He brought it up to his lips to brush a kiss across the top, and it was all I could do to keep the revulsion coiling in my gut out of my features.

Maybe the Fae Queen had performed some kind of shock therapy on me, making sure I'd never be happy because my fated mate and his family would always make me sick. I'd read about things like that happening before.

This all felt too fantastical to believe.

As far as I remembered, I'd lived a normal life with my mother. I'd gone to school. I'd played with friends. I'd hung out with my mother... The things that had allegedly happened to me over the past year seemed completely alien from anything I could comprehend.

"Rune?" Alistair's voice came from the doorway. His father finally let go of my hand in the presence of his son, and I sighed gratefully that he was here. The less amount of time that I could ever spend with the Alpha alone, the better.

"I went to look for you at breakfast, but the staff had said you'd already eaten," Alistair commented.

He was wearing a dark green shirt that complemented his eyes and his sable brown hair, and he was dressed in a suit, like he'd just come out of an important meeting... which he probably had. He was frowning as his eyes wandered down my body. "You didn't like the clothes I bought for you?"

I was aware of the Alpha walking back over to his desk, and I decided this was a good conversation to have somewhere else.

I threw out a polite goodbye, and then walked over to Alistair and grabbed his hand, pulling him from the room. His face was faintly amused once we got farther down the hallway. "Was my father mean to you? Is that why you're practically dragging me away?"

"He's just a little intimidating. As you know, I'd only met him once." I stopped, remembering the memory I did have. "Did I take a blood test that night?" I asked with a frown, glancing over to Alistair so I could watch his reaction.

He seemed to shift uncomfortably. "That is something that we do with all matches, to make sure both sides know the bloodline they're entering a partnership with." The words came out easy, but there was a tightness in his gaze... like there was more to it.

"Was there anything in my blood work that came out concerning?"

He shrugged. "I'm not sure anyone ever discussed the results after you were taken that night." He squeezed my hand. "But that's the last thing I care about after almost losing you. I can say with certainty that your blood and everything else about you is perfect for me."

I shot him a weak smile, because I almost felt bad... because nothing in my heart was telling me he was perfect for *me*.

"Now, back to the clothes...Was anything wrong with them? Are they not the right size?"

I tugged at the shirt awkwardly. "I just think that...my wolf wants your scent," I offered lamely.

That seemed to work, even if it was a lie. My wolf was actually disgusted at the fact his smell was all over my body.

"Well, as much as I love to see you in my clothes, I'm sure I could get my scent all over *your* clothes quite easily," he offered, in a way that would probably sound sexy for most people. He leaned towards me suggestively, and then kissed me, his tongue slipping into my mouth when I opened it in surprise. His kiss was wet, but not in a good way. It was too wet. And our lips seemed all wrong for each other as I tried to respond to his kiss.

He didn't appear to feel the way I did when he finally unlocked his lips from mine. He looked thrilled actually.

"We're having a dinner party to welcome you back tonight, just a few of my advisors and their mates. Do you think you're up for that?"

I didn't feel up for that. In fact, I felt a long way from that. But again, it felt like something I needed to do.

"Of course, and I'll make sure to wear one of my dresses. I'm sure it'll be fun."

Were other mates able to read each other better? Would another mate have been able to sense I was uncomfortable? Because Alistair wasn't sensing anything.

Alistair had more meetings, as he'd taken over many of the responsibilities of his father, and I ended up back in my room with a few books he'd had staff pick out from the mansion's library.

I was dreadfully bored, but it was probably better to stay in the room, then endure more awkward run-ins with members of Alistair's family.

At around four thirty, there was a knock on the door, and I opened it to see a very pretty, snooty woman standing there. She sniffed at the sight of me, like it offended her. She was wearing a skintight dress that was cinched so tight, her breasts almost came up to her chin.

"Alistair's asked me to help you get ready for the evening," she said, her voice annoyed.

My eyebrows rose. He hadn't made it sound like a fancy event requiring something like that, and the unease in my stomach only grew.

"I don't think I actually need any help," I said, moving to close the door. Her hand shot up and practically banged against the wood.

"I'm afraid I can't disobey his orders. I'm sure I can find

something to help you with," she sniffed, her gaze traveling up and down me disdainfully, and I didn't miss the hidden insult in that sentence.

"Of course," I answered through gritted teeth, finally opening the door so she could come in.

She strode directly towards the bathroom, like she'd been in here a million times, and I stiffened, watching the sway of her hips.

Because I suddenly had the sneaking suspicion that she *had* been here before.

The thought annoyed me, but surprisingly, I didn't feel jealous at all. I felt more insulted than anything else, that he would send one of his past girlfriends, lovers...or whoever she was, to help his mate.

Shaking my head, I strode after her, finding her rifling enviously through the clothes in my closet.

"So much in here that's getting wasted, while you wear *that*," she said spitefully, almost drooling over a red dress that was barely longer than a shirt.

"I don't think you'll be wearing this; the red's much too hot for you." She pulled out a hideous brown dress with cutouts all over it.

"I'm sorry—I don't think I caught your name." I began to look through the dresses as well...because the brown dress was definitely not happening.

"Carmen," she responded, like the question annoyed her.

"Carmen. Lovely. Well, I think you'll probably be able to give me a lot of help with the hair and makeup part of the evening...but I'm going to spend some time finding a dress myself."

I was proud, because my voice brokered no argument, and she sniffed as she straightened up from where she'd been bent over the rack—like I imagined she had been before—and trounced out of the room.

Why had I gotten out of bed this morning again?

Going through everything, I reluctantly admitted to myself that the red dress was probably the best option, even if it would draw a lot of attention. I decided to go with it anyway, and slipped it on, fidgeting with the hem as I attempting to pull it down further.

This was stupid. I was going to have to talk to Alistair about the clothes. He may like sexy clothing, but I liked my vagina covered. I'm sure there was a halfway point, some-where between our tastes.

I walked out, and Carmen's eyes flashed with displeasure.

"What did you have in mind for hair and makeup?" I asked, not putting it past her to make me look like a clown with the death glare she was shooting my way.

"Alistair wants an elegant updo. If you're capable of being elegant," she muttered under her breath, which of course I heard, because it wouldn't have taken wolf hearing to hear it. She pulled out the chair in front of the mirrored makeup area, and I sat down, ignoring her attitude. She grabbed her brush and started pulling it through my hair. I was a little afraid I'd be bald by the end with how hard she was tugging at it.

"A little softer," I murmured, deciding I wasn't going to put up with anymore shit from this girl. My mate was going to be Alpha, and with what he'd said at dinner last night it sounded like he was already assuming most of his father's role, which meant I was going to be the pack Luna. She may have gotten into my mate's pants many times before, but that didn't mean she could disrespect me.

Carmen begrudgingly softened her movements and

began to braid sections of my hair that she then pulled into the updo.

"Has your hair always been this white?" she quipped. "I've always heard that Alistair's into brunettes."

Boy, this was going to be a long afternoon. Of course, Carmen's hair was a dark, rich brunette.

"Yep," I clipped. "As far as I know, I was born with this color."

She continued to make little comments here and there, but for the most part I tuned her out, pretending to read the book I'd left on the counter before grabbing the dress. She finished with my hair, and she must've been scared of what Alistair would say, because it actually looked nice.

And then she started on my makeup.

"You know, I was with Alistair just a few nights before you were found," she said snidely.

The rest of what she'd said had been bad, but this one was going to cost her, because Alistair was suddenly standing in the doorway.

"What the fuck did you just say?" he snarled, and I did my best not to flinch, because the hate and fury in his gaze as he stared her down was terrifying.

She'd had an eye shadow brush in her hand, and she flinched at the sound of his voice, a pathetic whimper ricocheting out of her. She immediately bared her throat to him submissively, a pleading expression on her face.

"I'm sorry, Alpha. I was just jealous. I—"

"Get out of here, you fucking cunt. You're banished, and if I ever see you again, it will be your head."

"Please, no!" she cried as two hulking men appeared in the bathroom and grabbed her by the arms. They dragged her away as she screamed, pleaded, and cried. "I'm sorry," she screamed. "But you said you loved me. You said it..."

Her voice eventually faded, but I felt like I was going to be sick. Not because of the words she'd said, or that I was jealous, but just because of it *all*. The cruelty on his features, the way she'd just been pushed out of the pack without a second thought. It was all...a lot.

After the door slammed behind them, he rushed over to me, desperation flooding his features.

"I did sleep with her, my moon. But I was just lonely, and I was beginning to think I'd never find you. It was just a mistake..." he pleaded.

"There's nothing to apologize for," I said, just wanting the evening to be over, so I could go to sleep. "While I was imprisoned and probably being tortured, you were fucking your way through the pack because you missed me. Completely understandable."

What I'd said was meant to be sarcastic, but he somehow completely missed it. He breathed a deep sigh of relief as his shoulders straightened.

"I knew you would understand. I knew you would know that you're my one true love."

His words made me sick.

He hovered around me while I finished getting ready, his voice like a splinter in my brain. My veins felt icy, and I was getting another bad migraine. I found myself wondering if captivity by the Fae Queen had in fact been worse than this.

He was already dressed in a suit, and when I was finished, and had put on some way too tall heels, he led me out of the room and towards the dining room.

"You're the most gorgeous creature I've ever seen," he whispered in my ear as we neared the entrance, where I could hear the raucous din of voices coming from within, the guests already having a great time by the sound of it.

His breath was hot against my neck, but I didn't even bother to respond. He sighed when I didn't give a reaction, but plastered on a smile as he led me inside a room where every seat was taken except for the one at the head of the table and the one to the right of it.

I smiled and nodded as he introduced me to various members of the pack who appeared to have been invited based on how rich they were. There were a few of his betas there as well, and I tried not to cringe as they shook my hand, wondering why just the sight of them made me want to wash my eyes out with bleach. The smug grins on their faces, like they knew something I didn't...I hated it.

We settled into dinner, and I watched in disgusted amusement as they all practically licked Alistair's feet. Praise and compliments and conversation only directed at him filled the evening, and he seemed to soak it all up. I was very rarely asked a question, and Alistair made no effort to involve me. Tonight was obviously all about him.

Was this what I had to look forward to? I thought despondently. I couldn't imagine years and years of this. The night I met him, I was so excited. He'd seemed like such a gentleman, like the love of my life. Had he changed over the past year, or had I? I guess I couldn't really know since I hadn't known him at all before I was taken.

Why did I keep feeling like there was more to our relationship than what I remembered?

When the meal was finally done, after three hours I might add, the guests began to leave.

I stayed by Alistair's side, nodding and smiling and shaking hands as they wished us goodbye before leaving.

"Well, that went well," Alistair said happily.

"Yes," I muttered belatedly, after he shot me a questioning look.

"You look tired, darling," he said, examining my face.

"It was a lot of socializing for me," I agreed.

I meant my comment to try and gently point out that maybe it had been a little too much, too soon after getting back, but he obviously missed my point. I was going to have to be more direct with him, I knew that. I'd always struggled with speaking bluntly to strangers though, and Alistair still very much felt like a stranger to me.

He took a step closer and claimed my mouth in a hungry kiss, his hand sliding around my waist and then down to my ass where he squeezed. His hips churned restlessly against mine so I could feel how hard he was.

Fuck. Sex was definitely not on the table yet.

But just when I'd begun to panic, thinking I'd have to push him off once again, he shifted away from me. "I have a few more things I have to take care of tonight. You can go on ahead to bed, darling," he told me hoarsely.

I had no words, so I shot him a shaky smile and then left the room as quickly as I could, my pulse racing as I walked away. As I climbed into bed a little later on, I found myself wishing that Carmen hadn't been banished, and that she'd be here to distract Alistair from me.

What the fuck was wrong with me? What kind of mate ever had those thoughts?

Jolts of pleasure shot through me as he rubbed his cock against my clit. My breathing was coming out in gasps as our eyes met. His pupils were nothing but a pinprick, and there was a flush to his normally cold cheeks. I loved that he was just as turned on as I was. His hands were holding the back of my head and he pulled us closer until the tips of our noses were grazing.

"Tell me where you are," he growled as his lips pressed against mine, swallowing my moans as our tongues tangled together.

"Where I am?" I asked, between the brush of our lips, confused by his question. His tongue was stroking mine in long, explicit licks, and when his hands moved to my ass, he gripped the back of my pants, pulling the fabric so it was rubbing against my clit.

"I'm desperate for you. I need you. Now that I've had you, I can't live without seeing your face, hearing your voice...touching you."

I had no idea what my vampire was saying, I was too intent on feeling him. He moved one of his hands away from my ass, fiddling with my button until his hand was slipping inside and he was brushing his fingers against my clit. He got his fingers wet, and then pushed them inside me, and I arched into his touch.

He groaned as he watched me, plunging his fingers in and out. "You're so fucking wet for me," he breathed.

He slipped his fingers out and lifted them up so I could see my juices glistening on his fingers. He licked them and groaned, the sound sending goosebumps spiraling across my skin. His gaze was half-lidded and heavy as he watched me stare at him.

"You want a taste, Rune. Do you want to taste how much you want me?"

He dipped his fingers into my pants and through my folds again before bringing them up to my mouth this time. My tongue gingerly slipped out and I licked at the tips briefly before he put the fingers back into his mouth, sucking them in delight.

"I have to have you... Right now." He ripped the seam of my leggings and panties so that there was a giant hole in the crotch, and then he undid his jeans until his cock was jutting out. He

pulled me forward so I was straddling his legs, his cock positioned at my entrance.

"Fuck, you're so hot," he breathed, and I just whimpered, because I wanted him so badly. He fed me his dick, and I cried out, demanding his mouth. His thick head pushed into me, my core fluttering around him, pulling at it desperately.

As we devoured each other, he grabbed me by my hips and began to thrust up underneath me in quick movements.

"Let me in, baby," he said sweetly as he fucked me on his cock, the stretching ache feeling perfect. He buried his lips against my neck, his tongue darting out to taste my skin.

"I need you," he breathed.

"Yes, bite me," I pleaded, desperate for the pleasure I knew would come.

"Always."

He struck, his sharp teeth sliding into me, a climax immediately shooting through my insides as he continued to somehow fuck me perfectly the entire time. His exotic smell flooded my senses and I felt drugged, crazed, like he'd cast a spell over me. His thrusts were short and measured, giving me the exact rhythm that I needed somehow, like he could read my mind. Every thrust stretched me to the point of being uncomfortable, yet it was never enough. I wanted it to continue forever.

He sucked and pulled at my blood, his groans filling the room as he drank. I could feel my life force slipping into him... and it felt perfect. His thrusts grew harder and his cock jerked inside of me.

I cried as I came again, the world growing fuzzy at the edges as he continued to take my blood. When I was just about to pass out, he pulled out and licked at the wound, just a few drops of blood escaping down my skin.

I love you. Help me find you," he pleaded to me as he came.

"Where am I?" I asked breathlessly.

"Help me to find you. Help me to find you. Help me to find you." *His voice echoed as the world faded to black.*

I woke with a start, out of sorts and not knowing where I was for a second. I could hear the sound of the shower running in the bathroom, and I shivered as I laid back against my pillow, my body shaking with need. Already the dream was fading, but I could see the stranger's gaze in my mind. My hand slipped into my underwear and I began to press on my clit, just needing one small orgasm to take the edge off. I was so close that it took just a second for me to come, and the world darkened around me as pleasure flooded my veins. I had just finished when the shower shut off and a few seconds later the door from the bathroom opened up and light peeked into the room. I could feel his gaze on my skin, but I just pretended I was asleep, realizing belatedly he could most likely smell the scent of my arousal. I heard his footsteps disappearing further into the bathroom for a moment, and then he was back, extinguishing the light from the bathroom and prowling towards the bed.

He slid under the sheets, and his arm snaked around me, pulling me close.

"I can feel your desire for me, my moon. When are you going to let us both have what we want?" he murmured.

I desperately kept my breaths even, not wanting to give him any sign I was awake.

Finally, he huffed and let me go, rolling over to his other side so he was facing away from me.

As I lay there in the dark, listening to the sound of my mate sleeping, tears slid down my face, wetting my pillow.

It had to get better. There was no way I could live like this.

CHAPTER 7
RUNE

Thunder boomed, the walls of the manor shaking, and I rolled over in bed, curling up with the silk sheets as rain tapped against the window. Droplets slid down the glass pane. I'd always found rain calming, but the longer I lay in bed, the more I kept wondering where Alistair had gone.

Since he'd rescued me from the insane queen, I'd stayed safe with him, and he'd showered affection on me. One would think I'd be over the moon...And maybe I was still healing, but something just seemed off, like I didn't belong here, like I couldn't find the happiness I ought to have with my fated mate. I couldn't describe it, but I felt like one of those square pegs trying to squeeze into a round hole. And even though everyone kept telling me I fit, I didn't feel it.

Silence permeated the air, and I narrowed my gaze on my bedroom door. Why was it so quiet? Had Alistair gone out? The thought had me jumping out of bed with a desire to check out the manor and see what I could discover. Something to perhaps jog a memory.

It made me wonder if I was one of those people who

loved to snoop? Perhaps. I couldn't even answer truthfully because I still didn't remember large chunks of my memory, so for all I knew, I loved watching what my neighbors did.

Dressed in my pajamas, I changed into jeans and a loose tee, a concession from Alistair after I'd gotten the nerve to finally ask for clothes I didn't feel naked in.

I made my way out of my room, and down a few hallways, my gaze sweeping across my surroundings, with only the pitter-patter of rain outside keeping me company. The entrance to the kitchen was on my left, and I decided I needed a hot cup of coffee first to fully wake up.

It was only as I fiddled with the coffee maker that a thumping sound came from somewhere in the house. I paused, my ears perking.

The sound came again and again, leading me right to the steps down into the basement.

Unease curled in my gut as I reached for the door handle and pushed down. "Alistair?"

No response, but the earlier thumping sound came again and it was definitely from down in the basement.

Yellow light spilled down the wooden steps, fading into the murky darkness, and I floated the idea of just ignoring the noise. Except what if he was down there injured, or worse yet, what if the crazy Queen had broken into the mansion and was going to come up and get me?

Shivers raced up my spine, and I glanced over my shoulder, suddenly hating the silence in the rest of the manor.

Thump.

I flinched.

"Alistair. Is that you?" I swallowed hard and decided I would check or I would worry until I knew what was going on.

Slowly I descended, the steps groaning under my

weight. One would assume if anyone was down here, they'd hear my approach, which was exactly my intention.

Light spilled through the darkness as I reached the bottom of the steps, and I glanced around. There were boxes and shelves all over the room, but my attention was drawn to the thumping sound on my left where the basement extended deeper.

Wrapping my arms around myself, I stepped softly, my insides trembling. Just as I stepped past several boxes stacked on top of one another, I saw him.

But...

Alistair had his back to me, gripping a baseball bat, wearing what looked like a black raincoat. He was swinging the bat wildly, slamming it into someone who was tied by their arms to the ceiling.

I gasped, a scream pressing on the back of my throat. It was only then that I saw black garbage bags around the room like he was planning to divide the victim into bits before disposing of the poor guy.

I could barely breathe by this point, and yet I couldn't get my feet to unstick from the concrete floor. The man swinging from the chains had his head flopped forward, chin tucked into his chest, and I doubted he was still conscious. He bled profusely, the bucket beneath him splashing with fresh blood drops.

I heaved on an empty stomach, gagging at the sight, at the stench that reached me—blood and death.

I blinked, scared out of my mind. It was only when Alistair set a hand to his ear and adjusted the earpiece did I realize he was listening to music or something. That was why he hadn't heard me approaching. It was my saving grace, and I retreated quickly, dashing upstairs...barely able to breathe. Shutting the door as quietly as possible, I turned and ran, tears in my eyes.

Pausing outside the front yard, I wiped at my face, pacing, unsure I hadn't imagined what I'd just seen. Should I run? Where would I even go? There was nothing around the mansion, just open land and forests. The front yard was perfectly manicured with shrubs and roses.

Who had that man been down there? And why was Alistair hurting him?

The soft rain fell on me, and I tilted my head, letting it kiss my face. I closed my eyes, scared, confused...my whole body wracked with frustration that I still couldn't remember anything.

Please, make the visions stop, let me remember my past, and for heaven's sake, was what I just saw real? Is my fated mate a serial killer, or have I completely lost my mind?

"Little moon, what are you doing out here in the rain?" His voice danced in the air, and I jumped, my eyes flipping open.

I clenched my hands into tight balls, digging my finger-nails into the fleshy part of my palms to try to wake myself up, to not freak out in front of him.

"I-I..." I licked my lips. "Just needed some fresh air."

He closed the distance between us in three quick steps, and I lowered my gaze, unable to stop myself from scanning his clothes and shoes for any blood spots. He was clean, as were his neck and face.

My heart sped, savage breaths stealing my ability to act normal and not panicked.

"What's wrong? You look scared. Talk to me." He reached over, stroking the side of my face, and I cringed, and pulled away. I knew I shouldn't have, but my skin was crawling from what I'd seen. I was already struggling enough with not feeling attraction for my fated mate. That certainly hadn't helped.

Something was terribly wrong.

"Rune, baby," he groaned behind me, his hand on my shoulder. "Did something happen?"

I kept hearing the thumping sound in my head, of him striking that man. My knees shook, and I felt lightheaded, but his fingers squeezed my shoulder.

"I..." I swallowed the thickness in my throat. "Were you just in your basement? I saw something down there." I squeezed my fists harder, and a shudder washed over me as I finally turned to face Alistair.

Brows pinched, he stared at me with confusion. "I was in the study, answering emails. What did you see in the basement?"

My breaths drowned out my racing heartbeat. "You were hurting someone with a baseball bat," I whimpered, the words seeming to hurt me as they fell from my mouth. "I can't explain it, but I was certain of what I saw."

"Oh, I think you're having another episode from your captivity. I almost never go into the basement. There's nothing down there but boxes and dust." He brushed a loose strand from my face and tucked it behind my ear.

"I'm certain it was you." I recoiled from his touch, feeling stranger than normal around him.

He took a step after me, a fierce determination behind his gaze as he grabbed hold of my arm.

"You're scaring me," I whispered.

"You should never be scared of me, my moon. Come, let me show you everything is fine. I give you my word, there's nothing down there." With his hand around my elbow, he guided me back towards the house.

My palms felt slick, and I glanced down as I unfurled a clenched hand. Four moon-shaped marks bled from where I'd managed to dig my nails deeply into my palm, blood trickling over the edges of my hand and dripping into the soil at my feet.

Alistair hurried me inside, not seeming to notice the blood. I wiped it off my hand on the back of my jeans.

Dread filled me as he rushed me down the basement steps. Was he going to torture me like he'd punished that poor man?

He swung left, and before we took another step, I noticed the area was tidy. Normal looking. There were boxes stacked around...but there was no man hanging from the ceiling by chains, no garbage bags, and no blood. Even the air smelled of fresh citrus, rather than the coppery smell of blood.

"But..." I whispered, stepping forward in a daze. "How is this possible? I was so certain of what I'd seen."

Alistair stood behind me, his strong arms wrapped around the front of my shoulders, and he pressed his chest against my back. "I don't see anything down here, do you?"

I couldn't breathe, couldn't think. Was I losing my mind and this was one of the signs?

"Come, let's get you upstairs, and I'll make you a cup of chamomile. That'll calm you down. How does that sound?"

I didn't answer because only dark thoughts filled me. Images of the man being tortured, of me going slowly insane.

"I'll meet you in the kitchen," I said softly. "Just need to visit the bathroom."

"Of course, my moon. You know that you mean the world to me, and I'll look after you, protect you. You'll be with me forever and never have to worry about anything else. It will be just you and me."

I shuddered at his words. It was a particularly cruel twist of fate from the Moon Goddess that I feared and had distaste for my fated mate. That wasn't how it was supposed to be. I'd been told that when I was with him, I wouldn't be able to keep away. I'd crave him...beg for more. And yet I felt none of those things with Alistair.

Unsure of what was wrong with me, I stumbled into the bathroom alone and leaned over the sink. Hurriedly, I washed the blood from my hands, and then I splashed my face. Drying my face with the towel, I glanced at myself in the mirror. At how pale I appeared, at the shadows under my bloodshot eyes. I looked like I'd spent the night drinking.

Was I sick? Maybe with a brain tumor? That might explain my hallucinations and visions. Although I didn't know if wolf shifters could even have a brain tumor.

It was only when I dropped the towel in the sink and looked back up that I noticed a blushing mark on my neck. I tilted my head to the side, staring at a bruise. Or was that a bite mark? "What is that?" I murmured to myself. "How did I get that?"

Evidently, I had spoken right as Alistair stepped into the open doorway. "Let me have a look at that."

Standing beside him, he ran soft fingers along the length of my neck, the skin tender over the spot. "That was the mark I gave you, little moon, when I bit you to bond us together as fated mates. You don't remember?" He raised an eyebrow, appearing sorrowful.

I was shaking my head. "How can I not recall something so important?"

Turning me on my feet to face him, he smiled at me, his

hands on my hips. "It's perfectly okay, it will come back to you. Just give it time because I won't give up on us, on you remembering you belong to me."

His lips were suddenly on mine, and I let him kiss me, but I couldn't stop the disgust pulsing through my veins.

Fated mate. My skin crawled when he kissed me, and fresh tears burned in my eyes. Something was wrong.

It was as though I'd turned my back for a moment, and when I returned, someone had stolen everything I owned... including my memories.

I waited for the ache inside to ease, for his forceful hands to pull away from my body, but they never did and a tear slid out the corner of an eye. The tightness around my chest squeezed, and when he finally broke our kiss, he frowned.

"Why are you crying, little moon?" He wiped the tear away with his thumb.

"I don't know. I feel so lost, so scared. I must have slept terribly." I paused, my heart beating crazily. "If you don't mind, I just want to crawl back into bed and see if I can sleep some more. I can't believe I had a hallucination like that."

"Of course." The corners of his mouth pulled taut, but he just stared at me, and I wished I could read his mind and discover what he was really thinking.

He slipped his hand into mine, our fingers interlacing, and he walked me back to our bedroom. "I'll let you rest, and tonight, we'll go somewhere. Maybe being locked up in the house isn't good for you."

"Yes, I think I'd like that."

He pushed open the door to the bedroom and kissed my forehead before his hand slipped from mine. I stepped into the room, but not before I glanced back at him as he strolled away.

He glanced back at the same moment, and maybe it was the shadow falling over his face, but I could have sworn that for a second, his face soured, his lips thinned...and he was wearing an eye patch.

I blinked and he was back to normal, only stoking my fears that I was going insane.

I shook my head and hurried into the room, shutting the door behind me. The Fae Queen had broken me. That had to be it. Throwing myself back into bed, I didn't even bother to get changed or remove my clothes. I just wanted to hide away from the world that felt wrong.

Tugging the sheet up and over me, I curled in on myself and shut my eyes, calling for sleep to carry me away on its wings...as far as possible from this place.

We'd decided to attend a packed bar, the music thumping, lights dim. It could easily be mistaken for a nightclub with all the people around us on the dance floor. I'd insisted on dancing, much to his protest, and what started with something awkward as we joined the masses, morphed into me in his arms, my legs wrapped around his waist, our hips gyrating together.

"This is my kind of dancing, sweetheart," he purred in my ear, his hands across my back. "But I'd prefer if we had no clothes on."

I laughed at the gorgeous blond god I was wrapped around. "In front of everyone?"

A beautiful grin spread across the gorgeous man's face, and something sinful sparked behind his hazel eyes. "That wasn't a no. I can work with that."

Before I knew it, he was walking us off the dance floor, pushing through the crowds, the dim lights throwing shadows over everyone.

"*You're not telling me to stop,*" he said loud enough for me to hear him over the high-beat song that just started.

"*Who said I wanted you to?*" I teased, before kissing his neck, my insides filled with butterflies beating their wings. The attraction I had for him was constant. My panties were drenched from our dance alone, and when I looked into his gaze, I knew I was just as obsessed as he was...maybe I was even in love. I felt the sensation curling around my heart. I craved him with everything in me.

I left kisses all over his neck, unable to get enough of his masculine, woodsy scent. I loved his smell to the point of addiction.

When he gently pressed my back against the wall, I lifted my gaze to find we were in a dark corner of the bar with no one around us, and even if they did look...they wouldn't see much.

"*Look at how sexy you are,*" he purred once more against my lips before kissing me in a way that had me soaking my panties. I moaned as his tongue swept past my lips, and I drew him in, sucking on him, making moaning sounds. I imagined myself with his cock in my mouth.

His hand was sliding down my body, skipping under my skirt and he pulled at my thong. When he gave it another tug, he ripped it right off. He broke our kiss and lifted the panties to his nose, where he inhaled deeply.

"*Fuck, I love the way you smell. I'm fucking hard as a rock. I always am around you.*" He tucked my panties into his back pocket.

His hand was on my breast, squeezing and pinching my nipple. I groaned, my chest sticking out because I needed more. He never broke our stare. I wanted to imprint him on my soul, to never forget him because he was perfect, my everything.

Both of us were breathing heavily as he undid his belt and tugged open his pants.

"I've been dying to slide into you," he growled, then kissed me once more.

His cock pressed against my slick entrance.

Shuddering in his arms with need, he pressed in, spreading me wide. I moaned, pushing against him, our mouths and tongues tangled. He slid in deeper, growling in his throat, and I whined because he was huge. And he knew it. He took his time at first, working his way into me, sending me reeling into arousal.

Finally shoving all the way in, completely filling me, he paused and licked my lips. "You're so tight, I feel like I'm going to explode already."

"Don't you dare. Not yet. You need to fuck me...hard." I kissed him quickly while squeezing my walls around his cock.

He groaned, hissing, squeezing my ass. "Little Hellcat. Let me repay the favor."

He took a hard grip of my ass and drew out of me before slamming back in. I cried out from the sheer force of his movements. He studied me, eyes darkening–sexy as sin, and he thrust all the way into me, over and over.

I cried out, grasping onto his powerful shoulders, bouncing up and down on his cock. It was only then that I glanced out from our shadowy corner to the explosive dancers, to others chatting, drinking. But no one seemed to notice we were fucking right there near them.

"You wanted to be fucked. I'll always give you anything you desire. You're my girl." His voice was raspy, and I longed for everything he promised because it felt right. We felt right.

He moved and somehow managed to slam into me deeper, and I couldn't remember the last time I felt so completely full, so aroused that I begged for more. "Don't stop, I'm so close. Oh god, don't stop."

He grunted, rutting me in rhythm to the music, and I was floating, fingernails digging into his shoulders. I'd grown wetter, *and I was impossibly closer. And as my breaths escalated, his thrusts grew harder.*

I couldn't hold back, not when my entire body trembled, the buildup in my core losing control.

"Cum for me, sweetheart. Strangle my cock."

I came almost instantly with his single command, my body convulsing in his arms, white blinding light flashing behind my eyes. My pussy spasmed around his erection, sucking down on him as he snarled with his own explosion. Pausing, he gripped me hard, pinned between him and the wall, moaning, while he pulsed inside of me. Filling me with his seed. My head grew dizzy with how hard I'd just come.

He kissed me as we came down from my blissful orgasm. He held onto me like I meant the world to him, like it was so much more than a release to him.

For me, it was a need as much as breathing was, and I didn't think I could go another day without him.

"You're so beautiful," he said in a ragged breath. "I'm never going to let you go."

I woke up with a gasp, and tears came to my eyes at the heartache I felt, at the longing of having lost something I didn't understand. Something I couldn't even remember. And it left me broken.

I glanced across the bed where Alistair slept alongside me, an arm draped across my chest, and my stomach turned over itself.

These dreams, the visions. Alistair might be my fated mate, but I knew then, lying awake in the middle of the night, that I didn't belong there.

CHAPTER 8
ARES

The last few weeks had been torture. Absolute torment, and there I was in the city park, my knuckles white from the shovel I gripped. A bitter wind blew through my hair, the moon overhead illuminating the night. And I seethed because we still hadn't found Rune.

"It's a fucking waste of time. You've done this every day. It doesn't work," Daxon barked behind me, and irritation snaked up my spine.

"Then fuck off," I snapped over my shoulder, frustrated with his bitching. "We haven't found any leads yet. And even you with your mated mark can't find her, so I'm going to keep doing this. I'm bound to pick up something soon."

I spotted Wilder farther away from us in the park, stalking in the shadows, broodier than ever. He hadn't spoken most of today, but I wasn't there to babysit these wolves. They loved Rune, and I understood that. She was impossible not to love.

But I had hoped their searches through the city of Suceava would have tracked her down.

Every day I grew closer to losing my shit. And every day we didn't find her.

We'd scoured the surrounding towns and nearby areas, but with so much time passed, I worried she was too far away from the city. Maybe not even in the country any longer. I didn't have a clue where else to look.

"Okay, this is as good a spot as any," Daxon groaned and began digging into the soil in a clearing not too far from a path in the park. The old me would have been worried that late-night joggers might see us...but the new me...he didn't quite give a fuck.

I drove the shovel into the earth, my foot pushing down on the top and driving it deep. I kept on digging, just like the dozens of graves we'd already dug around the city. I wouldn't be surprised if the mysterious holes made it on the local news as we didn't bother to cover them up in our rush.

"This is what I've been reduced to. Digging fucking holes and I can't even bury you in them permanently," Daxon whined.

"You've dug a few in your time I'm certain, so this should be easy for you."

He shrugged, putting his shoulders into the job, but I knew from the first time I met Daxon that he had a darker side to him. And when he chopped me up and fed me to the pigs, that was when I saw the real him. The guy was a psychopath, a serial killer in the making if he just let himself go, but with Rune, he'd turned his devotion and all his possessiveness towards her.

I had no problems with that as long as I got to be by her side too.

Rune saw something in these two wolves, and their

devotion to her was admirable. I couldn't fault them because from the first time I met her, I knew she was different. Even though I tried to fight the inevitable, I still fell hard.

Shoveling more dirt out of the grave, we dug in silence, and my thoughts kept returning to Rune. On how I'd initially intended to kill her, how adamant I'd been that she was the long-lost princess of the Atlandia royal family after the blue stone drew me to her. I planned to finally gain my revenge for her father killing my parents...

But, I stood no chance once I met her. I'd lost my dead heart to her before I even realized it, and when I finally kissed her, bit her, tasted her, she'd made me just as obsessed over her as the wolves were.

We were a blood match, which was how vampires found their perfect mate.

There were no more revenge plans. Only a furious determination to claim her as my own, in whatever way she'd let me.

After visiting the Atlandia royal family castle, or what was left of it, I wasn't so sure what to think about her connection to the royal family. Her being back in the castle hadn't seemed to trigger any memories of her past.

The two broken stone pieces had merged together and healed her, but did that make her the lost princess?

I had no clue.

I no longer gave a damn as long as she was mine.

"That's enough. Get in the fucking hole." Daxon grunted, driving the shovel into the dirt next to him and propping a bent arm up on its handle. He wiped the perspiration from his forehead, staring at me with agitation. "I'm helping you for Rune, just to be clear. You and I are not friends," he continued. "I tolerate you because she likes you for some reason that is beyond me."

"I appreciate the honesty, but let's be clear here, I'm not going anywhere. One of us needs to stay sane for her." I threw my gaze over my shoulder at Wilder still in the shadows, doing who the fuck knew what. "Unlike the ticking timebomb over there."

"For a vampire, you talk a lot of shit. Get into the grave," he barked just as a human jogged right across the path, staring at us, wearing headphones. His gaze dipped to the grave we stood around, and his face blanched.

"Boo!" Daxon boomed, mock lunging at the guy, who in turn flinched so hard, he stumbled sideways and tripped over himself. "Get the hell out of here!"

Terrified half to death, the human scrambled to his feet and darted back the way he'd come.

"Okay, do this fast," Daxon stated. "The cops will be here soon enough now."

I stepped into the grave and lay down, Daxon already scooping soil over me before I got onto my back. He grinned like a demon every time he did this part.

"I've decided my new favorite thing to do is bury you, over and over. Now, if only you'd stay down."

"What fun would that be if I couldn't bring misery to your life?"

Just before he scooped more soil over me, he groaned, "Don't come back out unless you've found Rune." Then the dirt hit my face, and I clenched my jaw as some got into my mouth. Asshole.

He kept on working, the weight of the earth growing heavier, but it didn't take long for the earth's pulse to travel through my body. And with it came something else.

Something sweet...something I recognized instantly as Rune's blood.

A jolt hit me, and I shuddered.

Power raced through my insides, shooting right into my bones, and I hissed with the sting it brought. The heartache of never seeing her again faded, and in its place came her fear, her desire, her love.

My dead heart gave a jerk at the fact that I'd traced her, gained a clue, something to find her. I pushed my energy outward into the soil, seeking her sweet blood, and it came back at me in full force. The direction I'd find her was clear as day in my mind. Not the exact location, but it was close enough for me to track her now that I had her smell in my nostrils, and tasted her at the back of my throat.

I could almost hear her soft voice, her laughter. My fingers buzzed, my chest bowing upward with a feeling of brightness that she brought out of me.

Desperately, I burst up and out of the fresh grave, tossing soil in every direction, hope coming to life inside me.

Her scent still lingered in my nostrils, and all I could think about was tracking her down.

Daxon stared at me wide-eyed, Wilder was nearby too, frowning, saying, "You found her?" He approached me, his shoulder raised.

A possessive hunger pulled at my chest, and I dusted the dirt off, shaking it out of my hair. "She's still in the city. She's on the east side. I'll know more once I get closer."

"Fuck yes." Daxon threw his shovel aside. "Let's go get her."

But I was already moving away from them. "I can't wait a second longer. She needs me."

I turned and ran, hearing only their angry curses behind me.

Hey, I'd told them everything I knew. And right then, my priority was saving Rune.

And as I raced towards my love, I decided Daxon and Wilder could go get fucked. I was going to find her first!

CHAPTER 9
RUNE

I was in the garden hiding. It had been two weeks since I'd gotten here, and with every day that passed, I could feel Alistair's impatience growing.

Every night I was haunted by dreams I forgot as soon as I woke up.

Things were starting to sour between us. Alistair's expectations for me were lining up with the reality of the aftereffects of what the Queen had done to me.

Since he wasn't getting what he wanted from me, he decided to invite people over constantly, so I was forced to put on fake smiles in exchange for empty conversation with strangers until I felt like I was going to scream.

So here I was, in the gardens, trying to block out what my life had become with the beauty of the flowers.

Whoever Alistair's gardeners were, they were amazing. The gardens took up several acres and I could spend hours wandering in between the rose bushes and the dahlias and all the other flowers I couldn't name, pretending I was somewhere else.

"Rune," Alistair's voice came sharply.

I inwardly groaned and then schooled my features, turning to face my mate. He was dressed in a neatly pressed suit, per usual, and there was a tumbler of dark liquid in his hand, like he'd given up on the glass and decided to go straight to the source.

"Hi," I said, forcing a smile. His features were pinched and he didn't give me a smile back; his gaze just drifted up and down my form.

"You know that's torture, right?" he asked.

There was an ugliness in his voice that I did not like. My insides tensed as dread pressed down on me.

"What?" I answered, keeping my voice light.

"Having to hold your hot little body against mine every night, smell the arousal in the air, and not be able to even touch your cunt. And it's got me wondering, Rune. I'm not so sure that it's your fated mate that you're dreaming about every night."

My hands were trembling and I slowly crossed my arms in front of my chest to hide that.

"I don't know what you're talking about, Alistair. As far as I know, I've been trapped in a prison for the past year, and before that, I didn't have a boyfriend, so who could I possibly be dreaming about?"

I actually really wanted to know the answer to that question, because although I couldn't remember my dreams, I was very sure that they did not involve Alistair.

He seemed not to hear me; he just glared at me, heat in his gaze, a slight flush to his cheeks. Staring at him closer, I realized that he was drunk. Very drunk, I corrected, as he almost tripped over a small rock in the path.

I took a step backwards, even knowing that would probably incite him. And indeed, his eyes flashed.

"Why don't you want to be with your mate, Rune?" he growled, taking another long sip of his drink.

I held up my hands in front of me, because I could see where this ended, and I wanted nothing to do with it.

"This isn't something that just happens overnight," I pleaded softly. "I'm sure things will return to where they should be. I'm just... "

"Still being a frigid bitch?" he finished.

Anger poured through my veins. "What did you just say?"

His cheek ticked and his grip tightened on his drink. "I didn't mean that."

But I was angry so I didn't let it go, like I had all the other moments when I noticed something was off about him.

"I think you did mean it. You somehow thought that after a year of being tortured I should just eagerly climb into your bed, right? Especially because you don't have Carmen around to keep your sheets warm?"

His gaze hardened. "You know I thought things were going to be different?" he growled. "But maybe that's just how you are. Maybe I've been too nice."

I stared at him, a mixture of horror, confusion, and anger hitting me everywhere. Who was this man? Although I had seen hints of cruelty, *this* particular verson of him was not something I'd seen. I moved to turn around and walk away from him, done with the conversation and thinking he needed time to cool off, but as I swung around, my hand sliced across some thorns on the rosebush I'd backed too close to, and I squeaked as a few drops of blood ran down my hand and disappeared into the soil.

When I looked up from my hand, I realized Alistair had gotten even closer, now just a few steps away.

"What's it going to take to get you to offer that wet pussy to me?"

Without thinking, my hand darted out and I slapped him across the face. He roared in anger and moved to back-hand me, but right before he could touch me, a man appeared behind him in a flash, grabbing his wrist and stopping him just a few inches from my face.

Alistair growled in shock and turned towards the stranger...the absurdly handsome stranger might I add. His grip on Alistair's wrist tightened, until I could hear bones breaking as he crushed it in his grip.

Alistair was screaming as his hand was rendered perfectly useless.

"You must be the stupidest ass on this Earth to keep trying to get her when you've been marked as a dead man," the stranger said calmly, his tone at odds with the absolute fury flashing in his gaze.

"What do you want?" Alistair cried out, bent over and holding his broken wrist.

But I didn't have to ask him what he wanted. I knew what it was.

The stranger wanted me.

I turned to run and in the blink of an eye, he was standing in front of me. I froze at how fucking fast he was.

"You don't have to be afraid of me, Rune. Everything's going to be alright," he soothed like he was talking to a feral animal.

I tried to punch him, but he caught my wrist before it could land. But unlike what he did with Alistair, his grip was soft, just firm enough to hold me back. "Just give me a couple of minutes with the asshole and we'll get going," he said, as if we weren't complete strangers and I hadn't just seen him break my mate's wrist.

"Who are you?" I murmured, fear clear in my voice. He winced, like the sound of it had hurt him.

"Just a minute, sweetheart," he said warmly.

I turned to run again, but he didn't seem upset at all; he just snagged me around the waist and laid a hand softly on my cheek. Immediately heat flashed through me, the kind that I'd never even felt an inkling of with Alistair.

"Stay," he ordered Alistair, who'd started to slink away. Alistair was sweating, fear leaking out of his pores, but he stopped at the man's command, frozen in place.

My pulse quickened. How had he done that?

"Where'd you get that glamour you're wearing, Al?" the man spit at Alistair dangerously.

Glamour? What was he talking about?

"Sleep," he suddenly murmured to me, and no sooner had he said the words...And I was out.

————

I regained consciousness in a car, my cheek pressed against the cold glass as the world passed beyond it. Confused, I shifted in my seat and turned to look at who else was in the car, only to scream when I saw the gorgeous stranger sitting in the seat next to me. Glancing forward, I realized we were in the back, and there was another man driving the car.

"Let's not scare Armand, baby," he mused, his head tilted as he studied me.

I turned towards the door I was leaning against, frantically trying to open it.

Of course it was child-locked, and I didn't think it would be a great idea to use my wolf strength and break out the window.

And where was Alistair? "What did you do with my mate?" I hissed.

His eyebrows rose, confused. "What did that shit do to you?" he mused. "You don't remember anything, do you?"

My insides squeezed at the reminder of how big of a chunk of time I'd lost.

"I'm not telling you anything," I hissed. "Now where's Alistair?"

Sadness. Anger. They warred in his gaze. But it was the stark sadness that called to me. Like he was pining for me, like the thought that I didn't remember him hurt him right down to his soul, something I'd never felt with Alistair.

"That piece of trash is currently in our trunk," he said quietly, his dark blue eyes still studying me intently. "I plan to hold him, until you're ready to kill him."

"Kill him?"

He nodded. "When you get your memories back, I suspect that will be the first thing you'll do," he mused.

I thought back to his actions in the garden. It was becoming apparent that Alistair was an asshole, but certainly not enough of one to be killed for. "I can't imagine killing anyone...well, actually, the Fae Queen. I could definitely kill her if given the chance."

"There's the fire I know and love."

I scrunched up my face in confusion. Some of my fear was fading. This man was obviously dangerous...and powerful, but at least for the moment he didn't seem to mean any harm. And there was the fact he'd been so gentle with me in the garden, when it would've been much easier not to.

"What did you do to me to get me to fall asleep?" I asked, remembering the abrupt end to our interaction there.

He winced and rubbed the back of his neck sheepishly.

"Yeah, you'll probably want to murder me when you remember things, but I felt it was necessary under the circumstances. Just a little vampire thrall, nothing that will hurt you."

"You're a vampire?" I gasped, the fear returning.

There it was again. Sorrow. "Yes. And you're my perfect blood match," he announced solemnly.

Blood match, I didn't like the sound of that. I rubbed my forehead, another migraine forming because I was pressing it so hard to try and remember...anything. He clearly seemed to know me, but I had absolutely no memory of him. I only had this feeling...that wasn't exactly hate.

"What's your name?" I asked, deciding that would be the easiest to start with since he seemed to be open to answering questions.

"Ares," he said softly as we studied each other.

He...was beautiful. There was no denying that. In fact, Alistair's smooth looks were nothing in comparison.

After his midnight blue eyes, his hair was the next thing I noticed. It was dark, with a blue that almost matched his gaze running sporadically through it. His curls were haphazard, falling around his face like a frame for his perfect features. My gaze danced over him, thinking it was rather unfair for someone to be so beautiful compared to everyone else.

"Like what you see?" he asked wryly. My mouth opened and closed, heat flushing my face in embarrassment that I'd been checking out my kidnapper.

"What do you remember?" he pressed, leaning forward and touching my knee, sparks emanating from his touch.

"Why should I tell you anything?" I hissed. "You've got my mate in the trunk."

He shook his head. "I'm going to fucking tear apart whoever did this to you."

His anger seemed so...real.

It was so confusing. "I was told I've been in captivity for the past year. I remembered being imprisoned by the biggest bitch in the world...and then Alistair saving me."

"Daria?" he growled, his voice filled with dark hatred that was...extremely comforting. Even Alistair's attitude towards the Queen hadn't been like that. I frowned, thinking back to our conversations, and how little we'd actually talked about her. And every time we did, he'd never said her name, but the way he'd referred to her...it was almost deferential.

How had I not noticed that?

"That's convenient," he spat.

"The last thing I remember before that... was the night I was supposed to be officially betrothed to my mate."

The longer I was in Ares's presence, the more "mate" seemed to burn my tongue. It felt wrong, like it had since I'd returned, but somehow Ares made it even more noticeable.

"You don't remember anything," he breathed, closing his eyes. When he opened them, the dark blue looked pained. He glanced out the window next to him. "You don't remember *them*."

"Them?" I asked curiously.

Ares didn't answer me, and instead he straightened up in his seat. "Change of plans. Take us to Galeru," he ordered the driver...Armand, I guess.

Panic hit me again as Armand nodded and then came to a slow stop before turning the car around.

"Galeru? Wait. Where are you taking me?"

Ares turned towards me, reaching out and taking my

hand, and I didn't understand why I felt no need to yank it away. "We haven't gotten any time together. If I can just have some, I know everything will be different. I promise to make this right for you, just not right now."

His words made no sense to me, and my headache was growing to the point it felt like I was going to puke.

"What's wrong, pretty girl?" he breathed, looking concerned. His question pulled at my brain, like there was a memory there I should be recalling.

I leaned my head back, a tear sliding down my cheek. His eyes tracked it, his face pinched. Like it was offensive to him, but not in the way it had been to Alistair, who'd just been annoyed when I showed any emotion. Instead, it looked like Ares just hated the idea of me being unhappy at all. I realized then...I was still holding his hand.

"I've been getting migraines ever since I've come back. Every time I try to recall something... It just gets worse." I didn't know why I was telling him this, why I felt so ready to tell him this, but I did.

"I can help you with that. Anytime you have any pain at all, I can help you." I turned my head and examined him... he seemed to really mean what he was saying.

"How do you do that?" I murmured, finding it hard to talk with how much my brain was pounding.

"It's a blood bond gift. I can help you."

"I don't understand what that is, but if there's anything you can do..." My voice trailed off as his hand slipped to my cheek, resting there almost...lovingly.

Immediately the pain began to slip away, my brain getting relief for the first time since I'd opened my eyes that first morning in Alistair's bedroom. I straightened up and stared at him in wonder. "It worked. The pain's gone!"

He smiled at me fondly and my cheeks flushed again, because it only made him more attractive.

"Anytime you need anything from me. I'm all yours." The way he'd said that... It sounded like a vow.

"Can you explain the blood bond thing?" I asked, almost shyly. Because the moment we'd just shared felt so... intimate. I couldn't exactly explain why, but as my headache had begun to go away, I could feel how much he cared...somewhere deep inside of me.

I didn't understand *how* I could feel him so clearly while I couldn't sense Alistair at all. But I guess...I couldn't summon any emotions for Alistair either.

"I recall having this conversation with you before. It's almost nice to have a do-over," he mused.

"Did I not take it well the first time?" I asked, cocking my head as I studied him, still amazed I could do so without blinding pain shooting through my brain.

"Not exactly." But he didn't explain that any further. "The wolves have true mates...and regular mates. But the vampires, we have blood bonds. There's someone out there who's your perfect match."

I shivered. "You mean I'm what you have to feed on?" I asked, panicked.

He shook his head emphatically. "No...I mean yes. But no," he tried to explain.

"I have no interest in becoming a blood bag. Thanks for the offer though. Can you just let me out right ahead?"

"Fuck, I'm messing this up even more than I did before."

"Can you stop referring to 'before'!" I snapped, unreasonably angry because everything he said reminded me that we had some kind of past. At least with Alistair, there wasn't really any past to talk about. Just that one night, and evidently, it hadn't been that memorable.

"I can't do that," he said sadly. "When you remember..." He didn't finish; and his voice trailed off. Ares glanced down at his lap, thinking hard. And it seemed like forever passed before he met my gaze with his pools of blue.

"The most important thing for you to know is that I'm here for you," he said softly. My heart leaped in my chest at his words. I wanted that. I wanted someone to be there for me. Alistair had said he was there for me, but it was like a lie slipped from his lips every second. I realized it now. I'd never trusted he actually meant anything. But when Ares said it...it felt like I could.

"I will always protect you. I will always take care of you. I will always...love you," he finally whispered.

My chest tightened, and I felt a bit lightheaded, because I realized that my wolf was in perfect agreement with what he was saying. Everything inside of me was telling me he could be someone that I...loved. But what did that mean for Alistair? I'd been raised to know what a true mate was, and the horror that came when such a match was rejected. The Moon Goddess didn't take that lightly, her gift being thrown in her face, and it meant a lifetime of unhappiness and despair for whoever did that.

I bit my bottom lip as I stared out the window. It felt like that already though, didn't it? This time with Alistair, ending every day wondering if this was really it, if this was what I was going to have to deal with for the rest of my life.

I was so confused.

"I have a mate already," I finally said, and his features seemed to pale. "And however miserable of a person he is, I'm not sure I can damn us both to a life of torture because of his personality flaws."

He blinked, like it was taking him a second to understand who I was talking about. That was odd.

Finally, he shook his head, looking almost...relieved? "Alistair rejected you, Rune," he said gently. My heart lurched in my chest...as did my wolf. "He held you as a prisoner in his home, and he abused you. Horrifically from what I've gleaned through our conversations. You escaped, and eventually, I found you...and at one point, I'm pretty sure you rejected him right back."

"You're lying," I whispered, my heart in my throat.

He stared at me sympathetically, and I hated it.

"You're lying!" I screamed this time.

I didn't know why I was pushing back so hard. There was a rightness to his words, like my soul knew he was speaking the truth.

"Rune," he murmured soothingly, pulling me towards him. I began to beat on his chest, tears streaming down my face, and he just let me do it. He didn't even try to stop me until I was exhausted and I collapsed into him, my tears soaking his shirt.

"I'm so confused," I whispered. "I have no memory of anything from 'before'. Then I wake up and there's a sadistic woman torturing me for no reason...and then I wake up again, and there's my mate, and he's trying to be nice. The whole time I'm there, things start to seem not right. Like the night he sent the woman he'd been sleeping with to do my hair and makeup for our first official dinner as a couple." I laughed bitterly at that, anger threaded through me at the thought of it now that I was weeks past the initial haze I'd woken up with.

"How would you feel if you woke up one day and you'd lost a whole chunk of your life?" A hitched sob slipped from my mouth, and he stroked his fingers through my hair and down my back, whispering a litany of reassuring words.

"I don't know what the truth is. I don't know why I'm

okay with the fact he's in the trunk. I don't know why it feels like home laying against you like this," I confessed. He stiffened at my words, pulling me closer to him for a second before letting me go.

"Everything's going to be okay, Rune." But there was a hitch to his voice, and I wondered, was he telling me the truth? Would anyone I meet in this new life I'd woken up to, tell me the truth?

I had a million more questions, but we didn't say anything for the next couple of hours as we went to...who knows where. I hadn't even bothered to ask him about it.

I somehow drifted off to sleep, and what seemed like just a few minutes later, I woke to him softly murmuring my name.

"What?" I asked blearily.

"I want you to see this."

I sat up, wincing at the bit of drool on his chest that joined with the tears that had soaked his shirt. He didn't seem to care at all though, which was oddly sweet. I was sure Alistair would've had something to say about that.

When I glanced up, I gasped, because it seemed we were about to drive right into a lake. On the other side, there was a magical-looking waterfall that soared at least ten stories into the air. The color of the lake was crystal; you could see right down to the pebbled, sandy floor of it, and it seemed, even from here, that glitter and sparkles were emanating out of the waterfall.

It was like I'd stepped into some fantasy realm.

"Where are you taking me?" I gasped, even as we neared the water.

"Don't be afraid. It's not what it looks like. It's just protection I've put in place to protect my town and people," he explained soothingly. His eyes were dancing with happiness, and there was a broad grin on his face.

"Your town?"

"Yes, Galeru. My one good thing...until I met you."

Even though he told me we weren't about to drown, I still closed my eyes and tensed as we moved into the water. When it didn't feel like we were floating...or sinking, I opened my eyes, staring around in amazement as we drove on dry land right through the lake, like we'd become Moses parting the Red Sea.

"How is this happening?" I gasped.

Ares's smile grew, and I lost my breath for a second at how beautiful it was. I found myself thinking of other ways I could keep that grin on his face forever.

"Don't look at me like that," he growled. My eyes widened as I quickly glanced back towards the window, watching as a school of colorful fish swam by in the crystal clear waves next to the car.

"How am I looking at you?"

"Like you want to eat me."

My cheeks reddened, and I turned away from him, pretending to watch our surroundings. It seemed to take forever to get to the waterfall, but then, there we were, stopping right before it.

"What happens now?" I asked.

"A little more magic."

Armand pressed a button on his dash, and to my amazement, the waterfall began to part like a curtain, until there was a tunnel stretched out before us beyond the water.

"This is crazy," I whispered, my face glued to the window as I watched us pass through the waterfall and into the suffocating darkness ahead. The waterfall closed behind us, and the world went perfectly dark, none of the sun that should've been peeking through the water filtering into wherever we'd driven into.

"Ares," I called out, panicked, because I literally couldn't see my hand in front of my face.

"It's all right, pretty girl... It just takes a couple of minutes because the magic is making sure that no one followed us."

I tried to sit there patiently, but my mind was full of questions. I pinched myself.

"Why did you do that?" he asked.

"How did you see that?"

"I'm a vampire...darkness is kind of my thing."

"Right..." I drawled. I took a deep breath, feeling silly. "I did that because I'm not quite sure if I'm dreaming or not. Maybe I'm still back at the Fae Queen's right now, and my mind's cracked, and I just invented all of this."

Suddenly, a soft kiss brushed against my lips, and I jumped.

I could feel Ares's grin...even though I couldn't see it. "Still feel like you're dreaming?"

I didn't even know what to say.

Before I could embarrass myself any more, a wall opened in front of us, revealing a bright, sunny sky and a forest. We drove forward, and I glanced back to see the opening closing behind us. I peered around curiously, noting that we were surrounded on all sides by soaring mountains with evergreen pines and brightly colored leaves.

"Just a few more minutes and you'll see it," said Ares, a longing in his voice.

"When was the last time you've been back?" I asked.

He bit down on his lip, not looking at me. "Several years," he finally murmured.

"Years?"

"I had some...duties I had to attend to...and then I met you." There was a heaviness in his voice, and I sensed that there was much, much more to the story.

I opened my mouth to press him further, and he finally glanced over at me. "I'll tell you more later, Rune. I promise. Just not right now."

I nodded. I usually couldn't read the room right, but it was very clear he needed a moment right now.

We drove through the forest for a few more minutes, and there in front of me...was a storybook come to life.

The town stretched out in front of us, a paved golden road going through the center of it. The houses were all made of white stucco, with black shuttered roofs and balconies on most of the windows. There were flowers everywhere brightly decorating everything. Pinks and golds and purples adorned the balconies, and there were colorful flags and banners waving all over.

As our car drove through the town, people gathered in the streets, waving excitedly as we passed by.

Sliding down the window, Ares began waving right back...excitedly, I might add. His grin had somehow grown even wider.

Little children in sharply pressed school uniforms ran past the car, waving and jumping up with joy. "Ares, Ares!" they screamed happily. I watched him, and I watched them...remembering the past month and the fact that no one had seemed excited when Alistair walked into a room.

They seemed terrified.

It continued for the entire drive. Everyone must've been making calls simultaneously, because the whole town seemed to catch wind that he'd returned. Whoever Ares was to these people, they were excited.

"Earlier, you said *your* town... What exactly did you mean by that? Because they seem more excited than they'd be for just an ordinary citizen."

He waved at a passing couple and then turned towards me. "I mean it's *my* town. These people were all on the run. Under siege by the Fae King. They had no weapons. They had no food. I helped them all escape. All four hundred and twenty of them."

My mouth might have fallen open in surprise. I made a note to ask about the Fae King later.

"But I didn't know where to go. We wandered for a while until we set up camp right outside that lake. I heard rumors that the King was preparing to come after us, so I woke up anxious that morning. I got into the lake to try and clear my head, swimming all the way across it until I'd gotten to the waterfall. I could see something just beyond it, so I swam through. It wasn't closed like it was now, so you could see straight through to the other side where the forest began. I found this piece of paradise... And I knew it was going to be our home." His eyes glimmered as he remembered the moment, and I could just picture him, the relief he would've felt when he discovered this perfect place.

"And how did you get it protected like it is now? How did you even move everyone here?"

He waited for another passing couple and pointed ahead to where a large home sat directly in front of us. "Home sweet home," he murmured, his grin still there.

The house was a bit larger than the others we passed, but done up with the same white stucco and black roof as the rest. There were large white oak double doors in the front of it, and it looked welcoming and homey, nothing like Alistair's cold mansion that we'd left behind.

The only thing I would miss about that place was the roses.

As Armand moved around the side of the house where there was a garage, we pulled in next to a large black pickup truck and a white delivery van. Then the garage closed behind us.

"I still have questions," I reminded him. He reached out and stroked my cheek, amusement clear in his gaze.

"I would be worried if you didn't," he teased.

Armand opened the door next to me and I got my first good look at him. He was an older gentleman, probably in his sixties, with a very impressive mustache, and hazel blue eyes that just seemed trustworthy. His salt-and-pepper hair was neatly cut, and his skin was weathered and tan.

"Thank you," I murmured.

He nodded back at me. "Anything for Ares's girl," he said with a wink, more words than he'd said for the entire hours' long journey.

"His girl." I wasn't sure about that, but it was still shocking how right that felt compared to every time someone made a similar comment regarding Alistair and me.

Speaking of Alistair....I nodded back to the trunk as Ares joined us on the side of the car.

"What are you going to do with him?" I asked tentatively, still shocked, I was okay that he was in the trunk in the first place.

You did feel like he might rape you in the garden, a voice chided inside of me.

Yep, that was probably it. The lack of feeling gave credence to Ares's story as well, that somehow we'd severed the bond. I couldn't help but worry about my stroke of bad luck as far as the Fae Queen went, which he hadn't said was a lie; it was a reminder from the Moon Goddess that I did something wrong.

"I'll throw him in the dungeons until we're ready for him," Ares said calmly, studying my reaction.

I nodded, thinking there was no way I'd be able to sleep at night if we somehow allowed him to be locked up in a bedroom in this place. I don't know that I could sleep with him in the house at all, even if it was in a so-called dungeon.

Did this place even have a dungeon?

Ares must've read the question in my gaze, because he chuckled.

"He'll go into the town dungeon. We don't have any crime, but we built it just in case someone tried to invade from the outside, or a stranger made it past our protection somehow, and we needed to lock them up until we knew their intentions."

"Okay," I said, hearing the relief in my voice.

"You only have to tell me that you want him gone, and I'll do it myself. But something tells me, when you remember what he's done, you'll want the chance."

I nodded, not knowing what to say, and uneasy, because I wasn't sure I wanted to remember something so horrific that I'd want to kill my fated mate for it.

He studied me for a moment. "Let me show you something," he said quietly, popping open the trunk. "Look at him."

I bit my lip as I peeked inside, and then my mouth dropped open in shock. He was missing an eye!

"How—" I stuttered.

"He was using a fae glamour to mask his face since you

wouldn't have remembered him losing it and he was trying to get you to fall for him."

"How did he lose it?" I murmured, fascinated and horrified at the notion someone could hide their looks like that. It was also making Ares's story more and more plausible.

"I believe, my love, that you cut it out when you escaped from him."

My eyes must have looked cartoonishly large at that moment. I couldn't imagine doing something like that. He just chuckled at my response and slammed the trunk lid down.

"Armand will take care of him. Let's get you inside. You've had a long day."

My body actually felt somewhat refreshed from the short nap I'd taken on his chest. But my mind...that was another story. I followed him inside the house.

"I'm pretty sure I'm broken," I muttered to myself as I admired the white oak plank floors and the smooth white walls that gave a comforting, homey feeling to the place.

"What makes you say that?" he asked, leaning against a large island in the dreamy kitchen we'd walked into.

"Because you're still a perfect stranger to me, and I'm just wondering...is this where you turn into the Big Bad Wolf, and I realize you've been impersonating Grandma the whole time?" I mused.

He chuckled at that, and I couldn't help but grin in response.

"Sorry, just trying to picture myself in one of 'Grandma's' nightgowns and that ridiculous bonnet thing they always have the wolf wearing in those stories." He chuckled again. "But I can assure you–I have no problem assuring you every day for the rest of our lives–I am not the Big Bad

Wolf. I am the devoted lover who would walk through fire and give up his life to make the woman he loves happy."

My jaw dropped. I hadn't been expecting a confession of devotion like that. A thrill swept through me, and I tried to temper it down. I'd woken up, and Alistair had been there, pretending to be my knight in shining armor. It sounded like that had all been a trap, and I'd actually been sleeping in the bed of a monster. Would Ares turn out to be that way as well? I guess I had time to figure that out, since I had no idea where I'd come from besides Alistair's pack.

I was going to say something more prolific, but all that came out was, "We'll see," a statement that Ares didn't seem perturbed about at all.

I opened my mouth to ask another question, but then something outside the back windows caught my attention. I gasped, seeing a garden spread out as far as the eye could see. And not just a regular garden, like Alistair's, with his neatly trimmed rose bushes and the grass that had been kept at precision length the entire time I'd been there. This was a wild garden, one from a dream, brightly blooming blossoms popping up everywhere, no rhyme or reason to their growth except that it looked beautiful. It all seemed to go together though, like the person who'd designed it had been one of the most talented artists around, and he'd taken his paintbrush and mapped it all out. Organization in the chaos. It was hard to imagine that such perfection could have just been done by nature, but I suppose it could've been possible with how beautiful everything here was.

"One of my favorite places. And why I decided to build my house right here. I stood in the open field that used to be here...and I could just see it," he murmured, coming up to stand beside me. "Come on, you'll have plenty of time to explore the gardens later. Let me show you the rest of the house."

I nodded, reluctantly following him as he turned back towards the kitchen.

The kitchen really was a dream, the island stretching almost the entire length of it, and I could just imagine him hosting parties here with various townspeople, but I would bet that the invite list wasn't based on how much money was in their bank accounts.

Speaking of bank accounts... "How did you fund this place?" I asked, thinking not just about the beauty of the house, but also the beauty of the whole town and the logistics involved of keeping that many people fed.

His grin turned cocky at my question.

"The first six months seemed impossible. We were in this beautiful place, but we had just a couple of hammers, a couple of saws, nothing necessary to build a town with. And then I went on one of my walks...and I happened to find another cave just over there." He pointed at the mountain behind his house which was opposite from where we'd come in. "And in that cave was an abandoned mine full of emeralds."

"Wow."

"Everyone in the town takes turns working there in other positions. We have a bakery, a bookstore, a small grocery store...and many other places. But the primary livelihood for the town is the emerald mine."

I tried to picture it—all of them walking through the waterfall and seeing this picturesque little valley, and the work that would have had to be done to create this place. It was amazing.

"And how do you protect it?"

"This town is everything to me. And although I grew up a Hunter, my allegiance is with it. And I knew if things ever went sour, the Hunters would come after me, or any of the many enemies I happen to have. So I found a sympathetic witch, and I asked her to put enchantments on the entrance so there would be protections. We've never had a stranger actually make it through thanks to the lake and the waterfall and the room beyond the waterfall. It's all guarded with magic."

I was in awe. "Had I known about all of this before?"

He shook his head, staring at me intensely. "We hadn't gotten that far where I was bearing all of my secrets," he said slowly.

I cocked my head. He'd already declared his love to me earlier, so how far had we gotten?

"What was the status of our relationship before I got...taken?"

I frowned and stared back out the window after asking the question, realizing I hadn't gotten the story of how I had ended up in the Fae Queen's hands in the first place. I doubted a lot of my memory, but that interaction, that period of time, it lived in my mind like a living, breathing thing.

"I'd say we started as enemies, went to friends, and were well on our way to the lovers' part," he joked.

I snorted, despite the dark turn my thoughts had taken. "We wanted to cover the full breadth of tropes, then?" I asked lightly.

"Oh, for sure."

I was getting tired again. Whatever the Queen had done to me, I still hadn't completely recovered. I still found myself tiring more easily than I had before. Or at least what I remembered from before.

"So how did I get in the Fae Queen's hands? How long was I there?"

A dark shadow passed over Ares's features. "I will kill her for what she did to you," he growled, and his sharp fangs popped out with a hiss.

I gasped, because honestly... I'd forgotten he was a vampire.

"Sorry," he grimaced, retracting his teeth. "Do you know how long you were with Alistair?"

"I think it's been about a month since he first got me. I'd fallen asleep for a few days, but I'm pretty sure it's been at least a month since then. All I can remember were two days with the Fae Queen. Is that right?"

There was a tick in his jaw as he thought about it. "You've been missing for about forty days. So I would think that you were with the Queen for about four or five days on that timeline."

"So where have I been for the year before that?" I mused, mostly to myself.

"Amarok," Ares said, sounding reluctant. "It was my understanding that you drove around for a few months after you escaped Alistair, and then you found yourself settling in that little town. And that's where I met you."

I tried to grab onto any memory surrounding such a place, but not even the name sounded familiar. It was so frustrating.

I was sure there was more to the story, but my exhaustion was taking over so fast that I was fine saving my questions for tomorrow. Ares probably had a lot to catch up on anyway, seeing as how he'd been gone for years. My heart ached for him, thinking of him having this beautiful place in the back of his mind, but being unable to come here because he needed to protect the people.

"I'm glad you were able to come home," I said softly, watching the stress melt off his features, butterflies taking flight at the brilliant smile he gave me.

"Me too, sweetheart," he murmured. "But I'm most happy that you're here with me. I have a feeling it wouldn't have felt as it used to now that I've met you."

I blushed, not knowing what to say. At least it didn't feel as stilted and awkward as when Alistair had tried to make such declarations. The difference was that I believed Ares, even though I had little reason to yet.

"I know this may seem strange, since you don't know me from Adam, but you've become my home."

I stared at the floor, biting my lip as my cheeks continued to burn.

"Come on, let me show you to your room," he said gently, saving me from any further embarrassment.

Ares led me towards a wooden staircase which led up to a long row of doors. I noticed that everything was dust free and sparkling, obviously someone had kept up the place while he'd been gone.

Or he wasn't telling the truth, the snarky voice said in my head. But... I didn't think that was the case. He walked me to the second door on the left and opened it with a flourish, revealing a gorgeous bedroom, that while not as fancy as the one I'd had at Alistair's, was a million times more homey. It came with a deep red velvet comforter with red, white, and gold pillows, fluffy rugs on the polished wooden floor, and a comfy looking window seat with shelves on each side loaded down with books.

"This is gorgeous," I said softly, turning towards Ares. I blushed when I saw how intensely he was staring at me.

I shifted uncomfortably, "So...where's your bedroom?" I asked, a bit of dread seeping through my veins.

"Just down the hall," he responded, pointing to a door a little ways away.

"We're not sleeping together?" I asked, immediately slapping my hands against my face in embarrassment. I was just surprised. It felt like I'd had no choice but to sleep in the same bed as Alistair. But with Ares saying that we were blood mates, I guess I'd assumed it would be the same uncomfortable situation of us sharing a bed.

He looked surprised by my question when I finally peeked through my fingers, he asked, amusingly, "Do you want to sleep in the same room as me?"

"No," I immediately squeaked, before groaning as his delicious laugh filled the room.

Ares took a few steps towards me, until he was standing just a few inches away. I peered up at him and his hand went to my cheek, softly stroking it in that way I was coming to recognize.

"My hope is that you will someday soon. But above all, I just want you to be comfortable. So you let me know if you ever want to switch your bedtime arrangements?" he said with a wink.

My brain had ceased to function as he slowly licked his bottom lip in that sexy way of his.

"Good night, Rune," he whispered, and I swear my panties were drenched by the sexy way he'd said it.

Again, what was wrong with me? Should I have these reactions for a stranger...but nothing for my fated mate?

Maybe this was the curse? Or maybe this was how my reaction was supposed to be with my mate, and another confirmation that Ares was telling the truth.

If I kept thinking about all of this, I would get another headache.

Ares had left the room, softly closing the door behind

him, and I stared at my surroundings, feeling completely off-kilter...as usual lately. I decided to get ready for bed, and I was shocked to see that all of my favorite toiletries were on the counter, brand-new, making it clear he'd had them bought for me.

But wait...how did I remember that these were the toiletries I would have been using? These were not toiletries I had used in my mother's house. A glimmer of hope seeped into my veins. Did this mean parts of my memory were returning?

Before I could think anymore about it, that voice that had been haunting me filled my head, calling my name frantically in a tortured, broken tone. I fell to my knees, because his pain...felt like my pain. My head dipped forward as a shiver rushed across my skin. I waited to see if he'd say anything else, but my name was all he offered.

Despite the way things were slightly looking up, and the beautiful place I found myself in, I once again sobbed. He felt immeasurably important to me, whoever *he* was. So why wasn't *he* the one saving me? Was *he* even real?

Eventually, I dragged myself off the floor and into the shower. I realized I still smelled like Alistair, and I wanted to get it off right then.

The shower felt like heaven with gray marble stone on the floor and on the walls, and a giant waterfall shower-head above and in front of me, creating a perfect experience. After I got out, I finished preparing for bed, lathering on some lotion and brushing my teeth. When I walked into the closet, there were also racks filled with clothing still containing tags. But a key difference between Alistair's closet, and this one, was that these were all clothes I would love to wear, ranging from comfortable to tastefully sexy. Nothing that made me want to set my eyes on fire or threatened to show my nipples.

I found a sleep set with a tank top and shorts made of the softest material I'd ever touched. I dragged them on, sighing in relief at the feel of the fabric on my skin, and celebrating the fact that I wouldn't have to smell like Alistair, and I wouldn't have to wear lingerie.

I celebrated even more the fact that I didn't have to deal with his wandering hands.

For a moment, I wondered if he'd woken up yet, and realized he was in a cell. But as I searched my heart, I couldn't find anything that resembled pity for him. The side of him he'd shown in the garden...the side he'd shown glimpses of throughout my time with him, I knew for a fact he was a terrible person.

I slid under the covers, sighing at how comfortable it felt, and ignoring the way that my wolf was demanding I call Ares to the room.

And as I fell asleep that night, for the first time since that first night in Alistair's bed...I didn't dream.

CHAPTER 10
ARES

I didn't require much sleep, so my right-hand man, Connor, knew it was all right to stop in around midnight. I appreciated him giving me some time to settle back in, although the process wasn't quite as seamless as usual considering I couldn't stop thinking about Rune. Wondering if she was comfortable, wondering what she thought of the place...wondering if she was going to suspect anything.

I knew I was playing a dangerous game. But I couldn't help it. As I sat there in the car with her, her scent enveloping me, I felt like I was losing my mind. The idea of going back and sharing her with Daxon and Wilder, and them doing their best to push me away before I really had any source of standing in her heart...I couldn't do it.

A dark part of me wanted to keep her away from them forever, but if she did remember things, I could only imagine the pain she'd experience being without them, the same pain *they* no doubt were experiencing right now.

But something had told me this was my chance. If I didn't get her to fall in love with me now, I was never going to. That wasn't a chance I could risk. So I did what I had to, and I stole her away.

I assumed they would eventually find us, but I'd sworn to myself that after a couple of months, if it wasn't working, I'd return her back to them...and this time I'd let her go.

I knew that would mean spending my life pining for her, wishing and being miserable without her, but I would do that if it was what she wanted.

First, I had to give it one last chance.

"It's good to see you," my friend Connor said, hugging me tightly and slapping his hand on my back. "Look at you," he laughed, pushing back and holding my shoulders as he examined my face in that piercing way of his. Connor was a human, fifty-seven this year, with sky-blue eyes and salt-and-pepper hair. His skin was weathered, and he had laugh lines around his eyes.

There was no one I trusted more in the world.

"It's been too long," he said solemnly after he let me go.

I gave him a halfhearted smile, because it had been.

"You seem...different?" he mused. Walking over to the bottle of cognac he'd brought over, he poured two glasses quite full.

Different.

That was a way of stating it. Before Rune, this had been the only soft part of me, perhaps the only good thing I'd ever done in my life, the place where I could be someone else. After Rune, I felt changed, like I'd been reborn. For the first time...I wanted to be good for her, though I had no doubt I would do whatever it took to keep her safe and happy, even if it went against that new desire.

"I'm in love," I announced.

His mouth dropped open, because that was probably the last thing he would've expected to hear from me.

"She's my blood match."

"The woman who was in the car with you?" he asked.

I rolled my eyes, knowing he hadn't actually seen her today, and the town's gossip mills were in full swing. One of their favorite things to do was discuss my love life...or lack of love life as it was.

Everyone in the town was human, and although they knew I was a vampire, they never showed any care about that, and it seemed to be the women's main goal to try and catch my heart. I never slept with anyone in the town, not wanting anything to damper my relationship with these people, but it would be nice to actually confirm I was taken and stop the many advances.

"Yes," I said when I realized I hadn't answered. "Her name's Rune. She's...perfect." I knew I sounded like a love-struck fool, but I couldn't help it. I *was* a lovestruck fool.

"I'm happy for you, old friend," he murmured, handing me my drink. I grinned and lightly punched his shoulder, knowing he was telling the truth.

"But enough about me. You'll meet her soon enough. How are things?"

I kept a burner phone while out with the Hunters, and we had a code we used so that anyone reading the messages would never know what we were discussing–so I was mostly caught up with how things had gone. Connor still asked my advice for any major decisions for the town, even though I told him that I trusted him. But of course there were always things that would take too long to text. I cared about every part of this town, the important stuff... and the unimportant.

"Well, Kelly's getting married," he said proudly.

My eyes widened. Kelly was his twenty-two-year-old daughter. She hadn't been dating anyone before I left.

"Who's the lucky guy?" I asked, thinking he was truly lucky to be joining their family.

"Tanner Dawson," he announced. "He's a good boy, and I think he'll make her very happy."

Tanner was a quiet boy, but I agreed with his assessment. From what I'd seen, he had a very gentle, loving soul, and he was always helping out with the young children of the town.

"When's the big day?" I would have to figure out a way to be here no matter the date. And hopefully, Rune would be here right along with me.

"She's doing it at the festival celebrations next week. She wanted to make sure that you were there," he said, studying my face for my reaction.

I grinned at him, immediately feeling excited.

"She wants you to officiate."

"Over the reverend?" I teased, thinking of one of our less popular members of the community. The reverend was very passionate about our souls, or my lack of soul, as it were. I knew he had good intentions though, as ridiculous as he went about them.

Connor chuckled and shook his head before taking another sip of his drink.

"We'll have another shipment of emeralds ready to go by the start of the festival," he said more seriously.

I nodded. "Have the latest batch of supplies I requested been picked up?"

It was a bit difficult to get things into this place. Obviously, we didn't want to invite any strangers into the town, so the process for procuring supplies was complicated and usually included several hour-long trips and a million different cover stories. We grew our own fruits and vegetables, and made our own bread, but things like toilet paper goods that weren't easily handmade, clothes, etc., we got from the outside.

Connor nodded. "They didn't ask any questions," he assured me, and I breathed a sigh of relief I didn't know I'd been holding.

"Good, good."

"So what's the plan for tomorrow?" he asked, knowing that there would be a parade of people coming to see me if they had their way.

"I'm going to get Rune to fall in love with this place... and with me," I said with a wink.

He chuckled and shook his head. "I have no doubt that that's a battle you'll win."

He didn't ask more questions, and that was something I appreciated about Connor. He let me speak my mind when I *wanted* to. There was a lot I couldn't tell him. He knew that I'd been the leader of the Hunters, and that things had soured as of late, but the rest was on a mostly need-to-know basis, even though I considered him my closest friend.

We finished our drinks, chatting about random things before he left to return to his family a few houses down.

I stared out at the darkness, up at the moon, thinking about my plan.

I couldn't fail. I had to do everything I could. She couldn't leave this place before she was in love with me.

CHAPTER 11
RUNE

I woke up feeling more rested than I ever had at Alistair's. Staring out the window at the town laid out before me, I felt a bit like I'd stepped into a fairytale. The sky was a brilliant blue, seeming much brighter than at Alistair's. When I pushed open the window, I noticed it was chilly, but not uncomfortably so, and there were already people milling around in the golden streets.

I quickly got dressed and went downstairs, marveling at how much more comfortable I felt walking around the house than I had at Alistair's.

Ares was sitting at the bar, chatting with a plump, cheerful-looking woman with silver hair who was cooking something amazing smelling on the enormous stove.

"There's my girl," he said proudly when he saw me, his gaze filled with heat. I glanced down at the outfit I'd picked, skinny jeans and a sweater, but the way he was looking at me...I might as well have been naked. The woman at the stove turned and shot me a huge smile. I'd never seen anyone who looked so...happy. She kind of resembled Mrs.

Claus. And I immediately liked her before she even opened her mouth.

"Oh, my dear. You are more beautiful than he's been telling me. Come, sit down. I'm making breakfast, so I can make you whatever you want."

"Eggs Benedict is my favorite," I purred.

With her huge, excited smile, I felt like I had saved her life or something.

"Marcia is the second most important woman in my life...behind you," Ares said with a wink.

Marcia chortled and blushed, going back to work at the stove.

"Did you sleep well?" he asked quietly.

I nodded, my own cheeks flushing, not sure why the moment felt so intimate with another person in the room.

"I thought I would show you around the town today?" he offered.

I nodded eagerly, excited to get a look at everything without glass in between me and the view.

"I can even take you to the emerald mines, and you can mine your first stone," he teased.

"And in the garden. Don't forget about that."

He chuckled, sounding pleased at my obvious excitement, and I blushed again.

We talked back and forth with Marcia as she finished preparing breakfast. Evidently, she had been helping Ares out since they'd found this place. She also was responsible for how perfect everything looked.

"He makes it easy. I've never met a man so clean," she scoffed, like his cleanliness annoyed her.

I giggled and she winked at me, setting a perfect plate of eggs Benedict in front of me. I inhaled the deliciousness.

"Hand-carved maple ham, of course. But the secret...is my mother's recipe for tomato jelly, God rest her soul."

She made the Catholic sign across her chest and forehead, glancing up at the ceiling before directing her attention back at me.

Ares rolled his eyes and sipped his drink. Glancing at his coffee cup, I realized there was blood in there, and I gulped a bit, even as heat rushed through me. I couldn't help but wonder...how would it feel if he drank from me?

All right, pushing those thoughts aside, I took a bite of the eggs Benedict, immediately wanting to fall at her feet and worship her for how freaking amazing it tasted.

"I can die happy now," I moaned. "I found it. The perfect eggs Benedict."

They both laughed at me, not realizing I was actually pretty serious.

I inhaled her breakfast, and she promised to make it whenever I wanted.

Then it was time to go. We waved goodbye to Marcia, who was whistling as she cleaned up the dishes, and then we walked outside.

The air smelled so clean. And there was the mild scent of apples in the air, strangely enough. When I pointed it out, Ares smiled. "I'll let you in on that secret at lunch time. You're not going to be disappointed." He took my hand casually as we walked, and I marveled at how perfect everything seemed. We meandered the streets, the stones under our feet glimmering under the sunlight. Ares explained to me how they'd decided they wanted something other than asphalt, noting that everything had been carefully designed to look aesthetically pleasing.

"Well, you succeeded, because I don't think I've ever

seen a town so pleasing in my life," I said, admiring one of the shop's window sills, full of vibrant purple blooms.

Townspeople came up to us often, not shy at all about talking to Ares. I noticed the young women we passed stared at him like he was something of a rockstar though, and I couldn't help the flicker of jealousy at the way they were looking at him like they could eat him alive.

There was a large open area in the center of the town, with a fountain and a flagpole. There were children every-where, throwing footballs, playing tag, and just eating lunch while sitting by the fountain.

"This is where the school-age children have recess and eat lunch," he explained as a couple of them raced towards us.

"Will you play, will you play?" they pleaded, pulling on the dark blue shirt Ares was wearing that I couldn't help but notice outlined every perfect muscle in his body.

Ares glanced at me, a question in his gaze.

"Go ahead," I said with a laugh. His answering smile made me wish I had a camera, so I could capture it and keep it with me forever.

I watched as he played tag with them. Except the rules seemed a little bit different. Ares was always "it", and he was allowed to use his vampire speed to tag all of them. I realized they were playing freeze tag, because after he'd tagged them all, there were just a bunch of still, giggling children all over the square like someone had come in with a magic spell to hold them all in place.

It was hilarious to watch, but I found myself rubbing my arms around my chest, staring out towards the moun-tain where we'd entered, just imagining the Fae Queen or Alistair's father coming to attack this place. I'd only been walking around for a couple of hours and I'd recognized the magic of it. There would be any number of people...or creatures, who would want this place for themselves.

"Everything all right?" Ares asked suddenly, appearing beside me. His curls were wind-tossed, falling in his face, and he was practically glowing with happiness.

"Everything's perfect," I assured him.

I continued to watch as he played with the kids until their lunch break was over.

I couldn't help but think of how my mother would've liked this place. She'd always loved the sound of children playing. A pang of longing hit me as I thought about the small white stone that marked her grave. Alistair had kept his promise at least to take me to where she was buried. I'd tried to say goodbye that day, but most days, it still didn't feel real that she was gone.

"Your eyes are sad, my love," he murmured, taking my hand in his and bringing it to his lips. I shivered at the sensation, but this time...the shivers were the good kind.

"I was just thinking of how much my mother would've loved this place," I murmured. His eyes flashed, and for a moment he looked guilty.

"Ares...what aren't you telling me?" I scolded him, my insides tightening in dread.

"What did Alistair tell you about your mother?" he asked, leading me over to the now empty fountain. There were other townspeople walking around everywhere, but they were keeping their distance at the moment, like they recognized we were about to have a serious conversation.

"He told me she'd fallen ill soon after I was captured, that there was nothing they could do to save her." I took a deep breath. "Was that not the truth?"

Ares sighed and shook his head, still holding onto my

hand. "At some point after you escaped him, he got you back. And when you escaped again...she was killed."

I gasped, tears forming in my eyes. "He killed her?" I cried as anger and betrayal tore at my heart.

"Yes," he replied solemnly, his gaze filled with sympathy.

I might not remember anything about my time with Alistair, but the rage within me felt old, like it extended for far longer than what I'd just learned.

For the first time, the idea of killing my mate didn't seem so insane.

I took a few deep breaths, trying to let go of the bloodlust.

I finally got a hold of myself and glanced up at Ares. I could tell there was more to the story.

The smart thing to do would be to get everything I could out of him, but it had been a freaking hard month.

"How about you show me why everything smells like apples on the street," I said quietly, watching a woman push a baby carriage down the sidewalk.

"Are you sure?" he asked softly.

I couldn't speak then. I felt too choked up because I could feel how much he cared about me. So I just nodded.

He pressed another kiss against my hand and stood up, leading me to a small café on the other side of the fountain. Every step we took towards it, the apple smell grew stronger, until I was salivating.

Ares opened the door for me and I stepped inside, immediately in love with the quaint café. There was a line at the counter, and I could see a beautiful display of desserts and sandwiches sitting behind the glass. There were small wooden tables set up around the room, and most of them were full. I liked that people didn't automatically try to allow Ares to go first; it spoke to the ease that he had with them.

It hit me then...I was pretty sure that Marcia was human. Staring around the room, I was pretty sure that they were *all* human.

"Do they know you're a vampire?" I whispered.

"Don't say it out loud," he practically screamed, making sure that every person in the room was staring at us. "They can't know that I'm a vampire," he continued theatrically.

The couple in front of us snorted and rolled their eyes, shaking their heads fondly at Ares's antics.

Everyone else was laughing, and then they went back to what they'd been doing...eating their delicious food.

My cheeks were on fire. "You're an idiot," I murmured, my wolf agreeing inside of me.

Ares winked, and his arm slid around my waist until I was plastered against him.

But again...it felt so right.

"Everyone has known that I'm a vampire from the very beginning. I met them when I was out on a mission for a vampire group...'The Hunters'. They already knew that other creatures existed, since the Fae King was set on torturing them. So a vampire's existence wasn't a huge shocker. And then when I showed how much I wanted to help them...I guess they stopped caring about *what* I was and focused more on *who* I was." He examined me closely, because apparently, this was knowledge I would've had before, but I was just drawing a blank about now.

"And they weren't scared of you at the beginning?"

His face darkened. "They were terrified at first. They'd already been tortured by another fantasy creature, so they had high doubts that I wasn't just going to go on a rampage and eat them all. But eventually, they saw..." He shook his head, his eyes looking lost in the past. "The Fae King rules a completely separate kingdom from the bitch who took you. He makes Daria look like a pussy cat."

I grimaced at the thought of someone worse than her.

"Their community was attacked soon after I arrived... and I was wounded. They could've just left me there to die. But they didn't," he said softly as we moved up in line. "Instead, they set up a blood bank, so they could nurse me back to health. I guess we owed each other our lives, and that was the foundation for a beautiful friendship."

I stared around the room at the happy people, finding it surprisingly easy to picture them nursing Ares back to health.

"Where do you get the blood you drank this morning?"

"Oh, you noticed?" he said, rubbing his hand on the back of his neck.

I scoffed, thinking it would be impossible not to notice that someone was drinking a coffee mug filled with red blood.

"It's part of our supply runs. We get blood from a blood donation center, saying we order it for a hospital entity we made up. And it ensures that I always have food while I'm here."

I nodded, and something in the display case caught my eye. The sign on it said it was an apple turnover, and I immediately decided that it needed to be part of my lunch.

"The blood bag is not quite doing it for me now though," he remarked casually.

"Really?" I responded, distracted by another dish I saw in the case.

All of a sudden he was leaning towards me, his breath soft against my skin. "Now that I've tasted you, any other blood might as well be dirt."

That drew my attention away from the food, and I stared at him, a little surprised...and again, a little turned on.

"Um... Sorry about that," I answered, because what else could I say? Although the more time I spent with him, the more the idea of offering my neck to him didn't sound distasteful.

Before I could say anything, Ares was ordering everything in the display case, plus sandwiches and bags of chips.

Even if I tried my best, I wouldn't be able to eat it all, but by how good it smelled, it was worth giving it a shot.

We went to sit at a table and waited for our food to be brought to us.

"When you're up to it, my second-in-command, Connor, would love to have us over for dinner. He's...my best friend, and I leave him in charge when I'm gone."

Unlike the dinner parties I'd attended with Alistair, all of which I'd dreaded, the idea of this one made me excited... and intrigued, wondering what else I would discover about Ares around his friends.

A teenage girl came out carrying a tray loaded down with our food. She set it down on a stand and started passing out the plates, chattering enthusiastically to Ares about her new boyfriend, and the fact that her sister was getting married.

"Daddy says you said yes?" she asked him. She was a pretty girl, with spring green eyes, dirty blonde hair, and a cute button nose.

"I did. Now I gotta brush up on my wedding script," he teased. "This is Katie," he told me. "She's Connor's youngest."

"Hello," I said politely. But evidently, she knew all about

me already and her chattering was just as enthusiastic towards me as it had been for Ares.

"You should come over for dinner," she was begging after all the dishes had been laid out.

I nodded, a bit dazed by her enthusiasm as she darted away to assist more customers.

"Connor's oldest, Kelly, is getting married, and they've asked me to officiate the wedding," he explained.

"That's quite the honor," I told him, and he nodded, like he couldn't believe his good fortune.

"It's at the beginning of the festival at the end of next week, actually. It's been torture to miss the festival for the last few years, so I'm excited I've made it back in time. You're going to love it."

I took a bite of the apple turnover, ignoring my sandwich for the moment. I moaned in pleasure as the cinnamon apple taste rushed over my tongue.

Was there something in the water here? Because everything I tried ended up being the best food I'd ever eaten in my life.

When I opened my eyes, heat surged through my core... because of the way he was staring at me...

He adjusted his crotch discreetly. "Don't make those sounds while we're in public ever again," he muttered, sounding a bit cranky. "Now I have to get rid of this hard-on before we can leave the cafe."

I giggled, blushing furiously. I felt like a schoolgirl with her first crush. Giddy and nervous all at once.

It was hard to fathom that just a day ago, I was in Alistair's clutches, staring down a miserable life.

It was like I'd lost a five-hundred-pound weight I didn't even realize I was carrying.

I stared around the café, listening to everyone's light-hearted chatter.

But how long would it last?

"How long are you here this time?" I asked, and the humor in Ares's eyes died. He looked away, his jaw tense.

"I'd like to say forever, but that never really works out, does it?" he said, almost to himself.

"What do you mean?"

"You have a destiny, Rune. I believe that now. I just want to make sure that I'm a part of it."

I didn't understand what he was saying. Destiny?

"Like...the Fae Queen's going to return for me?" I asked, fear laced in my question. His eyes flicked to the necklace around my neck.

"Something much bigger than that, sweetheart," he said, just as vague as he'd been a second before.

My insides tightened, but I bit into my sandwich anyway, my mind turning. I was doing a good job of ruining my perfect day. I didn't want to be the girl that stuck her head in the sand, but maybe, it was okay to uncover things a little bit at a time.

After the best lunch I'd ever had, Ares continued to show me around the town. We ran into Connor walking down the sidewalk, and I immediately felt at ease with his calm and pleasant demeanor. So at ease, that I set up our dinner with him for the next night. Ares looked pleased at that, and a part of me wondered what else I could do to make him happy.

We set off for the emerald mine a little while later, Ares pointing out different paths in the forest you could walk.

We were halfway through when I heard a strange growl. I froze in place. "What's that?" I whispered, my gaze darting all around.

Ares groaned. "It's...my pet."

"Your pet?"

"Brace yourself." A second later, a creature stepped out of the woods. A monster, like something out of a horror movie, enormous with red eyes that glowed, and razor-sharp spikes running down its spine.

I didn't know what had gotten into me, but it was one of the cutest things I'd ever seen. It galloped towards us, heading straight towards me. I braced myself to be eaten, but instead, it began to lick all over my face with a warm, rough tongue.

"Down, boy," Ares ordered. It backed away, reluctantly, and its tail began to beat happily on the ground, the sound echoing around the forest.

"You're a gorgeous boy, aren't you," I cooed.

"You're not afraid of him?" Ares asked incredulously.

"Afraid of the sweetest boy I've ever met?" I scoffed in that same singsong baby voice that was probably grating on Ares's ears. He threw his head back and laughed, a deep belly laugh that I hadn't heard from him yet. The monster dog seemed pleased with the sound, his tongue hanging out of his mouth, making those rough, serrated teeth look cute somehow.

He whined then, and I reached out my hand and stroked his ears, making sure to avoid the spines that looked like they could cut me if I accidentally grazed them. His fur was surprisingly soft, and after a second of me rubbing him, he collapsed to the ground and rolled to his back, revealing his pink stomach.

"You want a belly rub?" I murmured, and Ares mock sighed next to me.

"That creature is a bloodthirsty beast. And you're going to ruin him."

"He's not a bloodthirsty beast. He's a cute little baby. Aren't you?" I cooed some more.

"His name's Aldo," Ares offered, his voice amused.

"Aldo," I repeated, thinking the cute name somehow fit him.

Aldo whined because I hadn't rubbed his belly yet, so I kneeled down and gave him what he wanted.

"How exactly did you get Aldo as your pet?" I mused, laughing again when Aldo's tail smacked my knee with how exuberantly he was wagging it.

"He found me, actually. He was scrounging around for food in a forest near the Carpathian Mountains about ten years ago and scared me half to death when he bounded out of the forest and started licking me. Aldo's as loyal as can be. The best monster dog you could ask for," Ares teased.

Aldo jumped up, almost impaling me on one of his spikes as he went to lick his master.

"He lives mainly in the woods. While everyone has no qualms about me at this point...he still scares them. Especially after he ate one of the kid's bunnies right in front of him."

I winced, just imagining how terrifying that would be to a child.

"Okay, Aldo, go play," Ares ordered sternly. Aldo nudged his hand once more for a pat and then he loped off into the forest, soon disappearing from sight.

"And he's okay?" I asked.

Ares laughed, lifting an eyebrow. "I would hate to find anything scarier than him in the woods."

That was true.

He took my hand, and I marveled at how it felt like we were a perfect fit. He pointed out some plants that were native to the area and told me some funny stories about the townspeople. The walk seemed to fly by.

Soon we were at the entrance of the mine. There was a team of five guards standing outside, menacing weapons in their hands as they kept an eye on anyone that would threaten the town's livelihood. As soon as they saw us though, they all had huge smiles on their faces, and they called out their greetings.

"Everything going okay today?" Ares asked.

One of the shorter men, his thighs the size of both my legs together, marched forward. "Right as rain. Evidently, they found a new pocket of stones...and there are some diamonds in there," he commented, raising his eyebrows up and down like a cartoon villain.

Ares clapped. "That's great news," he said, before patting the guy on the shoulder as we passed through. I soon forgot all about the armed guards though, when I saw what lay in front of us.

It was like an underground city inside. Nothing like I would expect from mines I'd seen on television or read about in books. There were lights set up everywhere, transforming the place from a dingy, depressing place to work, to one that was bright and cheerful. Up ahead were tunnels, but it seemed like most of their work was still taking place in this main area. Men and women were chipping away at the rocks, and there was rap music playing. There was a camp stove and kitchen set up in the middle, and three people were hard at work cutting up food. A man walked towards them, wiping his brow, and one of the women handed him a sandwich.

I watched in amazement as one of the women just a few yards away from me tipped out a particularly large green emerald that was almost the size of my palm. She tossed it into a bucket that already had its fair share of stones.

"This place is fantastic," I whispered as people called out greetings to Ares as we walked by. A lot of them stared at me curiously, but none of them looked hostile. And they all seemed so genuine. I glanced up at Ares, watching him wave to another man. It took someone special to create a community like this. The fact that I'd only felt kindness from everyone I'd met so far, was really saying something.

Ares was kind of...incredible.

We walked over to where a man and a woman were working side by side. "Think Rune can try her hand?" he asked, and the woman smiled as she wiped sweat from her forehead. There were fans going all over the mine, but I imagined the work could get strenuous.

"If you could take over for ten minutes, that would give me a chance to grab something to eat. It's 'roast beef sandwich day'. I've been dreaming about it," she said eagerly, handing me a small pickaxe, and something that resembled a screwdriver. I grabbed the tools and smiled at her as she hustled straight towards the food station. Ares patiently showed me how to work the rock, while the other man watched us, amused.

I found I liked the work, actually. It was almost soothing to do something so methodically, with not a lot of thought involved. Ten minutes passed quickly, and I'd almost unearthed my first emerald. I could see bits and pieces of it, but it wasn't free from the stone wall.

"Oh you've made my job so much easier," the woman praised me and handed the man a sandwich, before taking the tools back. I was kind of sad about stopping, but Ares assured me I could come back whenever I wanted to.

We talked to a few more people, and he checked out the

new area where they'd found some diamonds, and then we were setting off back to town.

When we made it to the house, I was thinking that Ares was indeed a dangerous man.

And not because he was a vampire with freakish super-powers to go with that.

But because everything about him called to me.

And I couldn't help but wonder if that was a terrible idea.

CHAPTER 12

RUNE

I'd been in Galeru for over a week, and every day I found myself eager to wake up and face the day. Time with Ares passed quickly, and there was so much to see and do in this place. We had dinner at Connor's, and his family was incredible. And today was the start of the festival. I'd heard all sorts of things about it, and everyone in the town seemed excited. Especially since it kicked off with Connor's daughter's wedding.

Marcia was in the kitchen, as she had been every day, and she already had eggs Benedict and a large fruit smoothie set out.

"You need your energy today, my dear. There are a lot of festivities planned. The whole town will be participating."

I'd offered to help with the wedding setup, but I was still tiring more easily than normal, which may have been related more to my lack of memories I was guessing now, and less to the torture the Fae Queen had put me through. Ares wanted me to sleep in, and just come when the wedding started.

Marcia and I chatted back and forth as I ate my delicious breakfast. She'd already given me eggs Benedict three times since being here, and I was half wondering if I'd actually died and gone to heaven.

"Ares had a dress sent for you to wear to the wedding party. Everyone will be in casual clothes after that, but the wedding is a dress-to-impress event."

"Just as long as the dress actually covers the parts it's supposed to, I'm game." I grinned. She looked a bit confused at the statement, but never asked me to clarify.

As she began to clean up, my thoughts drifted to Alistair. Ares said he was awake now, but he wasn't talking to anyone. He just sat there in the cell, looking miserable. Part of me wanted to march over and confront him about everything, but part of me also didn't feel ready.

I really wanted to have some of my memories back of what he'd done before I faced him. Ares and I talked about various things that we could try, but most of them would take a great deal of time to procure, like finding his witch friend who was a world traveler and almost impossible to find unless she wanted to find you.

I headed upstairs and was in the process of putting on the beautiful royal blue dress that Ares had bought for me... which did indeed cover all the important parts, when that voice came to my head again.

"I'm beginning to think I just imagined you," it whispered, so forlorn that it brought tears to my eyes. I pressed on my temple, hating that I was hearing it, but also hating that I couldn't give comfort to whoever's voice it was.

I'm here, I wanted to scream, but I knew that wouldn't help. I hadn't said anything to Ares yet, but...I was thinking I would say something soon.

I tried to shake off the pain and the sadness that settled over me every time I heard the voice, and I finished getting ready, twisting my hair into an elegant topknot, stepping into a pair of black heels that complemented the dress perfectly.

I stared at myself in the mirror, admiring the way my eyes seemed to sparkle, and the fact that the shadows underneath them had disappeared. There was a rosiness to my cheeks, and I looked alive...and happy. It was amazing the difference in me after just a week in such a beautiful place. What would it be after a month...after a year?

I quickly shut down those thoughts, because every time I went down that road...I thought of a relationship with Ares...and the idea of that only left me confused.

There was a car waiting for me outside, and I slipped in gratefully, nodding at Armand as we headed to the other side of the town. I would normally have walked, but trying to navigate the cobblestones in these heels would not have been fun. I was glad that Ares had thoughtfully arranged for Armand to drive me. That was just another example of how he always seemed to be anticipating my needs since I'd been here. Ten minutes later we'd reached the field where the wedding was taking place. There were white wooden chairs set up in neat rows and an archway set up in front of them, covered in vines, autumn leaves, and flowers. There was a garland of the same colors lining the aisle where the bride would walk.

It was an incredibly picturesque venue with the mountain stretched out behind it. I could only imagine how wonderful the pictures were going to be.

Ares had told me that the group for the ceremony was small, but the whole town would be at the reception afterwards to set off the festival. He was standing under the archway talking to Connor, but as if he could sense me, his gaze met mine down the aisle, and the smile he gave me made my heart stutter.

He looked somehow more gorgeous than he did normally, with his hair slicked back and the dark navy blue of his suit matching the blue in his hair and the blue of his eyes.

Ares gave Connor a pat on the shoulder and then immediately came towards me. He pulled me close, his hands grasping my waist. "You're the most beautiful girl I've ever seen," he whispered. And I felt a little lightheaded. He made me feel bubbly... free...happy. This was how I envisioned having a mate would be like when I was a little girl. This was how I should have felt with Alistair.

I just fiddled with his collar. "You look pretty sharp yourself," I murmured.

He was staring down at me intensely, as if he was trying to see straight to my soul. "Rune, I —" He was cut off by the start of music playing.

"Let's get you to your seat," he said with a soft smile. I couldn't help but wonder what he'd been about to say.

He sat me down on the second row, something I felt a little awkward about seeing as how I wasn't family, but as he strode back towards his position under the arch, I couldn't help but think that he'd given me a really good view.

A couple of minutes later, the wedding march started. We all stood as the bride walked down the aisle, arm in arm with a beaming Connor.

For some reason, I turned to glance at Ares, even as the bride came towards the arch. And I realized he was staring at me as well. We held each other's gaze the entire time, and I couldn't keep out of my head visions of myself walking towards him like that.

By the look in his eyes, he was having the exact same thoughts.

Danger. Danger. Danger. Abort mission, a voice inside me screamed, but it almost felt like it was too late, like somehow I'd already stepped over the line, right into the dangerous territory.

Connor and Kelly reached the arch, and I watched as the groom and Connor gave each other a hug before he excitedly took his bride's hand. Connor joined his wife in front of me.

Ares was a wonderful officiant. Funny at times, and then so romantic that I swore every woman gave an audible gasp. When the wedding was done, and the bride and groom were kissing and then running back down the aisle, they looked like it truly was the best day of their life.

Ares came and got me.

"Ready to start the festival?" he asked.

"You know, you were pretty amazing up there."

He flushed, staring down at his feet. "I've done some of those before, but this was definitely the best one yet. It's helpful when you actually have an idea of what the young couple are feeling."

My lips parted and I knew if anyone was staring at me, they would have thought we were in love. But I couldn't *not* look at him like that. Ares squeezed my hand, and together we walked to the large town hall where they held the gathering.

I changed in the bathroom into a pair of pants and a long sleeve blouse, and then joined Ares who'd also changed into a pair of dark jeans and a black V-neck that accentuated every one of his muscles.

If I ever got married, it was definitely going to be like this, I thought a few hours later.

This was a party, not something stiff and formal.

Everyone was laughing and talking, and the food was amazing. They were serving a spiked cider that tasted almost as good as the apple tart I'd had every day since trying my first one. There were booths set up around the room with different foods to try, and there was a face-painting station for the kids. I'd watched Ares bob for apples against a couple of teenage boys, raising his fist in the air in mock victory when he finally got one.

I had just stabbed my fork into my slice of maple-flavored wedding cake with cream cheese frosting when I hit something. Curiously, I fished out a small metal pump-kin. I picked it up, and tapped Ares on the shoulder. When he glanced over at what I was holding, a knowing gleam was in his eyes.

"You got the kissing pumpkin," Connor said from next to him.

"The kissing pumpkin?"

"It's a wedding tradition. If you don't kiss your date before you enjoy the cake, you'll have bad luck for nine years..." Connor explained.

I hadn't considered myself an overly superstitious person in my life, but considering the bad luck I'd had lately, I wasn't really wanting to risk it.

Or at least that's what I told myself when I turned expectantly towards Ares.

There was a question in his gaze.

"Yes, I want this," I whispered, with a smile.

His hand captured my face softly, and he leaned forward, our breaths dancing together right before his lips met mine. And then he was kissing me deeply, reverently, like this kiss meant everything to him.

Before I knew it, his tongue was pushing gently into my

mouth and I was responding. The kiss seemed to last forever, and then not long enough. It was only when the sound of people cheering and laughing nearby grew louder, that he reluctantly pulled away from me, my breath heavy.

I felt a little woozy, and not from the cider. That had been the most romantic moment of my life.

And he appeared to feel the same way, judging by the stars in his eyes.

Connor elbowed him and said something, but Ares only nodded, not taking his gaze away from mine.

A few minutes later, the music started up. The bride and groom did their first dance. We were welcomed to the dance floor after that, and I eagerly took Ares's hand as he led me forward. A slow song began to play that I recognized, but I couldn't come up with the name. I was too lost in Ares's touch, the way he was holding me, in his gaze. He had pulled me so close that every part of us was touching, his eyes on me the entire time.

Later on, so late in the night that it would actually be morning soon, we walked into his house, still holding hands. He led me up to my room, and we stood in front of my door, just staring at each other like we had been all night, tethered together.

"I had a good time, Ares," I murmured.

"The best night of my life," he responded, his thumb rubbing against my cheek. It made me feel fluttery inside. As he walked away, it was everything I could do not to call him back into my room with me.

...

The following week, the whole town seemed to be in recovery after the festivities. The day after the reception, there'd been carnival games and rides all day, followed by an enormous bonfire and feast that lasted late into the night once again. The next day there'd been a series of competitions, like who was the strongest and fastest. Of course, Ares didn't participate in any of those, because we all knew who would win.

The last day had been another enormous party, the carnival still set up with rides, and more amazing food. I couldn't remember ever laughing so much or having a better time. And Ares stayed by my side the entire time. It had been torture in its most exquisite form. We'd kissed a few more times, but he'd never pushed it further. Every brush of his hand against mine, and every time our lips met...I wanted more.

Today was actually the first time that we'd been separated since he brought me here. He was going out for a large supply run with Connor and some of the others, and I hovered anxiously in the doorway, watching as he drove away. Today was the first time it hadn't been sunny, and it seemed to match my somber mood in his absence. I felt like I was becoming addicted to Ares. Without him there, I wasn't sure what to do with myself. Finally, I decided I would get a ride to the mines, not wanting to walk through the forest with the impending storm.

Armand dropped me off at the entrance, and the guards nodded at me respectfully. I knew their names now, after celebrating with them for four days. The rest of the workers said hello when I came in, and one of the girls set me up with my own station. I went to work, doing my best to do it how Ares had taught me, but I was incredibly distracted. I kept anxiously checking the phone Ares had given me, looking for a message from him that said he was on his way back. He was only supposed to have been gone for a few hours.

I finally got into a rhythm when I heard shouting from

outside. Connor ran in, his face pale and his gaze frantic. "Rune, there you are," he gasped, his chest heaving as if he'd run all the way here. "You need to come quickly. Ares... he's hurt."

I dropped my tools and ran towards him.

"He's hurt?"

Connor grabbed me by the arm and led me to a waiting car. "We were attacked by some Hunters who happened to be passing by where we stopped. Ares was trying to keep them away from all of us, but he got distracted. Then one of them stabbed him."

A sob slipped from my lips. "Is he going to be okay? What can I do?" I asked frantically. I knew he had to have supernatural healing, but it didn't sound like it was working.

I noticed Connor's hands were trembling in his lap, and it only made my fear grow. "He was stabbed with a wooden stake, but it just missed his heart. The bleeding doesn't seem to be stopping though, and the blood he normally drinks isn't helping him to heal like it usually does." He glanced at me, a pleading expression in his gaze. "I think you need to give him some of your blood. It's the only thing I can think of. Your blood bond would have special power to help him."

"Of course," I murmured, feeling a bit dazed at the prospect of him feeding from me...but also willing to do whatever it took to help Ares.

I realized then...I didn't want to live in a world where he didn't exist.

Connor hustled me into a waiting car and we sped off down the road that led to town, taking curves far faster than was safe. My fear only grew as we got closer. We came to a stop suddenly in front of the town hall that had been the site of the town celebrations just the week before.

I jumped out of the car and ran with Connor inside.

My steps faltered when I saw Ares laid out on a table, a group of anxious townspeople gathered around him, talking quietly. There were a few different bags of blood hanging beside him, with some discarded tubes. But as soon as they saw me, they took out the one tube that was currently in his vein.

I ran to his bedside and stared down in horror at Ares. He was passed out, and there was so much blood gurgling up from the wound on his chest. Someone had cut his shirt away, and it looked like more than a stab; it looked like someone had stuck a stake in his chest and then moved it all around. His skin was as pale as death, and his breath was coming out in stuttered gasps.

"Ares," I whispered. I glanced over at Connor. "What do I do? Do you need to put a tube in me to feed him?"

He shook his head. "I think it will work best from the source. Here," he said, pulling a knife from his pocket. One of the women grabbed it from him and poured alcohol over it to clean it before handing it back to Connor.

"I'm sorry," he murmured before he took my hand and sliced it. That took me off guard, but I immediately brought it to Ares's lips, the drops of blood falling into his mouth while someone else held it open.

"I think you need to cut me more," I said worriedly when it didn't seem to be helping, and the wound was already starting to close from my supernatural healing powers.

I couldn't help but muse on that for half a second. I hadn't had that power before, because I hadn't had my first shift. You had to have your Alpha call your wolf out for you the first time. Had I shifted in the last year? And it was just another thing I couldn't remember. My heart cried at the thought.

Connor brought my attention back when he took a deep breath and then cut me even deeper. It hurt like a mother fucker, but I didn't make a sound. I just immediately put it back to Ares's lips as the blood trailed into his mouth. We all waited and watched with bated breath.

It seemed like a lifetime passed, but finally, I noticed that some color was returning to his cheeks.

"I think it's working," I cried out, listening to the excited murmurs around me. Suddenly, one of Ares's hands shot up and grabbed my arm, and his sharp fangs popped out. He plunged them into my wrist and I gasped, my knees buckling as he began to take deep draws of my blood.

"Rune!" Connor exclaimed, but I shook my head, staggering back up to my feet as all sorts of feelings rushed through me...not all of them painful.

"It's all right," I whispered, watching Ares's chest closely as the wound began to close up. If this didn't prove I was his blood match, or there was at least something special about my blood to him, I wasn't sure what would.

This moment felt intimate, even with his eyes closed. It felt like he was taking my life force inside of him, and we'd be connected forever after this.

Finally, Ares opened his eyes, and I was once again staring into his beautiful midnight-blue gaze.

He was confused for a moment, his gaze darting all around the room, before the hand that wasn't holding my wrist to his mouth felt around the ever-healing wound on his chest. He tried to remove his teeth from within me, but I held my wrist to his mouth.

"Just a little longer," I ordered, not wanting to stop until the wound was all the way gone.

He was still too pale.

His gaze came back to me, and there were so many emotions I was watching rippling over his face. Gratefulness, worship... And love that took my breath away.

Finally, the wound on his chest was completely gone and Ares slipped his teeth out of my wrist, licking across the wound so that the cuts would heal.

I was lightheaded, and the second he let go, I started to collapse. I was saved from falling by him leaping off the table and catching me in his arms.

"I was just testing to make sure you actually healed?" I said feebly. But he didn't smile at my joke.

"I took too much. Fuck," he growled, scooping me up into his arms until we were both on the table. He cradled me close to his chest as my body worked to recover. I noticed the way that my heartbeat had slowed. He'd really taken a lot.

"You are not allowed to ever put yourself in danger for me," he ordered fiercely before he took a shuddering breath. "But I love you so much that you did."

We sat there in silence, while I recovered, and just when I was about to ask him what happened, the crowd burst through the door, Connor leading the way. They gathered around us, all of them asking how he was feeling and fretting over him. Once again, it hit me just how much Ares was loved.

He reassured them for another ten minutes, but when I yawned, he immediately ended the conversations.

"I'll see all of you tomorrow," he said in a firm voice. "I love you all," he threw over his shoulder as he carried me out of the town hall. I peeked over Ares's shoulder, and

Connor mouthed "thank you" to me, bowing his head slightly.

I feebly smiled and laid my head back on Ares's shoulders as he carried me to a waiting car and we went back to the house. My body was so out of it due to the blood loss that I fell asleep during the five-minute ride home. I woke up to him carrying me to the stairs, and then into my room. He laid me gently down on the bed, taking off my shoes and adjusting the covers around me.

And then he went to leave.

"Stay," I croaked, needing him by my side after the events of the afternoon.

He sighed, seeming relieved by my request, and then he slipped his bloodied shirt off and crawled into bed with me. He still had dry-crusted blood on his skin, but neither of us cared. He pulled me into his arms and I laid my head on his chest, the sound of his beating heart...the sweetest lullaby I could imagine.

I was out within minutes, feeling safer than I could ever remember feeling.

———

My head still felt heavy when I woke up, and I was shocked to see that Ares was still lying in bed with me...sound asleep. He was always up long before me. Ares was facing my way, and I admired his beauty in the dim light of the sunrise caressing his face from the room's window.

He resembled a sleeping angel, a perfect creation I could scarcely believe was real.

"I can feel you watching me," he said in a sexy, sleep-ridden voice.

I blushed even though he hadn't opened his eyes.

"I was just wondering if you got up for me and brushed your teeth already, because your breath is surprisingly not bad," I teased.

His eyes flew open. A sexy grin stretched across his face.

"Just my vampire charm."

I laughed.

"How are you feeling, baby?" he murmured, his hand going to my cheek and stroking it softly. I pressed my face into his palm, soaking up the feel of him.

"Much better. Although a better question would be, how are *you* feeling?"

His face sobered. "Alive thanks to you. You saved my life, Rune."

I flushed, feeling shy under his worshipful stare.

"I wasn't about to let you die on my watch."

Ares continued to stare at me intensely, and my gaze darted away. "What happened?"

He stiffened and withdrew his hand, running it anxiously through his wild locks.

"You heard that I used to be head of a clan of Hunters..." he began, still studying me closely.

I nodded. "What exactly did you hunt?"

He visibly blanched, and dread reared its head.

"Wolves," he said. I flinched and flopped to my back.

"Remind me how we met?" I asked intensely, knowing what he was going to say even before he opened his mouth.

"I was hunting you," he said after a long silence. "I kidnapped you from Amarok, and I took you to the club-house we'd set up...and I was going to kill you."

His words were heavy, fearful even...I tensed, sure that what he was about to say would change everything.

"Go on," I whispered.

"I tasted your blood, and that's when I realized who you were to me. That's when everything changed."

I closed my eyes.

"But even before that, I started to feel things for you. I don't think I could've gone through with it even if I hadn't found out what you were to me."

In his voice, there was a plea for forgiveness. But as hard as it was to hear him tell the story, it felt like someone else's life he was talking about. I couldn't remember anything. He might as well have been reading out of a book. It was almost impossible for me to picture Ares wanting to kill me, the complete opposite of who he was right now.

"What happened after that?"

He sighed deeply. "I helped you escape and betrayed everyone in the organization. Although I killed everyone there, news had gotten out about what I'd done. I'm currently 'persona non grata' on the Hunters' list." There was a thread of sadness when he said that as well.

"How long had you been with the Hunters?"

Another long silence. "Practically my entire life. I was taken in by one of them when I was a little boy. It's been... an adjustment. I was lucky to have this place to call home as well, though."

"Did the Hunters know about your trip yesterday, or was it random?"

"As far as I could tell, it was random. They happened to be hunting in that small town for someone. And when they saw me in front of the store, helping load boxes... Well, they couldn't miss that opportunity to make me pay." He rubbed his chest, like he was still feeling the phantom pain of the stake they'd thrust there.

It hurt me to see him that way.

"Rune," he said, his voice trembling. "Has what I told

you ruined everything?" There was an air of finality in his voice when he asked it, like he didn't think there would be any other options for me *but* to hate him.

I searched his face for... I didn't know what exactly. Because it was hard to look past the love in his gaze, the way he'd made me feel so far, like I was his most priceless treasure. I fingered the necklace around my neck, his gaze dropping briefly to follow the movement before going back to my face.

"I can't imagine you that way. But I forgive you. It sounds like I went along with whatever Alistair wanted for a long time based on what you've told me, putting up with things I never should have, just because I didn't know it was supposed to be any other way. If you had been raised to hate me..."

"You forgive me?" he breathed, incredulous hope in his voice.

"Honestly, I'm not sure that there's anything to forgive in the first place."

For a second, something that looked like guilt flickered in his gaze, but I blinked and it was gone, the love that was always there shining out from his midnight blue eyes.

I tensed. "Are the Hunters still alive? Would they have followed you back here?" My mind raced, thinking of the town coming under attack and the innocent humans that would be caught up in such a battle.

Ares quickly shook his head. "I had already given them both fatal wounds when I was stabbed. Connor assured me that they're dead, and they didn't see any signs of others. He destroyed their cell phones, so it will be hard for anyone to track them."

I nodded, only feeling slightly relieved. The best-laid plans always seemed to go wrong, I knew that.

"I don't feel like doing anything today," he confessed.

I studied him, worriedly, but besides looking tired, something I realized I hadn't seen before, he looked healthy enough. Beautiful...as always.

"Well, I think since you almost died yesterday, you might deserve a day off. I'm still feeling rather tired today as well."

"How about we lounge on the couch all day? I'll let you pick the movies, and I promise to provide good snacks."

"Sounds good. I promise not to torture you with *Twilight* movies."

Ares scoffed and shook his head. "You know their portrayal of wolves is just as bad as their portrayal of vampires," he teased.

I shrugged. "I'm just disappointed that your skin doesn't sparkle."

He wrinkled his nose at me. "I'm sorry I can't fulfill all of your vampire fantasies." He hopped out of bed, and yesterday's events crashed through my head as I examined his chest, still covered in blood.

"I'm going to go shower," he murmured, his gaze tracing my figure as I sat up. "You're welcome to join me and save some water."

My breath hitched. His voice was teasing, but...his idea sounded pretty good. I flushed and fiddled with my sheets. Ares chuckled softly before he left the room.

I decided to take my own shower, so I went into the bathroom and started the water. Once I got under the hot spray, I sighed, the steam rising around me. My core was throbbing, and my breasts felt tight. I couldn't help but imagine myself in the shower with him, his hands stroking my body, massaging and pulling at my breasts. His fingers sliding through my folds.

"Rune!" The voice sounded in my head and my lust-filled daydreams faded like smoke. The voice didn't say anything else, but it was enough to make me finish my shower quickly. Ares was waiting for me on the couch with a huge pile of snacks on the table in front of him. There was also an oversized cup filled with blood.

"Is that going to help you at all?" I asked, gesturing to it.

He went stiff. "It will fill me up, but it probably won't help with my energy."

I opened my mouth to offer my vein to him again, but he shook his head before I could even get the words out.

"I took way too much yesterday. I could have killed you. I'll be fine. You just need to work on recovering. I'm so fucking sorry." He shook his head, his face distressed.

Surprising myself...and him, I slid onto the couch and straddled him, holding his gorgeous face between my palms. "I would do it for you a million times over," I whispered, unfamiliar emotions sliding through my chest.

Ares trembled under my touch. And then he closed his eyes as if he was pained.

"Thank you," he whispered. There was a long pause, and suddenly he was grabbing me and pulling me against him. His lips crashed against mine, our tongues tangling as he licked and sucked at my mouth. His hands traveled up and down my waist and my back, and my hands moved to his shirt, pulling him closer towards me, because it didn't feel like I could ever get close enough. When we separated, we were both breathing heavily. My lips felt swollen and bruised, and everything in me wanted more.

He shook his head as if he was trying to shake off the stupor.

"Let's get you fed, and that movie going, sweetheart.

When I finally take you, it's going to be when you're one hundred percent."

My chest and cheeks flushed as the mental imagery flooded my brain. And I realized...just how much I wanted that.

I snuggled into him as he turned on *Pretty Woman*—an oldie but a goodie, I thought—and we passed the day lazing about in each other's arms.

It was perfect.

CHAPTER 13
RUNE

The next week flew by. Ares made me take it easy for a few more days and insisted on taking care of my every need. I felt a bit spoiled...and cooped up by his imposed rest period.

And so was my wolf.

This was showcasing itself with the anxiety in my chest and the way the usually perfect eggs Benedict in front of me currently tasted like ash.

"Is everything alright, Rune?" Marcia asked, and I tried to make my body language less ridiculous.

"Everything's good."

"But you haven't eaten anything," she pressed with a frown.

I could feel Ares's frown as well, boring into the side of my head as he tried to read my mind.

"I'm not hungry," I groaned, sounding like a sullen child.

"What's wrong, baby?" Ares asked, his voice amused at my attitude because he seemed to find everything I did cute.

For some reason, I turned to him and stuck my tongue at him petulantly...

My wolf whined inside me.

Suddenly, it hit me. My wolf. She seemed like...she wanted to come out.

"Can we go to the forest today? With the memories I have, I don't remember transforming into my wolf, but I think...she needs out." My gaze automatically went to Marcia to see if she was going to be weirded out by that, though her boss was already a vampire, so a wolf shouldn't be that much of a stretch.

She didn't seem bothered at all by what I said...or shocked, for that matter. Ares had probably caught everyone up on what I was...but it was still strange.

"That sounds like a lovely idea, dearie," she said with a sweet smile before picking up a dish to wash.

Humans in this town were *very* different from the ones outside of it.

"I should've thought of that before now. Of course your pretty wolf would want to come out."

I'd forgotten he'd seen my wolf...because at least in my memories, I hadn't even seen her.

Marcia packed us a lunch, and we set out towards the woods, not bothering to use a car since my whole problem was I needed to expel some energy.

We mostly walked in silence, enjoying the beautiful, crisp weather and the scenery.

"Is Amarok like this?" I asked suddenly, gesturing to the majestic scene around us.

He shifted uncomfortably, just as he always did when I mentioned that town.

"It has its own charm," he finally said. "You're very close to many of the people there."

"I'd like to go back soon, try to pick up the pieces of my life. I probably have belongings there, right? Maybe that would help with my memory," I mused.

He didn't say anything for so long that I finally glanced over, stopping in my tracks by how tortured he looked. He tried to school his face when he saw me watching, but it wasn't fast enough.

"Why don't you want to go back there?" I asked quietly, walking again towards the forest.

He sighed and pushed some of his curls out of his face. "Because I feel like we're in a little bubble here, and I'm scared everything will change once we're out of it."

I cocked my head. "Why will it change?"

He glanced away. "It just will," he finally murmured.

Now I was the one sighing, frustrated he wasn't giving me more details.

But then I was distracted by the sight of Aldo galloping towards us, his tongue hanging out like the giant monster dog he was.

"There's my little baby," I cooed as he came to a stop in front of me, an inch away from knocking me to the ground.

I glanced over at Ares. "Is he going to be freaked out by me changing into a wolf? Did you train him to eat wolves when you were with the Hunters?" I asked the question with a tease in my voice, realizing at the end, though, that probably was the case.

"He'd never hurt you," Ares said firmly.

"You sound so confident about that." I continued to scratch behind Aldo's ears even as I envisioned him eating me alive.

"Because I love you. And he's part of me. He would never hurt anyone that I loved," Ares said the words almost challengingly, like he was daring me to refute them.

But I couldn't.

I wasn't confident of much in this new life of mine after I'd lost my identity and my past.

But I was confident that he loved me.

And I didn't know what to think about that.

"All right, here goes nothing." I stood still for a long pause because even though I must have transformed before, I just couldn't remember doing it. Surely, it couldn't be that hard.

"Everything okay?" Ares asked. "Sometimes it's better not to overthink these things and just give in to your wolf."

"That sounds easier than it is." But never one to not try a new approach, I closed my eyes, exhaled deeply, and reached down for my wolf, calling her to come out.

Something ignited in my chest, flaring over me with such a rush it scared me. But the feeling faded just as quickly because I knew it was my wolf. And it was exhilarating how easily she flowed out of me, just as Ares had said. Electricity zipped down my spine, and I was suddenly shifting, immediately having that out-of-body experience as my consciousness drifted inside my wolf.

I fell down onto all fours. The world looked sharper around me, more colorful. And when I looked up, I was blinded by how Ares somehow appeared even more gorgeous than usual. It would be nice to have this kind of eyesight all the time.

"You're beautiful, little dove," he murmured, petting me softly.

I tottered around on all fours, the sensation of being in my wolf so freeing, like I had endless energy and nothing could touch me. I went to speak to Ares, but a yelp came out, and with my excitement, I found myself breaking into a howl, my head tilted back. The song sliding past my lips was beautiful and full of longing.

My heart was beating so quickly.

I'd just transformed into my wolf and I wanted to scream it for the world to hear me.

Aldo stared at me as well, and he didn't seem like he was about to eat me—he actually looked excited, wagging his tail. Just when I'd thought that, he barked, and my wolf gave a warning growl that didn't seem to faze him at all.

"Stunning. Should we go for a run now?" Ares asked. "Do you think either of you can catch me?"

He suddenly took off like the wind—vampire speed was incredible—but my wolf was up for the chase. We raced off, silver glitter floating away in the wind behind us as I ran. This was heaven. In this form, I felt truly free. We spent hours running around chasing after Ares who never seemed to tire of having my wolf after him.

We were playing so hard, I didn't even notice the clouds rolling in. Not until the sky released a torrential rain shower, immediately soaking us to the core.

I yelped as I shifted back, completely freezing, covered in mud. My teeth were chattering. Ares handed me my clothes, not bothering to hide that he was looking.

I turned around as I slipped on my clothes, very aware of his gaze caressing my skin.

And then I got an idea.

As soon as I finished dressing, I leaned over and scooped up some mud...and then I turned and threw it right at his face, giggling hysterically as it splattered all over his shocked features.

"Did you really just do that?" he gasped, wiping mud off his lips.

I shrugged, giving him a daring stare.

"I'll give you a head start."

"A head start for what?" I asked.

"To run away before I get you back."

I ran as he scooped up two handfuls and tossed them at me, shrieking when the cold mud hit my neck and slid down my shirt.

Deciding playing defense wasn't working, I stopped and began to fling mud back at him.

Back and forth we went until we were absolutely covered.

And I was absolutely freezing.

"Truce? We should get you back before you freeze to death," he called over the wind and the rain. I nodded, because I was turning into a popsicle, I was pretty sure, and he could get us back much faster than I could run.

He pulled me into his arms and we took off. I buried my face in his neck as the wind whipped past us. By the time we arrived at his house, I no longer was *becoming* a popsicle —I *was* one.

"All right, a bath for you," he murmured.

I sat on the bathroom tile, the floor soon covered with mud and water as it dripped off of us. The sound of my teeth chattering flooded the room, and I stared longingly at the bath. As it filled up, the steam from the water caressed the air.

"I think I'm frozen," I stuttered, and he stared over at me, concerned.

"I should've been paying better attention," he growled.

I rolled my eyes. "I may do stupid crap sometimes, but I am a grown woman. I should've been paying attention as well. We were just having so much fun..."

He gave me a beautiful grin. "We were having fun, weren't we?"

I swooned at the fondness in his gaze.

We stared at each other openly, until my teeth chattered again.

"Call me if you need anything," he said before slipping out of the room. I struggled to get my clothes off, and then I walked towards the bath. Because my limbs felt frozen and stiff, I slipped on some water that dripped on the floor and fell into the bathtub, sending water everywhere, and my shampoo and conditioner crashed to the floor.

The door flew open. "Rune!" Ares exclaimed, staring around the bathroom like the enemy was about to pop up out of thin air.

I held up my hand, pushing my wet hair out of my face. "That was me just being clumsy."

"Oh, okay." But he was distracted, because there weren't any bubbles in the bath, so his gaze slid over my body.

He stood there, as if in a trance.

And...I decided to be brave.

"Stay," I whispered. "Better yet, get in the bath with me."

He stared at me, like he was wondering if this was all a dream. And I was wondering as well, because I was never this brave in asking what I wanted.

"Are you sure?" he asked, because we both knew where it would lead.

"Yes."

He slowly took off his dripping clothes, revealing inch by inch his beautiful, perfect body. I averted my eyes at the last second as his pants slid down, even though I was eager to see that part of his anatomy.

Baby steps in this bravery thing.

I was staring at my hands in the water when he slipped

in, sitting across from me, his legs on either side of me. I tingled all over from where we touched.

We just stared at each other, the soft light of the candles he'd lit on the counter flickering against his features. I took my time, taking every inch of him in.

———

ARES

"Sometimes I think I've just dreamed you into existence," I murmured, well aware of how besotted I sounded as I stared at her. Her eyes were closed and her head was tilted back as she soaked up the warm water.

I loved her body. Everything in me ached for, needed her. The way that I wanted her was going to drive me insane.

As much as the last month had been about getting her to fall in love with me, I realized that it had given me time too. The blood bond was strong, acting as an instant love drug, and while I'd already been well on my way to feelings before discovering who she was, this last month... Well, I'd fallen even more.

I thought I'd been in love before, but it was nothing close to how I felt now, after being around her every second. Everything about her fascinated me. I couldn't get enough.

"You're staring at me," she murmured as her head came up.

I knew I affected her. Her breath was hitched and her lips were parted.

And I wondered... Was she finally ready for me? I moved

forward and her eyes tracked me like I was a predator about to eat her up.

"How about we change the seating arrangements?" I murmured, moving slowly so she had time to say no if she wanted to.

But she didn't say anything. She just nodded her head, a small smile on her beautiful lips. I picked her up by the waist and slid behind her. Luckily the bathtub in this bathroom was big enough to fit several people, so it wasn't a tight fit at all. She was trembling against me as she laid her head back on my shoulder.

I started at her hands, keeping mine over hers for a minute before I slid them up her arms. Until I got to her delicious breasts. She gasped as I played with her tips, working her nipples until she was moaning. They were the perfect size. The most perfect breasts I'd ever seen.

She was staring up at me, her head still tilted back, with a half-lidded gaze, one that turned my cock to steel.

It was hard to go slow with her staring up at me like that, her hunger calling to me. I moved my rigid length against her back as I continued to work her breasts. She made a purring sound, and my lips were on hers, my tongue slipping into her mouth as my hips rocked against her.

Her breasts were heavy and hot in my hands, and I did everything I'd been dreaming about doing to her. Pinching, rolling, tugging at her nipples. She bucked against me, and I wanted everything. I wanted to consume her. I wanted to own her. I wanted her. I kept one hand working her breasts, and the other one slid down her stomach until I was parting her folds and settling on her clit with my finger. I studied her face, loving the sounds she was making as I applied the perfect amount of pressure on her.

"Sometime soon, I want to spend all day just tasting your perfect little pussy," I growled.

"Ares," she gasped for air as her hands came out of the water, and she put them behind my neck, fucking herself against my fingers. I let go of her breasts enough to grab her chin and plunge my tongue back into her mouth. She was my sole reason for living, having her like this was every dream of mine come true. I gently pushed in one thick finger and she cried out, her hips thrusting against me. I moved my other hand off her perfect face so I could massage her clit as I slipped more fingers into her burning hot core. She was tensing, and a red flush was spreading up her neck as her body prepared to climax.

"Give it to me, sweetheart. Come for me," I purred in her ear.

Her whole body stiffened when she came, writhing against me, her perfect pussy sucking at my fingers.

I wanted to own every inch of her, to mark every part of her.

"I can't wait any longer," I said as soon as she'd come down from her orgasm.

"Give me more," she begged, and I lifted and twisted her so that she was straddling me, my dick sliding between her folds, hitting against her clit.

"Are you sure?" I asked one more time, because I couldn't bear her having regrets after this. When she got her memories back, maybe regrets would be a given. For both of us. But at least today, in this world we'd created together, I didn't want her to have any.

She leaned forward and pressed her lips against mine, her hair soaked, sticking to her gorgeous face. "Fuck me," she whispered, and I almost came just from her pleading. I gripped my cock and lined it up, slowly pushing it in. Her core was so tight that even with the water, it was hard to get inside. Her small size was only making the torture worse.

"You're perfect. A goddess come to life," I groaned as I finally thrust all the way in, her cunt choking me.

"Fuck." I was becoming mindless, overcome with how much I wanted her. I grabbed onto her hips, lifting her up slightly until I looked into her eyes.

Reality brought me back and I stopped, scared that I'd hurt her if I went too hard.

"Don't stop," she asked, much to my delight. She pressed her lips against mine as I lost myself in her. I began to fuck her viciously as our lips moved against each other.

Her muscles were trembling and her body quivered as another orgasm approached.

"So good, baby," I whispered roughly as she milked my cock. Her hands gripped my neck, pulling me close as I continued to slide my cock in and out of her soft, lush body. Her eyes were dazed as I pounded into her, wanting the moment to last forever.

But of course it felt so good that there was no way for me to last forever, and a minute later I was cumming, the most intense orgasm I'd ever experienced.

Our heavy breaths filled the room as we continued to kiss lazily afterward. My hands slid all over her body, wanting to touch every part of her.

She moved her face away an inch, and I tried not to chase her, because I needed her body against mine. Forever.

Rune stared at me strangely, confused...and something else stirred behind her gaze.

Oh shit, was she regretting it already?

"Ares, I remember you..." she whispered.

Fuck.

———

Rune

It came back like a wave crashing over me, image by image of Ares. Seeing him on the sidewalk in Amarok, the dreams he'd given me, him kidnapping me...the moment he'd sunk his teeth into my neck and I thought I was about to die. When he realized I was his blood match...He'd given me my necklace...but I couldn't remember why. I couldn't remember why he'd been hunting me in the first place.

The memories felt so disjointed, and I could tell there were still large gaps, like I'd just gotten bits and pieces back, and I was still missing important parts.

"What all do you remember?" he asked, trepidation threaded through his voice.

I walked through the memories and he listened tensely.

Ares was still hard inside of me, and somehow it felt natural, like he was always meant to be there.

He was staring at the water in front of him by the time I finished, shame coating his features.

"Is that all you remember?" he asked quietly, still not looking at me.

"Yes," I answered. "Are there things missing? It still feels like there are."

He was quiet, his usual tell when he didn't want to answer one of my questions.

"There's a lot. But I'm sure you will get those back soon." He always made it seem like we were on a ticking clock. Like doomsday was just ahead.

As I went through the memories I remembered, they still didn't change how I felt in that moment...after spending almost every second with him over the past month.

"I'm still in love with you," I whispered, the words coming out shy and stilted, because it took a lot for me to get them out.

His head shot up so fast he almost head-butted me.

"What?" he asked incredulously.

"I'm still in love with you," I repeated, a huge smile stretching across my face, because it felt so good to say it out loud.

"I'm so fucking in love with you too," he breathed.

"I know," I said with a wink.

Our lips slid together like they were never meant to be apart.

And as he moved inside of me once again...I pushed all thoughts away of what I didn't know.

Because what I did know...was that I belonged to him.

And that was enough for now.

CHAPTER 14
DAXON

Pain flared in my chest like the point of a knife, twisting, scraping, pushing deeper the quicker Rune ran from me. And she was fast, darting through the woods, blurring in and out of the shadows. My gaze followed her long, white hair, glinting in the afternoon sunlight.

She glanced over her shoulder...eyes of shattering ice blue staring back at me.

I'd marked her as mine, and yet she ran from me. Instinct had me burning up with desperation, with unhinged craving.

Unraveling myself from my thoughts, I lunged after her.

Feet pounding the earth, I enjoyed the run, the exhilaration of the chase, and I ran after my sweetheart as I would hunt down my prey. And when I caught her, I'd devour her, starting with that delicious cunt. I'd spread open her legs, thrust my tongue into her, feel her wriggling under me, listen to her moans. She'd twist beneath me while begging me to take her harder.

"Fuck." She had me rattled with arousal, and I was ready to throw myself at her.

But first, I had to catch her and find out why the hell she was running in the first place.

I skidded around a tree to close the distance between us, convinced she was teasing me. She really had no idea what I had in store once I captured her.

"You won't get far, sweetheart," I called out after her, knowing she'd heard me, my footfalls thudding faster, harder as I scaled the hill. She moved fast like a rabbit, hopping about, and I was impressed.

I shoved faster, cutting her off as she swung left, and now she was directly in my sights. Her eyes grew huge as she glanced back at me descending upon her. My skin felt tight, burning me up with my wolf pressing forward to escape. He loved the hunt, except this was about her and me. About how I was going to remind her what happened if she taunted me.

Feet away, she released a small cry, madly scrambling out of my reach, swerving left and right past the trees.

Dominance roared through me with the hunger I held for my mate. I might have kept back my wolf, but his essence pumped in my veins, propelling me forward.

In a thunderous surge, I sprinted harder and snatched her by the arm with more force than I intended, but it got the job done. She flung back around, pivoting on her feet, and came flying at me from the momentum. I captured her in my arms, our bodies clashing, those gorgeous tits squeezed between us.

"You bastard," she wheezed, slamming a fist into my chest, yet the corners of her eyes smiled. Oh, she loved this.

"Rune, baby, did you really think you'd get away from me? I'd go to the ends of the earth to find you, fight armies. I'd die before I lost you. We are forever."

Breathing heavily, she lifted her gaze. "What if there's no forever?"

Words I hated to hear churned in my head. The ache of what she implied was devastating. I had no idea where they came from, but I refused to even tolerate them.

"That's not even an option," I said breathlessly, walking her backward until her back flushed flat against a tree where I ground my cock against her. "I've marked you as mine."

The sugary scent of her slick drove me to madness, all my blood rushing to my cock.

Our mouths clashed, and she tasted like heaven, leaving my whole body trembling with need. I was starved for my mate, to lap up her slick, to thrust into her tight pussy. She rubbed herself against me, her nipples hard, her hand sliding down between us, cupping my erection, and she squeezed.

"Fuck!" I hissed, lessening my grip on her as arousal ricocheted through me. But it was also the same moment she tore her lips from my mouth, ripped herself from my grip, and broke free. Then she ran from me.

"You can't find me," she said in a sing-song tease, laughing. She was sprinting so fast that she crossed the woods in seconds.

"Is that the game you want to play," I growled, slightly confused, my cock painfully hard, my hunger for her blurring my mind with my desperation.

I was a bastard in love who didn't hesitate to race after her, and that time I didn't hold back. I went full throttle, coming up on her so fast, she screamed from my determination.

Holding my gaze, she laughed at me.

My dick throbbed, and I threw myself at her that time, picking her up off her feet, her back flush to my chest.

She cried out, "Put me down."

"I can't wait a second longer. You're killing me, babe." I tore at her clothes savagely, her dress falling apart at my hands, her panties gone in seconds. Lush, heavy breasts bounced free, those dusty-pink nipples hard for me. Her scent thickened, flooding my senses. I could practically taste it at the back of my throat.

She bucked against me.

"You haven't told me yet you don't want this," I growled,

looping an arm around her thin waist while pushing my hand up her spine, forcing her to bend forward, while I brought us both down to our knees, her ass in the air.

She must have realized her escape was futile, because when I lowered her to her hands and knees, I pushed myself between her legs where slick dripped down the inside of her thighs.

"You are spectacular," I purred, lowering my touch to her core, my fingers coming back drenched and sticky. I couldn't help myself and stuck them into my mouth, and I groaned at her sweetness, at the heaviness of her scent fogging my brain.

She moaned, her hips rocking back and forth. My minx was aroused, craving what I had for her.

"Daxon," she cried, spreading her legs wider for me as her perfume swallowed me, placing me under her spell. She glanced at me over her shoulder, those blue eyes burning with desire. "Please, stop making me wait."

"I should make you wait as punishment for running from me."

Her eyes narrowed on me. "Would you be making me, or you, suffer if you did that?"

"I'll suffer to teach you a small lesson."

She giggled, wriggling her ass, sticking it higher, offering me everything, and fuck me, but I how could any resist the most beautiful pussy in the world?

"You're right, I shouldn't punish myself," I said with a smirk, loving the sound of her answering giggle. I guided my cock to her entrance, angling my hips for easy access, teasing her with my tip as I pushed against her swollen lips. Slick gushed over my dick from her arousal and she was pushing herself back to take me.

I grasped hold of her hips and rammed into her.

She screamed, her spine arching, her body trembling.

"Fuck, I love the way your body reacts to mine," I said

through gritted teeth as I tried to gain control of myself. "You've been a really bad girl, though. I should probably show you what happens."

"Yes, punish me," she moaned, pushing against me desperately.

Moving my hips back and forth, I thrust into her, my erection rubbing against her tight walls. The faster I went, the louder the sounds of me slapping against her drenched core escalated around us.

Waves of heat rolled from her body, her core gripping my cock, igniting into a burning blaze from the friction between us.

Her cries were beautiful. "I love you," I moaned, heat rising in my chest, while she writhed against me, shuddering, crying out for more.

Arousal pulled at my nerve endings, and I withdrew all the way before slamming back into her down to my base, my balls so tight, they readied to push into her too.

Her pussy tightened, squeezing me, and I hissed, gripping her hips harder.

With pink cheeks, she stared over at me, purring out, "I want to ride you now." Her tongue peeked out, dragging over her lower lip in that way that made me crazy. "Will you let me ride your big, thick cock?"

My chest rose and fell harder at her request. I was salivating.

"Oh, sweetheart, you're secretly my dirty girl, aren't you?" I groaned, pulling out of her as her pussy pulled at my cock, trying to hold me inside her.

As she moved, I caught sight of her swollen pussy lips, of her slick gushing down her legs. I was mesmerized by the view from back there, and I wanted to dive in...and lap it all up. My mouth watered, but she'd moved out of my grasp too quickly. She was standing in front of me, staring down.

I glanced up at her from where I knelt before my queen, at her stunning body, curves, her pert nipples just asking to be pulled, to that little pussy glistening with slickness.

"Come on," she moaned.

I in turn flipped to my back, needing my dick in her tight cunt before I went mad. I told myself I'd let her take the lead. I couldn't wait to watch her bouncing up and down on my cock.

Except it was that same second that she took off running madly away from me again, her laughter piercing the silence of the forest

What the fuck? I craned my head, staring after her incredulously as she raced completely naked through the forest.

"Sweetheart! Are you fucking kidding me right now?"

I threw myself up to my feet, my cock in pain, and charged after her. If she wanted to play this game, then I'd play...but next time I caught her, she'd end up with a red ass.

And so the chase started once more, but this time, frustration coursed through me. I usually loved my girl's playfulness, but there was only so much a man could take.

Choking on my own arousal, I ran, but somehow, she always moved faster than me. Just out of reach. There one minute, and then halfway across the glen the next.

I growled, fists curled into balls, my insides twisting.

"Come on, Daxon," she called out, sounding almost desperate herself. "Don't you dare give up on finding me. You promised me forever." Then she darted into the shadows, vanishing from sight.

I roared, my throat dry. Everything I felt for her was primal and so fucking raw. Every muscle in my body tensed, and I darted after her, needing to find her...

I shot upright in bed, a roar on my throat, sweat covering me, and my cock so hard, it hurt like a bitch.

"Fucking dream," I muttered under my breath, collapsing back into my bed, my muscles aching. It was the same damn dream I'd been having every day since we'd lost Rune.

It had been five fucking weeks since Ares left us in the park after he sensed Rune and took her for himself. The asshole had never returned and never sent word. We couldn't even be sure if he'd gotten her back. Although my guess was yes, judging by his disappearance.

The anger I had for him was like a sharp knife, embedded constantly in my gut. I knew I should have killed him. When had being the good guy ever turned out well for anyone?

Fury shook me, the fresh wound in my heart tearing open more and more each day that we hadn't found her. We'd searched every goddamn inch of Romania by this point.

And still no sign of my sweetheart.

We'd questioned anyone we came across, and even the bear pack, but no one had any clues.

I lived in a constant nightmare, one made of madness, where every day we did the same thing, and for some reason expected a different outcome. I was already teetering on the edge of insanity on a good day...and this fucked up situation was pushing me right off the ledge.

Tossing the blankets aside, I shoved myself out of bed, the crippling pain in my muscles getting worse. The longer I spent away from Rune, the more I hurt.

I stepped over my clothes that were strewn all over the floor. The mess did my head in, but I couldn't find the energy to fix anything. It felt like I barely existed, all my energy consumed with finding my mate and keeping back the darkness trying to consume me.

My chest tightened, and I unleashed raspy coughs that hadn't left me for weeks.

Our mating bond was slowly killing me. There was something dark connected to the bond I'd formed. The distance from her was slowly destroying me from the inside out, and I had no doubt how this would end for me if I didn't find her soon.

Making my way into my bathroom, I dragged myself into the shower. The only thing that got me out of bed most mornings was the thread of hope that today we'd find something on Rune.

People didn't just disappear, and we knew from our research that Ares had some kind of base here, somewhere he returned when he hadn't been out with the Hunters. It was just a matter of finding out where that base was.

Once I finished, I stepped out of the shower and wiped a hand across the fogged-up mirror. Staring back at me was a sickly-looking face, pale as fuck, eyes red like I hadn't slept a wink.

"I look like death," I groaned.

I never got a full night's sleep. And when I did sleep, I was constantly chasing Rune in my dreams. Her last words always stayed with me, playing on my mind, day in, day out. Driving me mad.

Don't you dare give up on finding me. You promised me forever.

"I'm coming for you, Rune. I give you my word. I won't stop until I'm dead." I gripped the sides of the porcelain sink until my hands hurt. Until a wave of dizziness washed over me, and I stumbled back into my room that looked like it'd been hit by a tornado.

I rubbed at my chest, staring at the mess in a daze. I was getting sicker. I felt the hole inside me expanding. How long before it inhaled me completely?

Getting dressed, I heard muffled voices outside my

room. Stepping into my boots, I raked my fingers through my wet hair and hacked out my lungs before I moved out into the corridor. We'd rented this place because it was central in the city and made it easier to go out and search.

The smell of blood suddenly assaulted my nostrils, slamming into me the moment I entered the main living room. I hissed as I came face to face with a scene right out of the show *Dexter*.

The furniture had all been shoved up against the walls, and a plastic tarp had been laid out across the room where three bodies lay, all dead. I could tell by the blood, pungent stench, and their blue faces.

Wilder was kneeling next to a body, staring down at him, wiping off his blood-covered hands with a cloth.

"Look, I'm all for you taking a page out of my book, but don't bring the victims right into the house where anyone can peer into the window and see them."

"The blinds are drawn," he murmured, and I glanced at the blinds that were in fact only partially drawn. Amateur. While I'd been losing my head and falling sick from my mate bond to Rune...Wilder had gone feral. One could say he was becoming me, furious with the world and ready to murder anyone who stood in his way.

I was rather proud of him because for too long he'd been a fucking sissy. Finally, he'd seen the dark side and came over.

"Who exactly are these assholes?" I asked, casually kicking at the tarp curling up near my feet.

"Well, fat head over there," he pointed to the one on the left with a head that did indeed resemble a fat melon, "pissed me off last night by smashing a bottle of beer over my head at a club. The second prick's a hyena shifter who said he knew where a vampire lived, but he lied and took me to his studio where he was gonna slice out my organs to eat them. The fucker had no idea who'd he brought home. Then the third guy..." He stared down at the blond man at his feet.

He was skinny and covered in blood from his throat sliced.

"This guy actually had some useful information for us."

I stiffened, my shoulders rearing back. "What'd he say?"

"There's a woman named Vrăjitoare somewhere in the city, and apparently she frequently deals with a vampire who lives nearby. I'm hoping that vampire is Ares."

I blinked at Wilder who went back to wiping his hands before getting up.

"How do we find her?" I growled.

"This Vrăjitoare chick, she's going to be at the night markets tonight. We'll make her tell us what she knows." When he glanced up at me, darkness slithered behind his gaze.

Hope flared in my chest.

"You did fucking amazing. This one is going to take us to Rune, I can feel it," I rasped, before breaking into a dreadful cough that felt like my lungs were literally trying to climb out of my chest and up my throat.

"You sound like you're dying." Wilder grunted as he started to roll up the bodies in the tarp.

"I am dying, shithead–" My words cut off as I watched him incredulously, finally rolling my eyes. "What are you doing? Everything about that is wrong. Have you never watched an episode of *Dexter*?"

He shrugged. "I didn't take you for someone who watched television, but I guess it would make sense that would be your favorite show, psycho."

"Pot meet kettle." I sighed. "You'd be surprised what I

do in my spare time. I binged the whole damn series and picked up some good ideas for disposing of bodies."

Wilder said nothing and kept on working, literally shoving three bodies into one giant burrito roll. "Dude, you need to be discreet, and you might as well scream to everyone you have bodies in there. How are you going to dispose of that huge thing now?"

"I've got this. You can go get fucked."

I shook my head. I'd thought he was moody before, but this was on a whole other level. "How long are you going to sulk over the mark with Rune? It doesn't change what you have with her."

He jerked around, his shoulders lifting, a snarl on his throat. "Like hell it doesn't. I saw what it did to her when you marked her, the devotion in her eyes, the absolute heartfelt love she had for you, the connection between you two so intense, it blocked out everything else. It's literally killing you from being apart from her." He wiped his mouth with the back of his hand. "It's destroying me how much I fucking want that with her."

"You want to feel as sick as a dog, like I have?" I tried to lighten the mood slightly because I'd been living with this moody wolf for weeks now and it was all I could do not to knock him out when he got like this.

"Yes," he snapped, his jaw clenched.

I stared at the ache in his eyes, at how deflated he looked despite standing tall. The man had lost part of himself since I'd bitten Rune. And while I wouldn't change a thing about it, and despite all the shit I'd gone through with Wilder all these years, something was changing inside me towards him. I felt actual pity for the guy. Of course, I'd never fucking tell him that, but it explained why I hadn't killed him yet.

If I didn't feel like crap, I'd be alongside him, slicing up every fucker in the city who crossed my path. Instead, I'd become a pathetic sick asshole who couldn't do much killing nowadays.

Swallowing the bitterness rising to the back of my throat and watching Wilder attempt to drag the three bodies across the room, I stepped towards him. "Let me show you how it's done."

CHAPTER 15
WILDER

"I've given a lot of thought on how I'd kill Ares," Daxon muttered as we strolled along the cobblestone street in the city of Suceava early in the night. The buildings we passed were of medieval constructions with varying designs I recognized from Renaissance and Neo-Baroque styles, mostly from books I'd read. I'd normally be enjoying the view, but instead, I hated everything.

"It's been on my mind every damned day," I rasped. "I've decided on skinning him first then burning his flesh, breaking every bone, then burying him on church grounds."

Daxon nodded, crossing the road, and I trailed alongside him. "Clever, though you're wasting your time with skinning and bone breaking. We saw he's going to come back together. Maybe we chop him up, then bury each part in consecrated ground across the world, which might keep him trapped."

"Fuck yes," my words poured out with a hiss. I licked my lips, almost tasting the victory of hearing him squirm. My hands itched for retribution, all while the cruel sting of

Rune's disappearance settled in my chest like a time bomb. I was barely keeping it together, anger lashing at me every waking hour.

A strange growl slipped free, sorrowful, tormented, broken. It was only when Daxon coughed like a six-pack-a-day smoker that I realized the growl came from me. I inhaled deeply the cold air around me, trying to get ahold of myself, all while the small voice in my head whispered to me.

You're not good enough for her.

She's not yours. She picked Daxon. Even Ares made her his blood match.

What are you? A fucking, pathetic loser.

No one has ever loved you.

I tensed, sweeping my hand through my hair several times, agitated to hell and back, shaking away the voice. It was going to be okay. I would find a way to mark Rune, to cement our connection, to make her see that we were meant to be together.

Hands fisted, I tensed and kicked an empty soda can across the sidewalk.

"Keep your shit together," Daxon murmured. "Don't kill anyone, and if anyone needs to die, leave it to me."

I actually laughed that time; it was impressive that I could find anything funny when my world was crumbling around me. "You're threatened because I'm doing a better job."

"The opposite," he said frustratedly. "You're sloppy, and you're going to get us both caught. Then I'll have to kill even more people to cover for your ass."

"It almost sounds like you care about me." Somewhere deep in my darkness, a thread of appreciation rose for

Daxon. I never thought I'd ever think those words, but we were both in a fucked up situation, and...I honestly didn't know what I would have done without him by my side.

"You're deluding yourself if you think that," he growled, then nudged his chin at the market up ahead of us, eyeing the food truck selling hot dogs. "But I'll get you one of those."

I grinned at his behavior.

Moments later, we were scarfing down the hotdogs that came with sauerkraut and mustard. I'd been starving and went back for another round, having forgotten to eat all day.

"Okay then," Daxon started, wiping his lips. "What does that virgin chick look like? How do we find her?"

I turned to look at him. "What virgin?"

"Man, earlier you said that guy you killed told you to visit the virgin or some shit like that at the markets. That's why we're here."

"It's Vrăjitoare, not a fucking virgin," I said, exasperated.

"Same shit. How do we find her?"

I shrugged, realizing in my haste to shut up the guy who'd been crying to be spared, I didn't get all the information I needed out of him. "Um, we're gonna ask the vendors. Someone's gonna direct us to her."

"Okay, get going and ask them." He nudged me in the back, his pissed expression twisting his face.

"If you're going to go into the killing game, you should at least watch *Dexter*," he muttered nonsensically as we walked. I shook my head, and we moved across the Suceava main square—the place where the markets were held. Stalls ran across two sides of the large cobblestone square.

Beyond the stalls were storefronts and lofty apartment buildings.

People were all around us, and I started asking them where I could find Vrăjitoare.

After getting a few strange stares, and people shaking their heads angrily at me to leave their stalls, I paused at one with a brunette in a fluffy blue jacket who pointed warily at an alleyway behind us. That was when I noticed the markets extended in that direction too.

But right as I started to leave, the woman called me back. "Sir, just be careful what you ask for. She is known for tricking anyone who doesn't do exactly as she asks." She spoke in a heavy Romanian accent, sounding slightly like Count Dracula.

"Thanks, I'll be careful." Unlike the rest of the others I spoke to tonight, she seemed to care, so I dug into my pocket and took out a fifty-dollar bill to hand to her as it was the smallest I had on me. She shook her head though. Instead she picked up a small rabbit's foot from her table of wares, handing it to me.

"You're going to need all the luck in the world if you so quickly flash your wealth here. She's going to rob you blind."

Daxon was chuckling to himself beside me. "Yeah, my friend here needs *all* the luck."

I ground my jaw, accepting the rabbit's foot because I didn't feel like I could refuse, and shoved it into my back pocket. "Thanks. I'm sure Vrăjitoare will be happy to help us."

"Sir, Vrăjitoare isn't her name. That's the Romanian word for witch."

I frowned, growling on the inside because I'd had enough of dealing with anyone who did magic.

"We love witches," Daxon exaggerated. "Let's go." He wrenched me by the arm, pulling me past the woman's stall.

"Wonder if this one is the real deal or just a fraudster? They have them all over the place here. Dealing with fae and their magic is enough for me. I'm not up for a witch at the moment." He coughed again, his face pale.

I cleared my throat. "We have no other choice."

The witch was easy to spot from a mile away, now that we knew who we were searching for. She sat at a stall decorated with wind-chimes made of bones, the tablecloth a deep purple, and she had several piles of tarot cards around her, along with a crystal ball. All cliché items I'd expect from a standard fraud, but as long as she had an answer for us, I didn't give a shit if she was claiming she could fly.

The alleyway had only three tables, the first two with customers, and the woman we sought sat the farthest away without any clients.

At her table, she raised her head, appearing to be in her late fifties, maybe older, her silvery hair pulled off her face by a black floral scarf that was secured at the back of her neck. She wore a thick, velvet-style dress with long sleeves, the top part buttoned up to her throat, the whole outfit black. She was definitely going for a theme.

"Share a drink with me," she offered upon our arrival, her voice croaky, as she made quick work of getting three small plastic cups and setting them up on the table in front of her. Then she retrieved a clear bottle from under the table, half filled with a pale yellow liquid.

"No thanks," Daxon answered. "I made myself a promise to not drink anything yellow from bottles," he mocked.

The woman started filling the cups to the rim regardless. Even from across the table, the overwhelming waft hit me, and I almost choked on its strength.

"I didn't ask," she pressed. "I hear you've been asking for me."

"We were told you could help us with the information we're looking for," I explained.

"Then accept my drink. I only help those who share a drink with me." She handed us the small cups, and Daxon sniffed, his nostrils flaring, then he gagged.

"What's in it? It smells like death," he muttered, giving me a quick side glance, all wide eyes and shaking his head slightly.

"It's tradition in Romania to enjoy țuică. A plumb drink. Noroc," she said, lifting her drink and then draining it in one gulp. Her eyes lit up and she gave a slight shake. "That warms the soul. Now you drink, quickly now, I have a busy night. Otherwise, you can leave."

Glancing behind me, I saw someone making their way to her table.

Daxon was huffing. "Fine, but if you've poisoned us or some other shit, I'm coming for you. Even if I'm dead."

She laughed. "Angry man. I know what you're after; I saw it in the cards, and yes, I know where the vampire's lair is."

I tensed at her words, but I also figured that after a month of finding nothing on Rune, I'd try anything. So I said, "Noroc," and pressed the cup to my mouth. I made the mistake of inhaling the spirit before I drank it, and I was coughing as I tipped it all into my mouth.

Fire.

That was the only way to describe how my mouth felt, the flames rushing down my throat as I swallowed it.

I coughed, smacking my chest with a fist because it felt like I'd just drank pure 100% alcohol.

"Fuck!" Daxon was choking next to me.

"What the hell was that?" I quipped.

"Shit, I think I can breathe fire after that," Daxon whined, slapping his chest for breath.

"Wasn't so bad," she murmured, grinning. "It'll warm you up in the cold and perhaps aid your friend with his dog-like cough."

Daxon heaved for breath.

"You alright?" I asked.

"Why does it feel like a fucking dragon is trying to climb out of my chest?"

The woman laughed at us. "Good, it's doing its job to heal the ache in your heart, boy."

That time, I stared at the woman, her words surprising me. The hairs on my arms rose.

"Now. You seek entrance to the hidden world of Galeru, which is located right here near our city. That is where your vampire lives." She tapped her crystal ball.

My mouth dropped open and I had to close it back up. Who was this woman and how in the world could she possibly know our purpose when we'd told nobody?

"Where is it?" I asked instantly, leaning forward, my hands on her table. "How do we get there?"

"I'll tell you, but first you must do something for me."

"Here it comes," Daxon croaked, an angry expression flaring over his face. "There's always a catch, isn't there?"

"Well, of course. I must make a living."

"Then name your price," I said warily. But we'd come this far, and I was thinking she had what I needed. I'd give her everything I had to find Rune.

"I'm in short supply of eyes. And you'd be amazed how many spells require human eyes." She spoke casually, while Daxon nodded his head alongside me. I should have been more disturbed by her request, but since I'd just killed three guys, it didn't sound so crazy.

"We can help," Daxon stated. "How does three pairs sound?" he added, sounding rather excited.

She eyed us, then nodded. "Bring them back to me tonight, and you'll have your instructions and crystal to enter. Don't turn up and forget coming back to see me ever again."

"Deal," I confirmed, then Daxon and I retreated.

Once we left behind the alleyway, we both launched into a race back home. We exchanged glances because we knew exactly what we had to do.

"We're going to find Rune. Fuck, we're going to find her." His voice boomed, and I couldn't remember the last time I'd seen so much hope and cheer coming from Daxon. He'd been in agonizing pain for weeks.

Joy and hope were beating in my chest as well, my heart close to bursting at the thought I'd have my wolf girl back. And this time, when I marked her, I'd do it right and it'd damn well stick. I just wanted Rune in my arms once more. My desperation was so great, that I refused to believe anything but that the witch was right.

Daxon was grinning, both of us running madly back to our house where we'd left the dead men in our basement.

"Are you glad I killed those three fuckers now?" I teased.

"Man, I could kiss you, but I'm saving it all for Rune."

We flew like the wind, and for the first time in too long, it felt like something was finally going right for us.

———

"Are you sure this is the way?" Daxon groaned, glancing back over his shoulder.

"She said keep north on the path."

"Are you certain?"

"Yes," I snapped. "You were practically dying from your coughing so you didn't hear half of what she said in her instructions."

We'd been hiking through the woods for the past hour, civilization left long behind us, and my gut twisted so tightly, I felt sick up to my eyeballs. At the same time, excitement and adrenaline pushed me to move faster through the trees...because Rune might be close.

"It's in that direction, can you hear it?" Daxon called out, picking up speed, and I followed his outstretched arm toward the grand waterfall in the distance. The crashing water called to me.

We took off at a sprint.

"That witch better have come through, or I'll be carving out *her* eyes," Daxon warned. I didn't care what he did to her as long as we found Rune.

Though, thinking back to us cutting out the men's eyes still churned my stomach. Daxon didn't seem to have an issue as he whistled to himself as he did so. I felt sick the whole time. I guessed I hadn't reached his level of psycho yet. That was only slightly reassuring.

On top of that, he'd barely coughed since we reached the woods, and he had more energy than before, more color in his face. All things that pointed to us getting close to Rune.

Soon enough, we reached an expansive lake, and beyond that stood a monstrous wall of rock. Its surface was covered in jagged stones. The waterfall glinted in all colors of the rainbow, the water below crystal clear.

"Galeru," I murmured. "A secret city. This has to be it. The witch had said once we reach the crystal waterfall, take out the crystal and walk into the lake and keep going until you pass the waterfall. Then we'll find the entrance."

"Well, let's find out if she was telling us the truth."

Collecting the crystal stone out of my pocket, I held it out in front of me where the sun shone through it, sending a rainbow of colors dancing across the lake's surface. I stepped down and the water parted for me.

"Whoa, did you see that?" I gasped, unsure how this was happening.

"Of course I can see, I'm not blind. Lead us forward, Moses," he joked. We started walking, the slick pebbles on the bottom of the lake grinding together beneath our steps.

Once we approached the waterfall, it opened up for us like a parting curtain.

That time, it was Daxon's turn to gasp. "How the fuck did Ares gain such magic?"

"He's been around for a long time. Let's move on." We scrambled forward and right into a cave. The waterfall fell back down, water splashing us, so we stepped deeper into the dark.

"She could be just on the other side of this," I whispered.

"Don't even get me started. I feel so tightly wound on the inside, that I can't tell if I'm going to go mental and kill the first person I see, or if I'm going to cry. Shit, man, I don't fucking cry, ever, and look at the shit that's coming out of my mouth. Forget I said anything." He was talking fast, his breaths speeding.

"Nothing leaves my lips," I added. "The anticipation to find her is killing me too."

He glanced across his shoulder quickly, a strange

expression on his face. "You're not such a bad guy, you know."

I grinned as that would be the closest to an acknowledgment of his acceptance I'd ever receive from him. Daxon had changed, his sickness slowing down his crazy, but once we got Rune back, I was sure he'd be back to his normal self.

I thought about how much I wanted Rune, how no matter what stood in my way, I'd persevere and make her mine. Agitation and desperation poured over me, and I moved faster, ready for this nightmare to be over.

A trickle of power danced up my arms as we reached an invisible barrier.

"This reminds me of the entrance to the fae world," Daxon muttered. "Hand over the crystal, and I can do it."

"Don't even mention that fucking bitch, and I've got this." I huffed and lifted the crystal towards the barrier that started to ripple in response.

The moment they touched, a zip of power snapped, curling up my spine, and every hair on my body stood on end. And just as quick, the barrier dropped and light shone from deeper in the cave ahead of us.

"That stung a bit," Daxon huffed, gasping for breath, and when I looked over, he clasped his chest.

"I'm guessing the crystal isn't the exact key to break into the city, so it's got some kickback when used."

"Whatever. We're in. Let's go get our girl."

We ran, both of us completely focused on what lay ahead. The anticipation, the ache of missing her, the worry that Ares had done something to her drove me to insanity.

One second we were in the dark cave, the next we burst out into daylight in a forest. Ahead of us stretched a wide path, the ground marked up by car tires. "This has to be the way."

We ran once more, my head thundering with uncertainty of what to expect, but if it meant finding Rune, I'd face Satan himself.

It wasn't long before the woods thinned and a different landscape came into view.

The dirty path became a golden paved road. Overhead, the sky beamed bright blue.

Then there were the blooming flowers in every direction, the golden path swerving amongst them, leading us directly to a quaint town with white houses and black roofs.

I paused, convinced we'd arrived in the wrong place. I stared incredulously at the sheer number of flowers...all the shades of pinks, purples, and golds. What was going on? Farther in the distance stood a mansion with brightly colored flags and banners. The flags and banners were all over the town, as though they were about to hold a festival.

There were a few people mingling at some shops in the distance. Were they vampires?

"Wait, you're seeing what I'm seeing, right?" Daxon blurted, turning on the spot. "I'm expecting the Munchkins from the Wizard of Oz to come rushing out to us any second now. Did that witch put a spell on us?"

"You've watched that movie too?" I was slightly startled for Daxon's sanity.

"Is that what you're worried about? I'm more worried about why vampires live in such a colorful world with all these flowers."

"I don't really give a shit. As long as we find Rune."

I kept glancing over my shoulder, expecting something

to jump out at us, but there was nothing, so we followed the golden paved road, scanning our surroundings. Mountains painted the backdrop, making the place picturesque. It just wasn't what I had pictured the home for vampires to be like. In my head, I imagined a dark, dingy castle with dungeons, where it rained all the time.

This place was the complete opposite.

As we got closer to the town, people spotted us. They immediately started to run away from us, terror paling their faces. They gathered their children and ran into their homes.

I stared over to Daxon, who shrugged his shoulders. "Maybe these vampires are vegetarians. I mean, look at all the flowers."

I shook my head. "Or they aren't vampires. Otherwise, why would they run when they saw us?"

Maybe I spoke too soon because that was when a dozen uniformed guards rushed towards us.

But it was also the same time I caught movement of someone with white hair fluttering near the mansion, and my heart stopped.

A second was all it took to recognize my girl. She stood in the middle of the field near the home, picking flowers. She wasn't hurt and was even smiling, but I ignored the ache in my chest at seeing her happy without us.

I'd found her. That was what mattered.

I missed her so much that I choked up.

The next thing I knew, I was running to her, my lips curling upward, and Daxon caught on pretty quickly as he was charging alongside me just as quickly, her name on his lips.

And behind us, the guards pursued.

She glanced up at our approach, flinching in shock, and started to back away, dropping the bunch of flowers in her hand.

I wouldn't lie that her reaction broke me. For all these weeks, I'd played scenario after scenario of how our reunion would go, and never once did it involve her retreating from us with in fear.

In seconds, Ares was at her side, and fury burned across my chest. Resignation sprawled across his face at seeing us. He threw up an arm and said something in a different language to the guards behind us. I glanced back to see they'd stopped their pursuit.

I reached Ares first and ripped him away from Rune before slamming him to the ground, crushing his stupid flowers.

"Found you, fucking asshole!" I snarled in his face, my body trembling with savage rage as I clipped his face with my fist again and again.

Daxon was there in moments, slamming into the vampire too, while Rune came at us screaming, slamming her small fists into me, then tugging at my shirt. The guards did nothing to my surprise, but Ares had always taken me off guard.

"Stop it, stop hurting him," she cried, tears flowing from her eyes. It broke me to see her distraught, and I pulled back, needing to understand why she was standing up for him, and why she hadn't batted an eye at seeing us.

Daxon got a few more jabs into Ares, before the vampire shoved him aside easily, then cracked his neck. "Feel better now, boys?" He climbed to his feet, wiping the blood from the corner of his mouth as Rune darted to his side, frantically examining where we'd struck him.

She stared at him with absolute love, and I couldn't tear my gaze away. It was destroying me. I wanted her to stare at me like that, to care for my wounds, to cling to me when she felt scared. Every second I watched her shower Ares with affection was a knife in my chest, and darkness shifted in me once more.

My mark wouldn't stick to her, and now she completely rejected my existence.

I stared at her, my body shaking, hands curling into balls. What the fuck did he have that we didn't?

"You fucking piece of shit, you dumped us and stole her for yourself," Daxon roared, his face red with fury.

"It's not that straightforward," Ares explained too casually, considering Daxon and I were about to explode.

"Rune," I said, reaching out to her, but she retreated from me, clinging to Ares's side. Her response to me was a blade to my heart, stabbing so deep, I lost my breath.

Daxon threw himself to his knees in front of her, pleading, "Rune, I was dying without you."

Her eyes widened, and for a moment, I expected her to embrace him.

Except she recoiled even from her mate, while the vampire slid his arm around her waist, keeping her pressed to him.

"What the fuck did you do to her?" Daxon roared, his body shaking. "Rune, sweetheart, what's wrong?"

"Ares." She shook, her gaze sweeping from Daxon to me, then back up at Ares, her grip so tight on his hand that I hissed under my breath. "Who are these men?"

A sting raced across my chest at her words, and my heart thundered in my ears. The reality of what she'd just asked shattered my mind, destroying me as I realized we were nothing but strangers to her.

What the fuck *had* Ares done?

"My dove, Daxon is your mate," he said, gesturing to Daxon. And then he turned towards me. "And Wilder's about to become one."

CHAPTER 16
RUNE

ies...Lies...Lies. The words sang across my mind.

"I already had one mate, Alistair, but now you're saying I have another?" My chin trembled, and I wasn't sure how many more surprises I could take.

These two men in front of me were gods, so gorgeous, that my knees shook, but I didn't recognize them. And they both stared at me with heartbreak in their eyes.

The man called Wilder stood stiff and looked like he might detonate, shaking, eyes locked on me. Black hair frayed around his face messily, bringing attention to those piercing green eyes that called to me, made me want to drown in them. Muscles rippled over his body, his skin tanned, and he towered over me.

Then there was Daxon with his sculpted face, screaming sex. But he carried an air of darkness about him. Blond hair, with pale hazel eyes with a crazy look behind them, the guy was just as big as Wilder, and there was something about him that made me keep staring. How could these men be so gorgeous?

And I didn't miss their hypnotizingly masculine and

wolfy smells. My wolf roused inside me, responding to their presence, to their wolves. She was actually drawn to them.

"Rune," Daxon kept saying my name, and the sound of his voice was so familiar to me, so captivating, so alluring. "How can you not remember me? I marked you as mine."

I blinked at him, wishing I could just recall everything. Anything, actually.

This was becoming too much for me, my mind hurt, and I just shook my head. The past kept rearing its head, and yet no one could help me gain my memories back.

"Why didn't you tell me about Daxon being my mate?" I asked, glancing up at Ares.

"Yeah, Ares. Why didn't you tell her?" Daxon's voice darkened as he got to his feet. "Why didn't you bring her back to us once you found her? Why the fucking hell have you been hiding out in this...this place, for weeks, all while Wilder and I have been going insane out there trying to find her?"

His voice boomed, and I was convinced the entire town heard him. But his words chilled me. Agony played across both men's faces. I felt sorry for them because I could tell they'd suffered a lot...because of me?

"Is what he's saying true?" I asked Ares.

The love of my life nodded, and it stung to see his confession.

"Why?" I croaked. A million questions in that one word.

He slid a hand across my cheek, the warmth in his eyes for me never extinguishing. I had no doubt about his love towards me, but there were so many things he still hadn't told me about my past. To be fair, I had asked him at one stage to stop talking about the past because if I couldn't remember it, what good was it? But now I was starting to think that wasn't such a good idea.

Staring into the faces from my past, two men who wanted answers, who had me curious to find out the same, I knew I couldn't pretend everything was fine any longer.

"Rune." There was an ache in his voice that made me flinch. "I—" He took a deep breath. "I've tried to think what I would say to you in this moment, but my only excuse is that I didn't think it would hurt to protect you here while you regained your memories. I just wanted some time with you...some time for you to fall in love with me without them around distracting you every moment. I was going to tell you everything. I swear to you...it would have happened soon." His gaze and voice pleaded with me, but a cold dread was floating through my veins.

"You fucking asshole," Wilder growled, his hands clenched. "You could have at least put Daxon and me out of our fucking misery and told us you had her safe."

"You would have taken her from me," Ares snapped matter-of-factly, to which Wilder lurched closer.

My heart bumped into the back of my throat at the fury in Wilder's gaze, and I threw myself between them, placing a hand out to stop him. I was furious with Ares. I felt betrayed. But whatever his intentions were...I *had* fallen in love with him, and I couldn't bear to see him hurt.

"I wish I could remember you both, but please, don't fight. Ares saved me from Alistair, the real monster in all of this. He and the Fae Queen kidnapped me. Ares has been protecting me."

"Alistair removed your memories?" Daxon barked, stepping closer, crowding in around me. "Tell me where he is. Fuck, I'm going to enjoy killing him."

"He's locked up for now," Ares stated, rather proud of himself as he grinned.

I wrung my hands, saying, "The Fae Queen suppressed

my memories. I've cried so much, I've been so confused. I've even learned about my mother's death...all over again. I—I guess I buried my head in the sand for a while here. I couldn't take any more bad news. Don't blame Ares, blame me for wanting to feel normal for half a second."

"Oh, Rune," Wilder whispered, staring at me with the same admiration I'd seen in Ares' eyes when he gazed at me. "I could never blame you."

"Daria," Daxon snarled, breaking the moment. "You've got to be fucking joking. She's in Romania too? Who the fuck else followed us here?"

Sorrow crossed Wilder's face, something that stole the color from his features. "This is my fault," he murmured. "She came for you because of me."

It was painful watching these powerful alphas crumbling around me, and as much as I wished to help them, I didn't know how.

"We need to find a way to break the curse and fast," Daxon stated, never taking his eyes off me, his attention dipping to my lips, burning me up.

"You think I haven't tried everything I know." Ares didn't appear happy, and he gave me one of his unreadable looks when I glanced over at him. "Rune, can you go inside and rest, and let me catch up with the boys on everything? I have an idea I want to run past them."

I wanted to scream at him, pummel his chest with my fists about the secrets he'd kept. But every time the anger sparked...the memories we'd had pushed to the surface.

"Is it something I should know about?"

"Absolutely. I may have a way to help with your memories of them, something that wouldn't work without them here. Get some rest while we talk though, little dove. You're looking a bit pale."

"Don't ever keep anything from me again," I said coldly, holding his gaze. Guilt flared in their depths.

"I promise," he vowed solemnly. And it was ridiculous... but I believed him.

With a lingering stare at the three of them, I retreated, tangled emotions weaving about inside of me.

Once inside, I rushed upstairs, my pulse galloping, my mind hurting.

And of course, I couldn't help but throw myself at the window, staring down at the three men outside. Staring at all of them...I couldn't help but think it wouldn't be so bad to have all of their attention.

I sorted through my thoughts, feeling like maybe I had my feet on earth again, like maybe their arrival would come with a solution to help my lost memories.

I peered out at Ares talking to the two men who were animated with their arms. The Wilder guy kept shoving his hand into Ares's chest.

I was pretty sure Ares could destroy him, and yet he just stood there, taking it. It told me that he didn't see them as a threat.

The longer I watched them, the more they almost felt... familiar to me. Unlike with Alistair, where something just sat wrong about him the entire time, these two left me curious to find out more about my past, and Daxon especially...my wolf seemed to recognize him.

As the three spoke, soon moving into the house, I pulled back from the window and went upstairs to my room, well aware that things weren't going to be the same anymore. Their arrival had changed everything, and I hoped for the better. I could feel the change in the air. I'd seen it in Ares' eyes.

But, what would happen with the four of us if I never gained my memories back?

————

The bonfire crackled in the night, embers shooting for the sky, giving off a magical appearance.

Ares had called for a town barbecue after a flurry of people grew paranoid with the arrival of Wilder and Daxon. It had been too easy for them to just stroll into town, without any sirens going off, or even guards noticing them.

Apparently, they'd gained a magical crystal from a witch in town that opened up the portal entrance and blocked the alarms.

Ares had gone out to pay the witch a visit and said he'd dealt with it. I didn't ask what that meant because he was in a rush once he'd returned, announcing the party for tonight.

He'd been busy assuring those who lived in town that they were safe. And that was why he insisted on having Daxon and Wilder attend the function, so people's worries were put at ease.

It also gave me confidence that these two alphas didn't pose a danger to us; otherwise, I was sure Ares would have thrown them into the dungeon.

I sat on one of the logs surrounding the outdoor fire, watching everyone mingling. Connor served food, while a group of women huddled around Wilder, chatting his ear off. It was a strange thing to feel a pique of jealousy at seeing them draping themselves all over him. Ares had said he was meant to become my mate, which left me intrigued. I tried to picture myself with him...and it surprisingly wasn't hard.

That was when I noticed Daxon sauntering towards me, and butterflies exploded in my stomach.

"Mind if I join you?"

"Sure," I answered softly, slightly mesmerized by the beauty this man possessed, how his masculine, woodsy scent washed over me each time the wind blew past him and into me.

With it came the haunting sound of his voice. The familiarity of it.

"It's such a perfect night," he continued.

And just listening to his voice brought the answer I sought. I knew where I'd heard it before...

He was the voice in my head. I straightened on the log as it became clearer.

Heat bloomed inside me, spreading through my chest at the man that had been in my head for weeks. It never made sense, and now, it seemed like the pieces of the puzzle were starting to click together.

If I had a close connection with him, a mating bond, it made sense that my head would try to remind me of it. It was a sign everything they'd said was true, but with that thought, I trembled because I wasn't sure how to deal with it when my emotions for them were absent.

Daxon took a seat next to me. "This town is something else," he said, his hands on either side of him, holding onto the log beneath us while stretching his legs out, crossing them at the ankles. Was it wrong of me to admire how perfectly well his jeans fit him?

"I love it here. It feels like I'm in a fairy tale," I answered, glancing over at the man who was studying me. I could tell he wrestled with the urge to move closer to me, to reach over and touch me. So, I appreciated that he contained himself. It was still so jarring and confusing to have him and Wilder in the village. To have a piece of my past right there, and yet none of my memories jogged.

"It reminds me a bit of our hometown, Amarok. It's quaint, tucked away in the woods, and it has incredible community spirit."

"Oh, are you the Alpha of Amarok?"

He nodded. "I am for half of the residents. I'm a Bitten breed of wolf, while Wilder is the Alpha of the other half of our town. He's a Lycan breed."

I must have looked confused because Daxon grinned.

"Let me explain. As a Bitten, I have the ability to change at will without the need of the moon, while Lycans are controlled by the moon's lure and can only transform those three nights a month. There are two other species, but they aren't that high up the food chain as a Bitten and Lycan. Wilder used to be bound by the moon, but you changed him somehow, and he's been able to shift when he wants lately."

I raised an eyebrow, wondering how on earth I'd done something like that. He was definitely mistaken.

I loved listening to him speak though, to hear about where I'd once lived. "Which one am I?" My wolf stirred deep inside of me, and she seemed especially taken with Daxon as she made purring sounds for him, pressing up against my insides to get closer.

He twisted toward me, rubbing his fingers across the stubble on his jawline. "That's the thing. We don't know. You're something different, sweetheart. Something special. Your wolf is the most stunning creature I've seen, and I love that you leave stardust with your paw prints."

I shifted, blushing in the light of the fire. "I don't hate that you think I'm special."

He grinned sexily at me. "You are. And your wolf is also

fierce and powerful. You're a real kick-ass, and I'm completely smitten by you. You have no idea how incredible you are. How broken I was when we first met and how you saved me."

My cheeks heated even more, and I glanced down to the lawn beneath my feet, at the small pink flower buds just starting to open. They reminded me of myself, with how shut off from the world I felt, and yet I had so much information inside me ready to be released.

"Tell me more," I said eagerly, completely turning around to face him. I loved the way he was staring at me like I was his world, like he'd do anything for me. Who didn't like to be admired by a hot, gorgeous alpha? "What am I really like? What interests do I have?"

"You're kind just like you are now, shy but strong, beautiful and captivating, and you wear your heart on your sleeve. You've also made a lot of friends back home, and let's see...you love jogging. I remember when you first arrived at Amarok, you were determined to go jogging into the woods, even when you were warned about it being dangerous."

I laughed. "So you're saying I'm stubborn."

"That's an understatement." He chuckled. "You also love pastries and coffee. We have a cafe back home where I can often find you enjoying one of their baked goods."

I laughed. "That definitely sounds like me."

Daxon shuffled closer to me, and the heat pouring from his body washed over me.

Finding my voice grew slightly harder. "Ares said you were my mate."

"He's right. I'd bitten you and marked you only days before you went missing. I'll be honest with you, it's been the worst time of my life to be away from you, and even now, keeping my distance is killing me. But don't worry, I won't push you until you're ready."

I felt hot and confused about how drawn I felt towards Daxon, when in my heart, I'd grown to love Ares with everything inside of me. It was all so painful to make sense of.

I glanced out around us where the townspeople were having fun, while night spread its wings across the land.

And that was when Ares and Wilder made their way towards me, two powerful men who again had me wondering how I managed to attract all three to me. I would have given anything to be with one of them, but three, I must be blessed by the Moon Goddess.

A few of the townspeople walked away from the area, and it was just me and the three of them around the log. Wilder kneeled in front of us while Ares took the empty seat at my side, his arm coiled around my back, our sides pressed close.

"Baby, I've been thinking about how to help you get your memories back for weeks now. I've researched all the books in my library, spoken to many people who wield power, and it all comes down to the fact that a fae's curse can't be undone by another's magic."

"Oh," I said, frowning. "So, what does that mean for us?"

"It means I may have another solution," he continued, sliding his fingers along my chin and jaw, before turning my head to face him. "You and I are a blood match. Daxon has bitten you with his mark, and Wilder is so close to bonding with you, that I wouldn't be surprised if your two souls aren't already intertwined."

"Okay," I said, leaning against him, curious about where he was going with this.

"And sometimes, the power of love can break a spell. I think that's what happened when we first made love."

Daxon and Wilder's growls surrounded me. I blushed under their gazes.

Ares didn't seem perturbed by their show of aggression. "So I'm proposing that you bond with all three of us, with the hope that it will break the spell."

I stiffened. "Wait, what do you mean by bonding? Like all of you bite me?"

He cupped my face, his lips on mine. "Much more than just biting, little dove. We'll all make love to you. Rune, you're meant to be with all three of us. And I am hoping this will weaken the curse so your memories return."

I blinked at him, unsure what to say. "I..." I licked my lips, looking around at Daxon and Wilder, both of who watched me intently with love in their eyes. And based on everything I'd learned, I'd had sex with all three men numerous times already. So what was one more time, right?

Despite being startled and scared...and awkward, there was also a level of excitement crawling through me.

How often did a girl have three god-like men insisting she belonged to them?

Was I imagining this and about to have the sexiest dream of my life?

Short of pinching myself, trepidation did sit in my chest.

"So, you're saying this might help me remember my past?" I repeated again, even though he'd already said that.

"We're hoping so," Wilder said, reaching over, his hand on my thigh, his touch burning hot, and when Daxon slid his fingers across my waist, I was starting to overheat.

Glancing up at Ares, I stared at him, trying to see deep

into his eyes and understand if this was exactly what *he* wanted.

"I absolutely love you, Rune, and this isn't a light decision to make, but I've also had you to myself all this time. And I wouldn't do anything that would hurt you. Daxon and Wilder are yours. Just like I am yours. Our relationship is just more equal now." He leaned in closer, our noses touching, and I loved it when he did that. "But this is only if you want to do it, of course. The decision is with you, okay?"

I was nodding, looking over at the other two who were in agreement. My heart was galloping, and having all their hands on me drove me slightly crazy with need. But that wasn't a reason to sleep with men who felt like complete strangers.

"And you're okay with sharing me?" I asked Ares.

"In my dreams, you're only mine. But you were Daxon's and Wilder's before I found you. I'm not a heartless bastard, my dove, and I understand the torture of losing someone you adore. I watched your suffering as you let go of Alistair. I never want you to suffer again. So, I'm completely fine with sharing you. It doesn't mean I love you any less. It just means I know they occupy a part of your soul, just like I do. But the final decision is always yours..."

I nodded and pressed against his chest, and he embraced me, kissing my head. "Whatever you decide, I'll support," he reassured me.

"I love you." And I remained buried against him, closing my eyes, trying to come to terms with what they'd just asked me. And if I was ready for this.

CHAPTER 17
RUNE

Two days had passed, and I still hadn't given Ares my answer. Instead, Wilder and Daxon were being shown around the village and introduced to the people. All seemed well on the outside, but when they were alone with Ares, it seemed to turn into an argument everytime. They were still struggling to forgive Ares for keeping me away from them.

I understood why he did it. I also wasn't completely happy about it, and I got why the other two were upset.

And it made me wonder if we tried bonding together, if the tension between them would dissipate. It also surprised me how hesitant I was to find out about my past. From everything I'd learned so far, it was chaotic, and I'd rather enjoyed being oblivious for a while.

The four of us sat around the dinner table, enjoying a meal while I still pushed the garlic bread around on my plate.

"Is everything alright, little dove?" Ares asked.

"Yeah," I answered and took a small bite, my stomach not hungry, my mind heavy with my thoughts.

"You've barely eaten anything," Daxon added.

I shrugged. "Guess I'm not that hungry."

"Is something on your mind?" Wilder asked, his bare feet under the table sliding over, bumping mine, and I didn't pull back.

The last couple of days had let me spend more time with them, talk about my past, discover who they were, and I found myself more attracted to them than I could have imagined.

"A few things have been on my mind," I answered, glancing up from my plate to the men who studied me carefully.

"Like what?" Daxon pressed.

"Um..." My throat dried up, and I reached for the water, drinking half of it, watching them over the tip of my glass.

"What is it?" Ares asked. "You can say anything."

Setting the glass back down, I felt a rush of heat climbing up my neck, and I didn't know why it was so hard for me to say this.

"Nothing you could say could offend us," Wilder murmured. His feet sliding against mine, his warmth was delicious.

"I-I was just wondering, when are we going to head to the bedroom?"

The clatter of cutlery hitting porcelain plates sounded, and all three men shot to their feet instantly.

I couldn't help but laugh at them, but they were taking this seriously. Ares was at my side in a second, lifting me out of my seat and into his arms.

We moved with speed up to his room, with the huge king-size bed, and he sat me down on the edge of the mattress and kneeled in front of me.

"Are you sure you're ready for this?" he asked, holding

onto my hands tenderly. "I will love you just as much with any decision you make."

Wilder and Daxon stood behind him, smiling at me, so much hope in their gazes. The fact that my body and wolf both reacted to them with such warmth, such desire, told me this was the right decision to make.

"Yes, this is what I want." My heart was racing. Those butterflies had returned, and with it came a strange awkwardness about how we were going to do this.

But Ares always had a way of making me forget everything and focus only on him. He tenderly took my hand and lifted me to my feet, then slid his grip to my waist before drawing me closer to him. He leaned in to kiss me, softly at first, tasting all of me, sucking on my lips. He kissed with such passion and devotion that I always lost myself to his affection. He unbuttoned my blouse and slipped it off my shoulders, never pausing our kiss.

My breath caught in my chest at the sensual touch of his fingers on my skin as he pushed the shirt down my arms and off me. "You're so beautiful," he whispered, standing where he blocked me from being seen by Wilder and Daxon.

His fingers traveled up my sides, up and over the lace covering my breasts. My nipples responded instantly to his touch, hardening, pressing against the soft fabric. I watched the way he studied me while pulling down the bra straps over my shoulders, then tugged down on the lace, releasing my breasts.

I gasped, heat burning me from the inside out, and he bent forward, wrapping his lips around a nipple, his touch tight on my other breast, rolling the soft flesh under his palm.

My gaze lifted to the hungry stares on Wilder and

Daxon's faces, studying me so intently. And I flushed all over.

Even though I kept reminding myself they'd seen me naked before, a sense of shyness still came over me.

It was Daxon who made the first move forward, his hand tucking loose strands of hair behind my ear as he towered over me. "You *are* so beautiful," he murmured, then leaned in and our mouths clashed. It was crazy how he immediately drew a moan out of me.

We kissed like our lives depended on it, like this was our first time, adding to my nerves and excitement. Ares moved onto my other nipple, tugging on it, and I moaned against Daxon's mouth from how instantly arousal drenched my panties. How turned on I'd become.

A large hand slid across my jawline, and I broke from Daxon to find Wilder on my other side, smiling at me. "You're going to be such a good girl for us, aren't you?"

I nodded because I discovered I loved being called a "good girl." Something about it awakened the primal instincts within me.

"Yes, I will be a good girl," I purred the words, and I reached over to grab his shirt and draw him to me. Our mouths collided and he kissed me like an animal. I loved his dominance, his desperation for me.

Daxon's lips were on my shoulder, and someone was pulling open the buttons of my jeans. Before I knew it, they'd been drawn down my legs along with my underwear, and I was suddenly completely naked in front of three starved men. They never released me, but they kissed me, sucked on my nipples, and warm fingers were sliding between my legs.

I shuddered with arousal, with the touch that pressed between my slick folds, finding me completely drenched. It all came at me so fast that I could barely hold myself up on my feet, and when a finger slipped into my core, I groaned, leaving me shuddering with desire.

My pussy was soaking wet, and that was when I felt a finger sliding to my ass, massaging me, leaving me thrashing for more. And we'd only just started.

When I finally came up for air, I was gasping for breath, my body tingling all over, and I fell back onto the bed, pulling free from their touches and dragging my feet free from my jeans still around my ankles. I scrambled away from them. Their pants were all tented, and their eyes glazed over.

And I decided then that I was going to enjoy being fucked by three men.

"It's only fair that you get naked too, seeing as I've lost my clothes," I teased, figuring that would help with my shyness and I would get to see what these alphas were packing.

Apparently, I didn't need to ask twice because they were stripping in seconds, not shy in the slightest. Even my gorgeous Ares did the same, winking at me, and I was so glad he was there with me, because I didn't know if I could go through with this without him.

And in moments, they all stood before me, naked, each with the biggest cocks I'd ever seen. I gasped at the sight because I wasn't sure where to look first. All those muscles, wide chests, strong legs, and long, thick dicks. I also noted that Daxon had an infinity symbol carved into his skin above his heart that intrigued me.

But was I really ready for all three of them?

"Do you like what you see?" Daxon asked smugly as he groped his dragon of a cock.

I swallowed hard. "Is that meant to be a trick question?"

Ares laughed, and I relaxed at the sound of it. He got onto the bed and started crawling towards me. Wilder and Daxon on either side of him, did the same.

My heart might give out from how hard it was beating as they approached. My core gushed with slick.

Ares slid a hand up and over my bent legs. "Show them, my sweet, why you smell so delicious. What they've missed."

I steadied myself as nerves and excitement rippled over me at his request.

"Let me see you," Wilder begged, Daxon leaning in closer, eager, hungry for me.

His nostrils flared as he inhaled the air ripe with my perfume. "You smell so fucking delicious. I've missed you so terribly."

With Ares's smile, I embraced my bravery and let my bent legs fall open. Ares pushed my feet wider too, exposing more of me, offering me to these alphas.

I sucked in a shaky breath, feeling shy to be sitting spread for three men, who were completely captivated.

"You're so wet for us. Such a pretty pussy." Ares reached over, his fingers sliding up and down my slit before pushing my lips open. Their eyes were locked between my legs. When he pushed two fingers into me, I lost myself, forgot about being embarrassed. Instead, I moaned, my chest pushing out.

I craved them, needed them. "Yes," I whimpered.

"Do you want us to fuck you, sweetheart?" Daxon moved closer, pushing his head between my thighs.

I moaned in response.

"I think I need a taste first...before I go insane. Then I'm going to stretch that gorgeous fucking pussy."

Ares removed his fingers, my arousal dripping from their tips. He stuck them into his mouth, savoring the taste, groaning with pleasure.

Daxon's mouth was on my pussy without pause, licking me, pushing open my lips for easier access. Wilder nudged up next to him.

"Did your mother never teach you to share?" he grumbled.

"Yeah, I prefer not to think of her right now." Daxon's breath danced across my core, just as Wilder pushed forward, licking my pussy as well.

I trembled, moaning for more.

"Lift your legs, baby," Ares said, sliding out from between the two mountainous men. "You're so perfect," he murmured, blowing me a kiss as he helped me get my legs up into the air, then spread them.

"Can you see how much they've missed you?" Ares explained, one hand on an ankle, another on my breast, squeezing, then pinching my nipple.

Breathless, it was hard to speak clearly with how hard I quivered. Wilder and Daxon were taking turns licking me, spreading me wider.

They didn't mind sharing and were moving faster, unable to get enough, pulling at my inner lips, gently gnawing around my clit. They were going to completely ruin me.

My legs trembled, and I was crying out at this stage, so close I knew I wouldn't last much longer.

I had no idea if this would work to bring back my memory, but it would be a moment I'd never forget. But when one of them kept teasing my rear entry, then pushed a finger into my ass, I knew I couldn't hold on any longer.

"I'm so close now," I cried out, but the words had barely left my mouth, when the building orgasm crashed through me.

Screaming out, I squirmed beneath them. Ares leaned over and kissed me, his tongue so fierce, it knocked me right off balance. He stole my moans while the two men between my legs savagely licked up my cum, pressing to get closer. Two tongues dipped inside me. Even when I came down from my euphoria, the men were still licking me, taking every last drop.

Ares pulled back and stroked my brow. "You were incredible. Are you ready to be fucked?"

"I can't wait," my response came out a bit too eagerly, because he laughed.

"You heard her," he responded, glancing down at Wilder and Daxon who finally released me from their carnal pleasure. Their lips and chin glistened with my cum, and they licked it with those dangerously sexy tongues.

As if they'd done this before, Daxon threw himself onto the bed alongside me, his cock upright like a flagpole, his grin devilish, his eyes promising me the most sinful experience.

"Why do you get that position?" Wilder moaned.

"Because I was faster than you." Daxon never stopped smiling at me, his hand reaching up to stroke my cheek. "I've missed you so much. I'm still struggling to believe that I've finally found you."

"I really hope this works. I want to remember you." Glancing over at Ares, I didn't see any jealousy or judgment in his gaze. Just acceptance. I clearly had something wonderful beforehand seeing how well these men were getting along.

With Ares's help, I got up and rolled over onto my hands and knees, before crawling over to Daxon. I pushed a leg over his hips and shuffled to find a comfortable position. His erection instantly slid along my folds.

"I want you to take my cock deep, to suck down on it."

His words took my breath away.

"Me too, gorgeous," Wilder said instantly, his tender hands on my back as he shifted to position himself behind me, the tip of his dick sliding over the slick on my ass. I mewled with renewed urgency to have them claim me, over and over.

"Lean over me," Daxon purred. "Kiss me and taste yourself on my mouth."

Pressing myself over him, my breasts against his chest, I kissed Daxon. My scent was intoxicating, my taste sweet on my tongue. And he kissed me hungrily all while Wilder pushed a finger into my ass, working it in and out.

I felt like I'd been through a whirlwind already, and that was just the beginning of the fun.

Daxon's cock found my entry with ease, like we were meant to be one, and he pushed inside. I stiffened from him stretching me slowly, his mouth still on mine.

Wilder was doing the same, replacing his finger with his cock, the urgency for them to claim me incredibly sexy... and kind of scary.

There was no rush from their end and they seemed to find a rhythm, sliding slowly deeper into me. I moaned against Daxon's mouth, while Ares stroked my hair.

"You're doing so amazing, my dove."

It felt a bit weird to be praised for fucking two other men, but it was also incredibly sexy.

They rocked in and out, finding the perfect rhythm to make me catch fire.

When I broke from Daxon's lips, I moaned loudly, feeling completely full as they both jammed their huge erections all the way inside of me at once.

Ares was there, stroking me, kneeling closer, his cock right in my face. I trembled with desire, licking my lips, eager to take him.

"How are you doing?" he asked softly.

"Amazingly full, and it feels incredible. But I need you as well," I purred, and I slipped my lips over his cock. He tasted deliciously musky, salty, and intoxicating. I took him deeper, licking the underside of his shaft, all while Wilder and Daxon fucked me.

It was incredible to be in the center of such a carnal dance. They moved faster, quicker, and I gasped against Ares's dick as I worked my mouth back and forth over him.

We growled and moaned, our bodies in sync. There were hands all over me, and I couldn't comprehend the level of adoration I was feeling at that moment. Like nothing I could ever dream of.

As we moved faster, our bodies grinding together, I noticed something flashing from down my chest, the blue light catching my attention from the corners of my eye. And I knew instantly what it was, though I wasn't the only one who saw it.

"Your necklace is glowing," Daxon murmured. "Us together, we've activated it. This is going to work, it has to."

I wanted to scream with joy, but instead, I sucked Ares' cock harder, his tip bumping the back of my throat, my eyes tearing up from how deep I took him. He groaned, his hand in my hair, guiding me, his hips rocking back and forward.

Wilder and Daxon were moving faster now, the fuck

fest spurring all kinds of arousal in me. Every nerve ending was about to burst, my body tingling, and even though I'd just come, I knew I didn't have long for my second climax.

"I love you, little dove," Ares hissed as I took all of him into my mouth.

"You have no idea yet how much I love you too," Daxon added, his hands on my breasts, his grunts like a beast, growing louder, faster.

"Rune, you are my life, and I'll always love you," Wilder breathed heavily, his fingers digging into my hips as he hammered into me.

I didn't know how to respond because I loved this moment more than I could express in words, but I barely knew these men...if it worked though, very soon, that would change. And with that single thought, with the blue light pulsating faster and faster, my climax ripped through me.

It tore me right out of my existence. One second I was being fucked, shuddering with a climax, the next, my soul was somewhere else. I floated right above the house I called home for the past many weeks.

I stared down at the village, at the black roofs, at how far the secret world stretched outward in every direction. And around my neck, the blue stone no longer flashed...it remained a bright blue glow. Its light speared outward from the center, reminding me of a lighthouse, guiding ships back home safely.

In a heartbeat, the blue light rushed out over the land. I blinked as it shimmered, at the way the land seemed to be changing before my eyes. For a moment, I could have sworn I saw another town cradled between forests, a river dividing the place, a bridge joining the two sides, and there were people everywhere. Seeing the place brought me a deep joy I didn't quite understand, but I knew that it belonged to me.

Just as quick, the blue vanished, the world disappeared, and I was back in the bedroom with three huge cocks inside me.

I shook with a delicious orgasm just as the men growled, flooding me with their seed. Ares pumped into my mouth, and I took it all, swallowing down everything he gave me.

By the time I'd been filled to the brim and we finished, the men pulled out of me, and I collapsed on top of Daxon, completely exhausted, gasping for air. My head was spinning, my body trembling with how incredible I felt.

"Hello there, sweetheart. You are spectacular." Daxon kissed me. "Do you feel any different?"

I paused for a moment, trying to make sense of what I was feeling, of the strange vision of me floating in the sky. I stared at Wilder. At this beautiful man who studied me as he waited with bated breath for the words he longed for.

Wracking my brain, I concentrated, trying to remember our time together.

Wilder was stroking my back. "Anything?"

"Don't rush her," Ares added.

But the longer I tried, the more I came up blank. We'd failed, and sorrow slithered through me. With it came a sharp pain in my heart, and tears.

"It didn't work," I whispered, my voice shaky.

Daxon's face fell, the sadness in his eyes destroying me. Wilder sighed heavily behind me. I felt like I was breaking apart, and I rolled off Daxon, my tears refusing to stop falling. They fell for their loss, for everything I'd never know again. I cried because I didn't know what we were supposed to do now.

Ares quickly gathered me into his arms. "It's okay, everything will be fine. We just give it time and try again. We'll find a way to bring back your memories."

I cradled against him, unable to stop crying or stop feeling like a disappointment. Heaviness and exhaustion rattled through me, and I closed my eyes, wanting to disappear. I couldn't bear to look at the heartache in Wilder's and Daxon's eyes again.

CHAPTER 18
RUNE

I must have fallen asleep because when I opened my eyes, bright morning light streamed into the bedroom. Warmth cradled around me, a strong arm looped around my middle from the alpha hugging me, breathing heavily across the back of my nape. My first thought flew to Daxon because, ever since he'd marked me back in the Atlandia castle, he'd insisted on sleeping next to me every night.

Just thinking of Daxon, my mate, warmed my heart, but with it came the worry for Wilder and how distant he'd been since his mark failed. We had to try again...this time it had to work.

Blinking a few more times and pushing up and out of bed, it became obvious quickly that this wasn't our room back in Amarok. And when I turned, I saw it was Ares who embraced me. Behind him, Wilder and Daxon slept. My mind fluttered with images, with events, with memories like a movie reel in my head.

I stumbled as every memory came back, rippling over me...me arriving in Amarok, meeting Wilder and Daxon, living in their town, falling in love, meeting Ares, arriving in Romania, being cursed again, Alistair stealing me, and spending a month with Ares. Everything came at me, all the way to last night having sex with all three of them to try and get my memories back.

A small yelp spilled from my lips, and I burst out laughing at the reality. There was so much to unpack, to deal with, but right now I just wanted to yell that I was back to normal.

I must have been loud enough to wake up the three men, as they all stirred, glancing around in a daze, Wilder and Daxon shoving each other, seeing as they were snuggling.

I jumped back into bed with them, squishing them. They moaned, looking dazed and confused, but I straddled Daxon as he was the one in the middle, smiling crazily.

"Are you okay?" Ares asked.

"I'm more than okay. My memories are back!" I beamed and ended up cheering, my hands thrown into the air as I did a small wiggle dance. Of course, I realized then, I was still naked and I'd just jiggled my breasts for the three men who were suddenly very distracted from my words.

I shot my hands back down and said, "It's all back, all my memories at Amarok, us traveling to Romania to bring back my wolf, and then being spelled again...and everything in between to now." I was laughing hysterically at this point.

Everyone scrambled out of bed at that stage, me in Daxon's arms, and they were all surrounding me, crowding close, hugging me, kissing me. If I thought I was the luckiest girl last night, I was mistaken. I was now with three men I loved, who loved me. I'd gained all my memories back. And I knew that with my men by my side, nothing could stop us.

I kissed them all back, fresh tears threading down my cheeks. Tears that came from pure happiness. They were peppering me with kisses and I couldn't stop smiling.

"It's good to be back," I murmured, kissing Daxon on the lips.

I turned to Ares and hugged him as I slipped out of Daxon's arms. "Thank you for helping me fall in love with you."

Wilder's hands were already on my hips, pulling me towards him, twisting me around to face him.

"Rune, I'm ready to make you mine, finally, as well." His voice broke, and I understood the agony he'd been going through.

"Of course," I answered, because I couldn't stand to have him suffering a second longer. "This is a special morning." I fingered the blue stone around my neck, feeling how it gave off a small buzz. This had to work.

"We'll leave you two alone," Ares stated, nudging Daxon to join him since Daxon didn't look like he was going anywhere.

I turned my attention to Wilder who slid his hands around my waist, bringing me closer to him. "I love you so much, Rune. But I'm worried that something's broken inside of me and that's why I can't make our bond complete. If this doesn't work…"

I was shaking my head, placing my palm against his bare chest. "You are mine, and no matter what happens… that won't change."

"It matters to me," his voice slightly rose, his grip tightening. "I want what you and Daxon have, the connection that bonds you both to your souls. To have you forever, knowing that you would keep on wanting me."

"Wilder, please..."

"No, hear me out. I've given it a lot of thought. I think I've been cursed ever since Daria spelled me. When I forgot about you and believed she was my fated mate." His eyebrows pinched together with agony, sorrow etched across his features. "Ever since then, I've been different."

I remembered the moment he spoke of because it had shattered me to pieces. I'd found him and Daria strolling along a trail in the woods, laughing, holding each other like they were soul mates. For a long time after that, I believed Wilder had left me for that bitch. And it hurt to see him still suffering because of it.

Pushing my hair away from my neck, I offered myself to him. "There's magic in the air and a miracle has just happened, and I know this is going to work."

"You are my everything. My stars, my sun, my existence." He leaned in and kissed me slowly. I pushed myself up on my tippy toes to reach him, to show him he meant the world to me too. "But I'm not enough for you if I can't even claim your soul as mine."

His words hurt, and I clung to him, wanting desperately to show him we were meant to be together.

His mouth left a path of kisses across my cheek, then down my neck. There was no pause, only the heaviness of his breath, then he struck. His teeth sank into the curve of my neck.

I flinched at the rawness of his bite, at him tearing skin. Pain swelled over me, and I clutched onto him, shaking, but I swallowed back how much it hurt.

Please let it work, please, it has to work this time.

But the longer I waited, the more dread filled me. There

was no overwhelming love, no possessive feeling, no grate-fulness for the bite. I couldn't feel Wilder's feelings rushing over my senses... there was nothing but excruciating pain from his teeth.

And nothing hurt as much as the realization that we weren't bonding. I wanted to cry, to scream as my chest tightened.

When Wilder pulled back from me, my blood on his lips, he was destroyed.

"Wilder," I whispered, reaching for him, shaking at seeing him that way.

"I told you, it's me. I'm the problem." Red burned across his face, self-hatred battering in his gaze. He brushed right past me, darting out of the room.

My knees buckled and I fell to them, tears falling. I sobbed into my hands. But the longer I cried for him, the more a fierce anger rose through me that he'd let something like a bond stand between us.

That same fury had me getting to my feet. I dressed quickly and darted out of the room, needing to talk sense into him. To make him see that nothing else mattered.

Just as I ran out the open, front door, a shiver ran down my spine, a feeling that something was really wrong.

Panicked, I burst down the golden paved road, searching for Wilder.

It didn't take long for me to spot his dark hair fluttering in the breeze, but a second was all it took for me to know something was wrong. He was on his knees, facing away from me. In front of him stood a woman with flowing black hair and a matching gown. She glanced up, grinning.

My heart stopped beating and dread spiked through me.

Daria.

My veins turned to ice and I screamed, throwing myself toward them just as she vanished into dust, evaporating out of sight. She was obsessed with Wilder. That fucking bitch would never leave him alone.

I reached Wilder just as he collapsed onto his side.

Blood was all I saw, his hands clutching the wound right above his heart. Ribbons of blood spilled from between his fingers, his eyes fluttering, his breaths raspy like each inhale was a struggle.

I couldn't breathe and dropped to my knees in front of, pressing my palms to the stab wound. But there was so much blood already.

"Wilder, hold on, please, we'll heal you. God, please don't die." I then screamed for Daxon and Ares.

But Wilder grabbed my hand, his strength feeling weak, and he croaked my name, "Rune. I know now why we can't bond."

"Wilder, forget about that. Just hold on, please." Tears were soaking my cheeks, and my chest was about to crack in half as I shook uncontrollably.

"You have to let me go, Rune. Because I can't fix what's wrong with me here. The answer's in the afterlife. Maybe there, I can be the mate you need."

And just like that, his head flopped to the side, his eyes rolled back, and his breathing stopped.

No, no, no. I shook him hard, my insides going cold. "Wilder. Get up, get up."

I screamed hysterically. "Don't you dare die on me."

But he never got back up.

Turn the page to preorder the final book in the series!

WILD FOREVER
BOOK 7

Real Wolves Bite. Continue the Wild series...

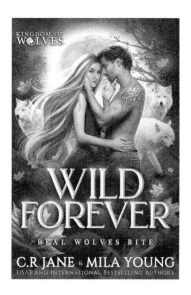

Get your copy of Wild Forever today!

WILD SERIES

Wild Moon

Wild Heart

Wild Girl

Wild Love

Wild Soul

Wild Kiss

MONSTER'S TEMPTATION

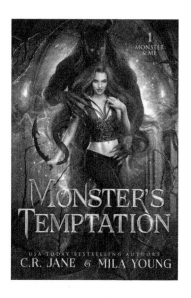

The Monster King wants to play...

It's been 1097 days and 14 hours since I've been locked in this place.

And they've come to me every night.

The monsters in my dreams worship my body.

And when I wake up, I'm desperate for more...

But they're never there to finish me off.

Dr. Adams says I can leave the asylum if I start to take my meds, but I've always hated how they made me feel...and I'm not sure that I agree with them that I'm actually crazy.

Because dreams don't make you crazy, right?

I've got to start living someday though...so I finally take the plunge and obey so I can get out.

My dreams stop, and the monsters disappear. I'm finally starting a new life.

And that's when he comes...the monster king.

Evidently my little dreams, weren't just dreams. And he and his demon horde were feeding off my lust.

Their glowing eyes, sharp teeth, and big...

They're all real.

The Monster King wants me back. I'm their favorite plaything after all.

And I just might want to play.

AUTHOR'S NOTE

Well I would say I'm sorry...but the screaming is so delicious. Poor Wilder.

One of the things we knew we needed to do, was make you and Rune fall in love with Ares. I mean, Wilder and Daxon are kind of pushy, and that would be a hard relationship to form with them around.

That being said...we were the ones who fell in love with Ares in this book. And we hoped you did too.

It's going to be so hard to say goodbye to these characters...but we promise to make it worthy of them. See you in Wild Forever...

Acknowledgments

Caitlin-My bff for life. Thanks for always being there for me, you make me life so much better and allow me to do what I love to do!

Jasmine-you're a goddess. I tell you this every time, but your efforts are seen and appreciated. Thank you for what you do for our book babies!

And last...thanks to you. I wake up every day, in disbelief of the gift you've given me of reading our words. I never take it for granted. Not a single day.

ABOUT C.R. JANE

A Texas girl living in Utah now, I'm a wife, mother, lawyer, and now author. My stories have been floating around in my head for years, and it has been a relief to finally get them down on paper. I'm a huge Dallas Cowboys fan and I primarily listen to Taylor Swift and hip hop...don't lie and say you don't too.

My love of reading started probably when I was three and it only made sense that I would start to create my own worlds since I was always getting lost in others'.

I like heroines who have to grow in order to become badasses, happy endings, and swoon-worthy, devoted, (and hot) male characters. If this sounds like you, I'm pretty sure we'll be friends.

I'm so glad to have you on my team...check out the links below for ways to hang out with me and more of my books you can read!

Visit my **Facebook** page to get updates.

Visit my Website.

Sign up for my newsletter to stay updated on new

releases, find out random facts about me, and get access to different points of view from my characters.

ABOUT MILA YOUNG

Best-selling author, Mila Young tackles everything with the zeal and bravado of the fairytale heroes she grew up reading about. She slays monsters, real and imaginary, like there's no tomorrow. By day she rocks a keyboard as a marketing extraordinaire. At night she battles with her mighty pen-sword, creating fairytale retellings, and sexy ever after tales.

Ready to read more and more from Mila Young? www. subscribepage.com/milayoung

www.milayoungbooks.com

For more information...
mila@milayoungbooks.com

Printed in Great Britain
by Amazon

23649908R00163